Souls

A Demon Trappers® Novel

Lost Souls

A Demon Trappers® Novel

Jana Oliver

Nevermore Books

Published by
MageSpell LLC
Porto, Portugal

This novel is a work of fiction. Names, characters, places, and incidents are the product of the author's imagination and are not to be construed as real. Any resemblance to actual persons, living or dead, events or locales, is entirely coincidental.

Lost Souls
A Demon Trappers® Novel
ISBN: 978-1-941527-16-0
Copyright © 2021 Jana Oliver

From Hell with Love
A Demon Trappers® Short Story
Copyright © 2019 Jana Oliver

Cover Art courtesy of Yocla Designs
Angel Wing Graphic used with permission of
Macmillan Children's Books

All rights reserved.
No part of this book may be reproduced or transmitted in any form or by any means now known or hereinafter invented, electronic or mechanical, including but not limited to photocopying, recording, or by an information storage and retrieval system, without the written permission of the Publisher, except where permitted by law.

Demon Trappers is a Registered Trademark of Jana G. Oliver

To

Steve Wood

a devoted reader and

a lover of the written word

&

To our dearest Dali

who will always be with us,

deep within our hearts and our souls.

Requiescant in pace

Had I not fallen, I would not have arisen.
Had I not been subject to darkness,
I would not have seen the light.

~ Midrash

ONE

May 2019
Atlanta, Georgia

Simon Adler glanced at the address in the text message, then compared it to the white mailbox at the end of the driveway. It'd taken longer than he'd anticipated to find the right house. Sometimes the confusion was the fault of the subdivision, but usually it was Hell's trickery. Since he was a lay exorcist for the Vatican, Lucifer, and his infernal minions, went out of their way to make his life difficult.

Stepping out of his car immediately introduced him to a full blast of late May heat, along with a side order of body-drenching humidity. Sweat obligingly popped out on his forehead. With the thermometer marching toward 94 degrees, the heat index would be stifling.

A quick visual check proved the neighborhood was as he'd expected: two-story houses, probably built in the eighties, some four-side brick, others not. Most had well-manicured lawns with discrete, though wilting, flower borders.

Not the house in front of him. The lawn hadn't been mowed and children's toys were scattered in the grass. A few more days and they'd be lost from view entirely. Now that Simon looked closer, he realized the rain-smeared chalk marks on the driveway were crosses, along with three equally faint ones on the garage door. More dotted the concrete stairs leading to the front porch.

"There we are," he said.

With the homeowners safe in an extended-stay hotel,

word would have spread that this house was possessed. Even if they'd tried, it would have been hard to hide that news. The upstairs windows were blown out, curtains hanging limp in the non-existent breeze. Scorch marks rose onto the roof from the openings. There had been no earthly fire involved and that's why he was here.

Lay exorcists were a recent development, at least when it came to a church with over two thousand years of history. As the demand for exorcisms increased, Rome began to recruit and train men who were not in the priesthood. Simon had been in the Vatican's first class, spending months learning the intricacies, and the dangers, involved in exorcising fiends from people and buildings. After graduation he immediately returned home because Atlanta was Ground Zero in the fight against Hell.

He could feel eyes on him now, no doubt some neighbor watching his every move. It came with the territory. Often, they would venture out of their house to tell him about the horrors they'd witnessed. Most of the time they remained locked inside, murmuring prayers. He preferred the latter.

Simon took a deep breath, already feeling sweat wicking into his white shirt, making it stick to his skin. Coupled with his black slacks and the large wooden cross he wore on a thick leather cord around his neck, he knew he could easily double as a door-to-door missionary.

After running a hand through his hair—it was considerably shorter than usual courtesy of a feisty demon and its hellfire—Simon opened the rear driver's side door and removed the black suitcase holding his exorcism equipment. He didn't like leaving it in plain sight even with the doors locked, but the case heated up too much in the trunk. After setting it on the driveway, he reached in for an ornate metal container. It wasn't a big box, just ten inches square, but it was engraved with crosses and would hold the demon after its exorcism. Just as his hands touched it, someone cleared their throat.

As Simon turned, the hairs on the back of his neck rose. This was not a nosey neighbor, not with those bottomless eyes and coal-black hair that nearly touched his shoulders. Ori looked to be in his early thirties, which was ridiculous. Most likely he'd been alive since the universe had been created. If not longer.

The angel wore all black—jeans and a short-sleeved T-shirt that revealed his muscled arms. His wings were hidden, as well as his flaming sword. At least for the moment.

"Simon Michael David Adler," he said solemnly.

"Fallen," Simon replied, trying to keep his voice from showing his surprise, and failing.

He'd last seen the angel at Riley Blackthorne's wedding. According to the master demon trapper, Ori was no longer on Hell's payroll, and that he'd become his own master, if there was such a thing for Divines.

"Some reason you're lurking in suburbia?" he asked.

"You are not as trusting as you once were," the Fallen observed.

"Neither are you," Simon shot back.

A knowing nod returned. "If you prefer that I leave, just tell me. If not, I will remain."

Simon knew this Divine's story almost as well as his own. Ori had swallowed Lucifer's magnificent lies and followed him into exile where he had served as the Prince's executioner for millennia. That job had eventually sent him to Atlanta where he'd seduced Paul Blackthorne's daughter and claimed Riley's soul. That should have been the end of it, but this Fallen was different. In the end, Ori had sacrificed himself to save Riley, and she'd regained her soul. Simon gave thanks for that miracle every day.

It was time to do some probing. "Is it true you're on your own now?" he asked. "Not allied with Hell or Heaven?"

"That is true."

"How's that going?"

One of Ori's black eyebrows rose. "About as good as you'd think," was the sharp reply. "Though I find I now have certain informants in Hell who are eager to cultivate my favor."

"Why?"

"They think I intend to overthrow the Prince."

Simon's heart double beat. "Do you?"

Ori's eyes weren't meeting his. When they did, he shook his head. "I have wasted enough of my existence on *that one*. I have my own goals now."

"Which are?"

"You are incredibly inquisitive for someone who has been offered Divine assistance."

Simon huffed. "Somehow I missed the *Divine assistance* part of this conversation. I certainly have legitimate reasons to be skeptical: I once had a Fallen's 'help' and almost lost my soul because of it."

"It would appear we both learned much-needed lessons." A pause, then, "My personal goals are variable, but I seek to destroy my former master's Hellspawn wherever they are found. They are my enemies . . . *for eternity*."

"Then I'd appreciate any assistance you are willing to give me."

In response, Ori claimed the small metal box from the car while Simon picked up the case.

"Have you seen Riley lately?"

"I enjoyed her and the grand master's hospitality just last week," the angel replied.

"Do that often?"

"Every now and then. Grand Master Beck makes excellent pancakes."

"Yes, he does." Simon had been the recipient of a few of those himself. "She's happy now. With Beck, I mean."

"Yes, she is."

They shared a moment of reflective silence. Simon had once dated Riley, had even begun to think of their future together. At least until nearly dying at the claws of a demon had caused a crisis of faith, and led to his betrayal of her. It'd been a lying Fallen that had lured him on that path, yet another of Lucifer's devious angels. Riley eventually forgave Simon, but he still carried the guilt. Always would.

A poorly spray-painted cross greeted them at the front door. The paint had been applied so quickly that it had run and made the sacred symbol appear to be bleeding.

Simon shuddered at the thought, then knocked. He hadn't expected a response, but you never knew. He held his hand close to the doorknob to ensure it wouldn't fry his flesh—Riley had learned that lesson during one of their joint exorcisms—and then tried the knob. It was unlocked, which was often the case when the homeowners ran for their lives. It was that or be possessed. At least they'd all escaped unharmed.

He was about to push the door open when Ori touched his arm. "Prepare yourself out here. You may not have the chance once inside this dwelling."

Simon let that sink in. "Is this a demon, or something worse?"

"I'm not sure. All I know is that I felt an urgent need to join you here today. Since my instincts have been uncannily accurate as of late, you should heed my warning."

"Getting help from . . . " Simon pointed upward.

The angel shrugged in return.

Simon moved a desiccated geranium off a wrought iron table, sending a rain of dried yellow petals to the porch. He placed the case that held his equipment on top of the cleared space. Popping open the lid, he began the ritual he performed before each exorcism.

Clearing his mind, Simon focused on the task ahead, intoning a prayer for guidance, and for protection. Then he anointed himself with the freshly consecrated Holy Water that had arrived from the Vatican late last evening. Papal Holy Water—it didn't get any more potent than that. On impulse, Simon turned toward his companion and offered the small vial just to see the Divine's reaction.

Ori shook his head. "I have no need of it, Simon Michael David Adler. You're forgetting who created me."

The angel did have a point.

"Just Simon, okay? Hearing my full name makes me feel like I'm getting chewed out by one of the nuns in elementary school."

"As you wish."

Since it appeared the case would have to remain outside, Simon removed the large wooden cross from its cushioned niche. He usually employed a brass one, but it often grew too hot sitting in the car so the wooden version would do. It was the symbol, not its construction, that mattered.

Though most of the Vatican's lay exorcists continued to conduct their exorcisms exactly as they'd been taught in Rome, Simon, much to his own surprise, had begun to change-up that formula. Unless he was working with a priest, he no longer used the aspergillum to sprinkle Holy Water. He'd streamlined other portions of the ritual as well. Time was not always on your side in the real world. It appeared that Hell's strategies changed constantly, at least when it came to him, though not so with the priests. He still wasn't sure what to make of that.

In many ways, Riley had been an inadvertent catalyst for some of his alterations, others had occurred the longer Simon exorcised Hellspawn. As long as the fiends continued to change their tactics, so would he.

The angel opened the door to the house, though he allowed Simon to enter first. The moment he stepped into the entryway, Simon felt a blast of heat and inhaled the thick stench of brimstone. The foyer in front of him undulated, like heat rising off the sands in a desert, casting red and yellow shadows on the once-white walls. For some perverse reason, the fiends loved to show him their home.

"Some things never change," Ori murmured. The stench of the Pit seared his nostrils. Had the reek of brimstone always been that strong or had he become accustomed to it when he'd served the Prince? No matter, it was rank now.

A quick glance at the exorcist told him his companion wasn't as stunned as he'd expected.

"It's been this way lately—lots and lots of Hell," Simon

explained. He looked over at Ori now, thoughtful. "What kind of backup can you give me?"

"My fiery sword and a whole lot of attitude."

A particularly grim smile claimed the exorcist's face. "Then as Riley would say, let's go kick some demon butt."

A low laugh rolled through the house now, rattling the windows.

Ori frowned, searching. "There's more than one." He let his senses roam, but something was blocking him from visualizing every part of the structure. That was unusual. "Still want to face them?"

"Yes," was the instant reply.

"There is no dishonor in stepping back," he said, testing Simon's resolve.

"I step back, then next time they'll bring even more fiends. It'll only escalate. We do this here, *now*."

Simon had barely finished speaking when the front door slammed shut behind them. To his credit, the exorcist didn't flinch. If anything, he appeared more determined.

"If I tell you to flee, heed me. Do you understand?" Ori demanded.

"I'm not suicidal."

"Curiously, neither am I." *Not anymore.*

The mortal next to him had changed. A year ago, Simon Michael David Adler seemed convinced of his own moral superiority. That he, alone, could stand against evil and prevail.

That Simon was gone. Now he looked older than his years, battle-hardened, no longer a naive young man who believed everything was strictly good vs. evil. He had witnessed death, faced it firsthand, and learned life-changing lessons because of that naivete. Simon the Exorcist was a force to be reckoned with, someone who merited protection.

They made their way through the stifling atmosphere, entering a room with a brick fireplace and a big-screen television mounted above it, the screen shattered. Furniture had been thrown around, each piece scorched, the cushions shredded. The stench of urine filled the air. The owners would weep when they saw their home violated in such a way.

"This room is too big for this size house," Simon said. "Is it an illusion?"

"Yes. Its purpose is to disorient us, making us question everything we see."

"Can you work inside a Holy Water circle?"

Ori wasn't sure, so he hedged. "I would prefer not to."

"Then I'll set a circle for me and—"

The first demon swooped out of nowhere and flew at them like a demented bird, mouth gaped open, teeth in abundance, its hands tipped with studded claws. Even before Simon could react, the flash of Ori's blinding sword cut the thing in half. As it fell, it melted into the carpet in a stinking black puddle before it turned to ash.

With an abrupt change in pressure, the kind that heralded the arrival of one of Lucifer's higher-level fiends, the air in front them boiled and a Hellspawn stepped forward. At least seven feet tall, it had golden skin studded with spikes, two broad eyes that glowed with amber fire, and massive arms that ended in sausage-shaped fingers tipped with claws.

"Traitor," it hissed, eyeing him. Then it abruptly turned its attention to the exorcist as if Ori posed no threat.

That wasn't good news.

"Simon the Betrayer," it said, smirking. Like most of the more powerful fiends, the voice was riddled with cunning, sliding across your skin like oil. "Do you believe you can cleanse your sins by wielding your pathetic faith? I am of Hell, I am all powerful, I am—"

"Lucifer's lapdog," Simon spat back.

He touched a finger to the still damp Holy Water on his forehead and then bent to touch that same digit to the carpet. As he rose, he murmured to himself, and to Ori's astonishment a flash of light heralded the near instantaneous creation of a sacred circle around the young man. A circle that would keep him safe if he remained within it.

Very clever.

He sensed Riley Anora Blackthorne's hand in that, though there was no magic to it. No matter how the circle came to be, it meant the difference between remaining alive, or being impaled on a demon's claws.

Ori settled into a fighting stance, blazing sword in hand, waiting to see what horrors the fiend had in mind.

With a deep breath, Simon raised the cross. "Abomination, know that I am Simon Michael David Adler, child of God. I command you—"

The fiend's eyes narrowed, and with a wave of a clawed hand three figures appeared, kneeling on the carpet to its right. They were boys, probably fourteen or fifteen years of age, their eyes filled with unimaginable terror. An iron collar encircled each kid's neck, and standing behind them was a single demon, holding the thick metal chains that attached to those collars.

"I know of you, Simon the Betrayer," the large fiend said. "You do not fear death. But what of these mortals? Do you fear for them? Are you as righteous as you claim?"

"I claim no glory for what I do," Simon replied. "All glory goes to God."

"Then let us put your faith to a test." The fiend glowered, its eyes riveted on him. "How much courage do you possess?"

"My courage is endless because of whom I serve."

The demon slapped its thigh, as if Simon had made the best joke. "We shall see, we shall see," it hissed. "I will send Hellspawn against you until the stroke of midnight this day. If you defeat each of them then you will face *me*. If you can defeat *all* of us, I will release one of these mortals."

You *never* bargained with a fiend. *Never*. It was the first rule he'd been taught in Rome. And yet if Simon didn't, he'd likely lose all these souls.

"No," he said, shaking his head. "You have no skin in this game." He paused, thinking it through, carefully choosing his words. "I defeat all the demons you send to me, and only one of these boys will be set free? That's hardly worth my time."

He heard Ori's sharp intake of breath, followed by the angel's urgent voice in his mind. *Be very careful. Your soul is in jeopardy.*

"All three," Simon said, ignoring the advice. "I will defeat each of the demons you send, *one by one*, by midnight, and you will release *all of your captives at once*." He sucked in a deep breath. "If you lose three potential souls your master will take notice, and you know that's never a good thing. All three. Take it or leave it."

The demon's eyes narrowed even further as it glanced toward Ori, then back to him. "No help from this traitor, or Blackthorne's Daughter, any grand master, or the Killer of the Fallen, cursed be his name forever."

Which sidelined Ori, Riley, Grand Masters Stewart and Denver Beck from this battle.

Damn.

"By midnight your mortal time, beginning now," the demon pressed. "If you violate those rules, all of these mortals' souls will be mine. And, because you dared to bargain with me, your soul will be mine as well. My master will be pleased to hear your screams of agony . . . for eternity."

Even before Simon could refuse that outrageous bargain, the fiends and the teens vanished in a swirling cloud of brimstone.

"I can't believe you did that!" Ori shouted, his voice echoing off the walls. "Are you insane?"

Simon glared at him. "And what, O Wise Angel, should I have done? Waited until you killed that lesser demon while that big one took off with the kids? Or maybe I should have tried to exorcise *both* of them, like *that* was going to work. Playing the fiend's game bought me time."

"Playing the fiend's game bought your way into Hell."

"Had any of the kids given up their souls yet?"

As his sword disappeared, Ori's furious expression lessened. "No. They retain their souls."

"Then I still have a chance to save them," Simon said. He dragged his foot across the Holy Water circle to break it, astounded at what he'd just done.

Demons lied. Even if he pulled off the impossible, there was no guarantee those souls would live, or that he would retain his freedom.

The angel shook his head in dismay. "The Hellspawn will hold you to the letter of the agreement because you accepted part of its bargain. Your mortal soul is in peril, Simon."

"I know." *God, I know.*

"I cannot help you."

"I know."

"How could you be so stupid?" the Fallen demanded.

"How could you be so stupid to follow Lucifer into exile?"

Ori reeled back in shock. "You mortals never learn," he said, then abruptly vanished.

Simon's hand shook so badly the cross quavered in midair, so he lowered it. His eyes tracked back to where the boys had been. Did their families know they were missing? How had they been captured? Why three of them?

With a whispered prayer, he made his way to the front of the house. The fiends were gone, but there was no reason they would not reappear here. He would anoint each room, clear it of Hell's taint, beginning at the top of the house. Once he was done, he'd go to Mass and pray for help to free those innocent souls.

If God were merciful, he might even save his own.

TWO

Master Riley Blackthorne's stack of official paperwork seemed to grow daily. Another form here, another report there, it all added up. Her superior was happy to hand it all off to her. If it'd been anyone else but Master Harper, she'd think him giddy at the prospect, but the grizzled trapper wasn't wired that way. He claimed her handwriting was neater, which was true.

Because this was her lot in life, she chose where to conduct this Herculean task. As was often the case, it was her favorite coffee shop in downtown Atlanta, the Grounds Zero. Unlike her usual hot chocolate, she sipped on iced coffee because it was toastier than Hell outside. Well, not quite as bad as that, but close. Riley certainly knew the difference.

The coffee shop was always busy on Saturdays, and it being Memorial Day weekend only added to the crowd, a chance to escape the heat and enjoy some conversation and a cool beverage. Or in Riley's case Form NDTG04-1090-E. She set aside a lengthy trapping report—why would a Biblio-Fiend think tearing apart a mobile lending library was a good idea?—when a sensation slid over her, one she knew well.

Riley looked up and smiled. "Ori."

The Fallen angel sat in the booth opposite her, his brows furrowed and his expression intense. As was often the case, he was dressed in all black. That alone said he wasn't a native of the Deep South.

"Uh-oh. What's up?" she asked, knowing that look.

The angel waved a hand, muting their conversation from their neighbors, then delivered the news in crisp tones. Unfortunately, that news matched his grim expression: Simon, an all-or-nothing deal with a powerful demon who had kidnapped a trio of young mortals. Three souls, and the exorcist's, were on the line.

"That's nuts. It sounds like something I'd do," she grumbled as a pensive nod came her way. "I'm guessing since you're here you want me to help."

"No. The fiend's terms don't allow either of us to aid the exorcist. If we do, it'll claim we cheated and take those souls."

"It might do that no matter what," she said, frowning. "How strong is this thing?"

"You would consider it an extremely powerful Grade Four."

To keep track of their enemies, the trappers had devised a simple sliding scale of demonic power: The higher the number, the bigger the danger. Grade Four Hypno-Fiends were known for co-opting your will while draining your life force. However, in the last year or so some of the Fours had become more formidable, bulkier, and layered in armor. This one sounded like it was one of the warrior Fours.

"The fiend is more powerful than it should be," Ori added.

"Someone augmenting its power? Our Infernal Pest, perhaps?" Riley asked. She refused to use the L word in public because sometimes the Prince just loved to drop in for a visit.

"Maybe, maybe not. Hard to guess."

"His Infernalness played that game with me at the airport last week. At least there wasn't too much damage." She sighed. "When does the challenge start?

"It's already started. Simon has until midnight to best any demons sent his way. Then he'll face the more powerful fiend, because it will try to collect his soul, or kill him."

"Or both." Riley put the paperwork into a tidy pile, thinking through the problem. "What about Beck? Can he help?"

"No, none of the grand masters may be involved. The fiend isn't that stupid."

"Of course not."

A barista approached and set a cup of black coffee in front of Ori. He gave her money, though exactly where that had come from was a mystery. With a wide smile—he'd included a hefty tip—she thanked him and departed.

"You're supposed to pick that up at the front counter like everyone else," Riley said.

The angel ignored her, taking a sip of the brew. "The exorcist needs someone who breaks the rules, like you do," he advised. "Someone the demon can't intimidate. Who can you recommend to help him?"

Riley frowned now. "I'm not sure who—"

"Master Blackthorne?" a voice asked.

At Ori's startled expression she looked up to find a young woman standing near their table. She was older than Riley's eighteen years, with chin-length asymmetrical ebony hair that looked like she'd cut it herself. Her skin was tanned, her cheekbones sharp, as if she'd recently lost weight. Two small silver studs were tucked in the cartilage of her left ear, none in the right.

Dark circles sat under her brown eyes and she wore a long-sleeved shirt even though it was blisteringly hot outside. She pushed a small piece of worn luggage out of the way with a foot, and then readjusted the strap to a stained denim bag.

"Yes, I'm Master Blackthorne."

"Some guy named Jackson said I'd find you here. I'm Breman." She kept twisting a silver ring on her left thumb.

Her name meant absolutely nothing to Riley. "I'm sorry, am I supposed to know you?"

The young woman sighed as if somehow this wasn't a surprise, then dug in her bag. A stack of paper came Riley's way.

Accept her help. She's been sent here for a reason.

Riley blinked at the mental intrusion, her eyes connecting with the angel's. *You sure?* He nodded.

A quick skim of the first document revealed that Katia Allyson Breman, age 24, was from Lawrence, Kansas, had passed her journeyman trapper's exam three months before, but had been transferred to the Atlanta Demon Trappers Guild because of discipline problems. A terse note at the bottom of the page indicated that Ms. Breman claimed to see things that weren't real. The master who signed the report felt she didn't have what it took to be a trapper, but had been "reluctantly" persuaded to give her one more chance.

What he didn't say was that the Atlanta Guild was known to take in the oddballs, the ones that didn't fit the mold, and that was why she was here. Someone at the National Guild had approved this transfer but had failed to pass the word on to her and Harper. Not a surprise.

"So, who did you piss off?" Riley asked, folding the papers and dropping them into her own trapping bag for future reference. From the frown on Breman's face, she amended her question. "Or maybe it would be better to ask who *didn't* you piss off?"

The frown vanished and there was a faint spark of a smile. That also quickly evaporated. "When I said things weren't like they thought they were, they didn't believe me."

"Been there, done that." *Far too many times.*

Breman finally glanced over at Ori and her eyes widened. "You're . . . oh, man." She frowned in confusion. "You're not as bright white as the other angel I saw today."

Ohhhkay . . .

The insubordinate trapper from Kansas could spot a Divine on sight, and somehow knew that Ori wasn't like those on Heaven's payroll? That was indeed a gift, one Riley would have loved to have had last year. No wonder Katia Bremen unnerved the guys back in Lawrence.

"Can you see through illusion or glamour spells?" she asked. No reply. Riley knew this drill. "Look, I'm not going to kick you out of the Guild just because you can see things others can't. Okay?"

Breman blinked. "Then yes, I can sometimes see glamour spells. Illusions are harder."

Yes, they are. "And you can tell if someone is a Divine."

"Yes."

"That didn't go down well back home?" A short shake of the trapper's head. "Well, that's just dumb on their part."

"She's been sent here for a reason," Ori said, then took another sip of his coffee.

"Got that. Just not sure whether it's a good thing to dump her into this mess or not. It is going to be ugly."

"I don't see that you have a choice."

"Can you two stop talking like I'm not here?" Breman asked.

This trapper had a backbone, and from the pinched look to her face, not enough to eat.

"Would you have any problems working with someone from the Vatican? A lay exorcist?"

Ms. Breman pondered that question. "Is he okay? I mean, not a creeper?"

Riley snorted at the thought. "Far from it. I'd trust him with my life, which should tell you everything you need to know about him."

The young woman's posture relaxed. "What do I have to do?"

"Keep him alive," Riley replied. Ori frowned over at her, clearly wanting to talk this out. "How's about you get yourself something to drink while I chat with the 'not as bright white as the other angel' dude across the table. We need to come to a decision and it's not going to be an easy one to make."

"About me and this Vatican guy, right?"

"Exactly."

Katia hesitated in a way that felt so familiar.

"Did you drive over to Atlanta?" Riley asked, suspecting why the trapper hesitated to head to the front counter.

"No. Don't have a car. I took the bus."

"From *Kansas*?"

"Yeah. Took almost a day."

"Okay, then let me buy you a drink to welcome you to Atlanta. We have our share of jerks, but we make it work. You might find a home here, you never know."

Breman's expression remained dubious. That changed to relief when Riley handed over a twenty and a five.

"Get some food if you're hungry."

A nod, then the newest addition to Atlanta's demon trapping family headed for the counter at top speed, leaving her luggage behind.

"She's definitely hungry," Riley said. "I remember what that felt like."

"You were never that thin," Ori observed. "Her previous assignment was bad. Did you notice how she kept scratching her arms?"

"Think those long sleeves are hiding a few scars?"

He nodded, then finished up his coffee. "She's been sent here for a reason."

"You've said that like three times. I counted even."

"I'll say it three times more if needed. You *have* to pair her up with Simon Michael David Adler."

"Why her?" Riley asked. "She's half-starved and clearly has issues, if you know what I mean."

"She is all of that, but something's going on and it's not just demons playing games."

Trust wasn't easy to give, especially when the individual was a Fallen angel. This Divine was different. This one had saved her life, taught her how to fight Hellspawn, given back her soul and helped Beck defeat another Fallen. If Ori said something was going on, it was, and Katia Breman was in the middle of it.

Riley gave in. "Fine. I'll see that she is paired up with Simon for today, at least. What else can we do?"

"You, nothing. I'll keep an eye on them without giving the fiend any reason to say Adler cheated. If we're lucky, we'll be able to reclaim those captive mortals, and the exorcist will retain his life, and his soul."

"Or we could lose all of them."

Ori's expression saddened. "Or we could lose all of them."

THREE

Though she'd not wanted to act that needy, Katia had ordered a big bowl of oatmeal, two breakfast sandwiches, and the largest cup of coffee they offered. Then she'd wolfed down the food like it'd been the only meal she'd had in the last two days. Somehow Master Blackthorne had guessed this was the case. But how?

She wants me to call her Riley.

Katia wasn't quite sure how to handle that degree of familiarity. She sure hadn't had it back in Kansas, at least not with her second master. Besides, in the trapping world Riley Blackthorne was a freaking legend. Everyone knew about her and her dad.

Master Blackthorne's hair was longer than in some of the videos, and more auburn than brown. She wore a pale blue T-shirt and bleached jeans. These weren't the expensive kind, but what happened to denim after repeated encounters with Hellspawn. At least hers had fewer holes than Katia's.

If she'd met Riley on the street, she'd guess her to be in college, the kind of girl who would hang with her friends in the evening, just having fun. That ended when you looked into Master Blackthorne's eyes and knew she'd survived more than her share of Hell. Some might say the same of her.

"You okay over there?" Riley asked, after turning onto a side street. They were on their way to the office of some guy named Harper, the most senior trapper in Atlanta.

"Yeah. I'm just . . . digesting." *And not just the food.*

Riley chuckled. "So now is when I give you my Master Harper speech, the one I deliver to every new apprentice."

"I'm not an apprentice."

"No, you're not. You're also not used to Harper, and that's why you need to know what he's like so he doesn't roll right over you."

"He does that?" Katia asked, eyeing her companion.

"He can. Master Harper is naturally gruff and has a wicked temper. He's also had a lot of bad stuff happen in his life. You'll see the evidence of one of those when you meet him. Harper is brutally blunt and takes crap from no one."

"An abusive asshole then?" Katia asked, testing the waters.

Riley shrugged. "At one time, yes, but not so much now. No matter how much he growls, he will have your back if you're straight with him. Not all the masters are like that."

"Yeah, met a few of those. They're fine if it's you getting hurt."

"Is that why you're wearing long sleeves when it's in the 90s?"

Katia couldn't stop the full body tremor. She opened her mouth to answer, then closed it, unsure.

The master turned into a parking lot in front of what looked to be a car repair place. "I have scars myself. We all do. Some are even visible."

Their eyes met and for a second Katia wondered if she'd found a kindred spirit. But that couldn't be for real.

Riley pulled up next to a dusty red pickup truck with empty demon cages in the back, then turned off the engine. Katia undid her seatbelt, then just sat there. Maybe it would be good to tell the truth. At least a little of it.

"My arms are all . . . ripped up," she admitted.

"Personally, I prefer the term 'battle scarred'."

"Same thing."

"I'm proud of mine: They tell the world I'm faster and smarter than Hell's hounds. Not everyone is."

Maybe that was what she thought, but for Katia, her scars spoke of pain, and the debt she still owed.

Riley opened her car door. "Remember, no matter how bitchy Harper is just let it slide off you. If he asks for details about what went on in Kansas, tell him all of it. Leave nothing out."

"Why would he want to know that?"

"Because he cares. Hard to see it sometimes, but he does." As they headed for the door, Riley added, "And yes, this used to be a tire shop. There's a personal reason why this is our office so don't make fun of it, no matter what you do."

A blast of cooler air hit Katia as they entered the structure, along with it the smell of old motor oil and the distinctive stink of demons. The latter were housed in cages where the cars had once been serviced. They immediately began an eerie chorus of "Blackthorne's Daughter!" in their deep, rusty voices. Riley ignored them.

The actual office wasn't fancy, just as you'd expect for a trapper, though the walls did appear to have received a coat of pale beige paint recently. There were a pair of bulletin boards which held the National Guild notices every trapping office was required to display, as well as the state and federal notices. Katia always thought that bunching them together made them easier to ignore.

The floor was dark-brown linoleum, shiny in places. There were only two desks, both of which had seen some use, and in the corner were filing cabinets and a cheap metal table with a computer, monitor and printer, just like any other office. On the back wall was a door that led to a kitchen, and in the opposite corner, one that led to a restroom.

Master Harper sat behind the larger desk, and he was not what she'd expected. Probably in his mid or late fifties with short hair and a thick white scar on the left side of his face that immediately drew attention.

"Getting a good look at it?" he asked, his eyes riveted on hers.

Before Katia could stop herself, she'd undone the button on her left cuff and pushed up the sleeve. The telltale ribbon of scars scored up her arm like some intricate tribal tattoo.

"Ouch," Riley said, grimacing.

"Matching set on the other side?" Harper asked. Katia

nodded. "Then you know how damned bad this job can be." He set down his pen. "Blackthorne says you've been turfed here from Kansas. Tell me why."

As she opened her mouth, he waved her off. "Not the official bullshit. Tell me what really happened."

She sent Riley a panicked look.

"Lay it all out," the master replied. "Now's the time."

Closing her eyes, Katia took a deep breath and when she reopened them, she found Harper watching her intently.

"Can I sit down?" she asked, her knees beginning to shake. What if he thought she wasn't worth the hassle? What if he kicked her out of the Guild? Where would she go?

"You can stand on your head for all I care, just talk."

"Here," Riley said, dragging a chair over for her. Katia sank into it. To her surprise, the master brought another over and sat nearby, as if to lend her support.

So many words not to say.

"My brother was attacked by a demon. He and his buddies thought it'd be great to call one up; to see what happened. It actually worked."

The two masters traded looks.

"Go on," Harper said.

"He's sixteen now. He's in a coma. The doctors aren't sure if he'll ever wake up." She swallowed, weighing her words. "I was an apprentice when it happened. My parents demanded I quit, but I wanted to . . . make those bastards pay. I trained with the Lawrence Demon Trappers Guild and my master was a good man."

"Was?"

"Master Griffin died in a car accident a week before I took my journeyman's exam. I barely passed."

"They should have postponed it, given you time to deal with his death," Riley said. She'd leaned back in her chair, arms folded over her chest, frowning now.

"Yeah, well, the master I ended up didn't want me. Master Kelly wasn't happy that I knew things other people didn't."

"Like what sorta things?" Harper demanded.

Riley jumped in. "When Katia arrived, I was talking to Ori at the coffee shop. She knew he was an angel just by looking at him."

"Oh great, another one," he muttered, shaking his head.

"What?" Katia said, not understanding.

"Anything else? Your soul still your own?" he asked.

"Yes, it's still mine."

"We'll test you anyway." Harper leaned back and abruptly shifted directions. "You have enough money to hold you until next payday?"

She had to be honest. "Ah, no. I have about five bucks. I haven't been paid in the last few weeks."

Riley muttered under her breath as she headed toward a computer in the corner of the room. "Your ID number?"

Katia rattled it off and watched the master access the National Guild's database and her account. There was silence as Riley skimmed the recent history of her trapping runs, payments due and paid. A low whisper of Hellspeak swear words colored the air. In any other situation that would have been impressive.

"How bad?" Harper asked, without turning around.

"Bad. She was paid regularly until she passed her journeyman's exam, probably because her first master was on the level. After that she's getting only a third of what's owed her."

"What?" Katia blurted. "No, Master Kelly said it took time for the payments to go through once I was a journeyman."

"That's bullshit," Harper said, thumping his fist in the middle of his desk, startling her. "The demon traffickers would have paid for each fiend when they were surrendered, and a portion of that money should have gone to you, *weekly*."

"Damn it," Katia muttered. She'd been starving, and couch surfing for nothing, because her parents refused to let her come home as long as she was a trapper. Worse, none of the other trappers had told her she was being screwed over, probably because they feared Kelly.

A printer kicked off somewhere in the room, and when it

was done Riley retrieved the printout and placed it in front of the master. "You want me to call them?"

"No, I'll deal with this," Harper said, his eyes like flint.

"How . . . much?" Katia stammered.

"At least two thousand dollars, probably more," Riley replied. "Since it'll take time to get this straightened out, you'll need a place to stay. I'd offer you crash space, but we just don't have it now that Beck has to have an office at home."

"Stewart's?" Harper suggested.

"That was my thought. I'll check with him," she replied, and headed for the kitchen.

Katia tried to button her cuff, but her fingers were shaking too much. She gave up. Two thousand bucks was a fortune when you had nothing. She'd been there when the traffickers paid for the fiends, but just accepted Kelly's word that it took time for her to get paid. Looking back, she'd been an idiot.

"I'm not a fan of weird shit, Breman," the master said, his eyes meeting hers.

"If you don't want me here, just tell me. I'll figure out how to get back to—"

"I'm not fond of martyrs, either. Blackthorne," he tilted his head in the direction Riley had gone, "showed me that sometimes weird gets the job done." He leaned forward on the desk again. "This ain't Kansas, Breman. You had demons there, but Hell plays big league ball here. The Prince believes this town is his, and we're not going to let that happen." He leaned back again. "Listen to Blackthorne, learn from her, and you might still be here in a couple weeks."

Master Harper ignored her from that point on, reading through the documents on his desk, accompanied by the occasional 'F' word.

"What the hell are they doing?" he grumbled. He shuffled more papers. "Did you get a travel allowance?"

"Yes."

"How much?"

"Twenty bucks and a paid bus ticket."

He stared at her. "That's it?"

"My master said that's all I was entitled to." Now she felt like an idiot. Why hadn't she done more research?

Because it wouldn't have mattered.

"Blackthorne!" Harper shouted.

Riley ducked her head out the kitchen door. "You bellowed, Fearless Leader?" she said.

Katia swore she saw the hint of a smile in the old master's eyes. It quickly vanished.

"Those Kansas assholes screwed this kid over big time. I need you to audit her runs and see how much they pocketed. Once you get that done, type it up into some neat little report, the kind the pencil necks at National love." Harper's expression looked downright gleeful now. "Then I'm calling Kansas. I haven't reamed anyone in a day or two. Way past time."

At Katia's stunned expression, Riley winked. "Told you. Come on in here and let's get the Holy Water check out of the way."

To her relief, the liquid felt cool against her palm, but did nothing else.

"Just as you said, your soul doesn't have Hell's brand on it. Always good news," the master replied. "I have some money for you, and a place for you to stay for the time being."

"At the Stewart guy's place?"

"Yup. And no, he's not creepy, either," Riley said. "I stayed with him after my dad died. You'll be fine there."

After the master gave her an envelope of cash, a half dozen power bars and offered her a drink from the refrigerator—Katia chose a soda—they were back in the car, pulling out of the parking lot.

"How much money did you give me?" Katia asked, thinking it would be rude to count it in front of her.

"Two hundred dollars. Figured that will get you started. Once we have a full audit, you'll get the rest."

Two hundred dollars? It was like winning the lottery.

"Master Harper will really call the Lawrence Guild?"

"He'll do more than call. When he gets done your former asshat of a master will be going to the closest burn center for the scorch marks. Harper hates people like that. Then he'll call National and my nice, neat report will back up everything he's going to tell them. Screwing a trapper out of their earnings and stiffing you for travel expenses is a big no-no. It'll go nuclear from that point on."

Katia stared at nothing for a time, then finally whispered, "Wow."

"Yeah, wow. In case you haven't noticed, we do things differently here. So . . . welcome to Atlanta, Journeyman Breman. It sure isn't going to be boring."

If the last hour or so was any indication, it was going to be unreal.

FOUR

Master Blackthorne's plan to introduce her to the exorcist had hit a snag: As they were trying to find a parking place, Riley had been called to a trapping gone wrong. The *injured trapper* kind of wrong. After pointing her toward the church, the master had driven off at top speed. Despite her worry for the unnamed trapper, once again Katia was on her own in a city she didn't know. At least this time she had Riley's phone number and some money.

After waiting for a break in the traffic, she rolled her suitcase across the street. Built of red brick, the church in front of her was curiously asymmetrical with a taller tower to the left than the one on the right. Master Blackthorne had said it had been built after the Civil War, in the late 1860s, and that the homeless frequently hung out on the church steps to avoid the Hellspawn downtown. Katia couldn't imagine a city so big it had one area known as Demon Central. Her hometown certainly didn't rate that kind of attention from Lucifer and his servants.

She made her way up one flight of steps to a landing and settled on the worn concrete, then tucked her suitcase next to her, uneasy. Master Blackthorne had said she'd contact this Simon guy so there wasn't much else she could do but wait and try not to fall asleep. That was going to be the hardest part.

Across the street from her, a massive glass and stone building dominated the entire block, the windows reflecting the church's spires like a mirror. Three police cars were parked in front of it, so Katia guessed it might be the courthouse, or maybe a jail. She'd was just about to dig out her phone to check the time when she heard a series of barks, followed by a wet nose to her hand.

"Hi, you!" she said, beaming at the collie who sat in front of her now. Black and white fur mixed with a bit of cinnamon brown, the dog's equally brown eyes were eager and happy, its tail moving so fast she could barely see it.

Katia knew this dog, and its "owner."

"You get around, don't you?" she asked the figure who stood a few steps from her. A nod returned.

To anyone else, this was a homeless guy in ragged clothes with a weathered face that spoke of years of deprivation and disappointment. Katia saw all that, but there was more—the white glow that hovered around him. He'd been at the bus station when she'd arrived early this morning and had given her directions on how to catch a city bus downtown. At first, that white aura hadn't been visible, not until Katia had wished him well and placed a very precious dollar bill in his hand. Even if she was broke, and didn't know when her next meal would be, she had more than him.

The instant she'd wished the man well, the Light had poured from him, nearly blinding her. She'd been so shocked, she'd just stared in wonder. Finally, Katia'd given him a big smile in return.

How many people walk right by him without knowing he's an angel?

"A very large number," was the reply. His hair was brown, long, curly, and looked like it hadn't been washed recently. It was his brilliant blue eyes that held her attention.

He looked up at the church, then back at her. "You're here for the exorcist."

"Yeah. He's okay, right?" she asked. Master Blackthorne had said he was, but trust wasn't something she gave easily.

"He's very okay, but he needs your help," was the solemn reply. "He's facing an unholy challenge."

"I hope I can help."

"That is why you are here."

That made her uncomfortable, so when a weird question popped into her brain, she asked, "What do you do with the money you collect?"

"I give it to those who are in need," the angel replied.

Katia reached into her trapping bag, found the small wallet inside and removed two ten-dollar bills, part of the cash she'd received from Master Blackthorne.

"I have more money now. Please give this to anyone who needs it."

The angel nodded, took the bills and tucked them into a pocket. "You see more than most, Katia Allyson Breman. Be of the Light. Trust it, and trust yourself, for you, too, will be mightily challenged this day."

After that pronouncement, the Divine headed up the stairs, the collie in tow. He sat near the entrance, the dog curling up at his feet, just another homeless soul in this huge metropolis.

Did he follow me here on purpose?

Katia certainly wasn't going to ask that question, so while she waited, she unwrapped one of the power bars and ate her second breakfast of the day.

†*‡*†

Crossing himself, Simon remained seated as the other parishioners filed out. The interior of the old building was cooler than he'd expected, and the light seemed to strike exactly on the ornate white altar. He looked up, seeking the paintings on the ceiling, then looked back down at his hands. His rosary hung from the right one, a gift from Father Rosetti when he'd graduated from the exorcism course. He rubbed his fingers over the wooden beads, remembering how proud he'd been that day. How he'd felt he'd been called to this job. He still did.

This wasn't his parent's church, and he appreciated the anonymity. No family members watching his every move. Simon regularly attended Mass, seeking solace, but there was none to be found today. He'd made a deal with a demon, skillfully maneuvered into that "bargain". It was ironic: He'd been personally invited to become an exorcist by Father Rosetti. He'd even had a private audience with the pope, and yet he'd fallen for Hell's trickery, once again.

I'm a fool. If he'd expected a heavenly voice to dispute that, he'd have been disappointed. At least the time in this sacred space had allowed him to accept that he was willing to spend eternity in Hell as long as those boys were free.

That was what the demon was hoping for, the boys were just bait, with Simon the ultimate prize. Someone in the Pit, maybe even the Prince, had put a price tag on his head. In some ways that pleased him, because it meant that what he was doing here in Atlanta had meaning. That would all end if the fiend won.

As he reached the front doors, he turned on his phone and it instantly buzzed with a voicemail from Riley.

> *Hi, Simon. There's a trapper waiting for you outside the church. Katia Breman is a journeyman from Kansas. She just arrived here this morning. Ori insists she's been sent to Atlanta for a reason. We can't help you with the demon, but he thinks she can. Sorry I couldn't be there to introduce you. Journeyman Kilburn got jumped by a Three and I'm headed to the hospital to see how bad he's hurt.*

Riley added some personal details about the trapper, then repeated that he should trust Ori's instincts. With a sigh, Simon clipped the phone back into the holder at his waist. Exiting the church, he paused on the front steps. Horns blared on the street as people headed to and from work. A few of the older parishioners greeted him, having seen him off and on, then went their own way.

A man sat near one of the doors, his expression neutral as if life had nothing more to offer him than living rough. Simon hadn't seen him here before. The dog at his side looked up and bounced its tail on the concrete step.

Simon placed money in the battered paper cup in front of them. "May God Bless you."

"Thank you." The man's bright blue eyes seemed out of

place with the grubby clothes.

"You're welcome. What's your dog's name?"

"Elijah," he replied.

"Named after the prophet?" A nod returned as the collie banged its tail faster now.

"He is a good companion," the man replied. "We should all have trustworthy companions on our journey through life."

That was the truth.

"Are you new in town?" Simon asked. Another nod returned. "Then if someone hasn't already told you, if you're not staying in a shelter, it's best to be on church property or in a cemetery at night. Someplace that is holy ground. We have a lot of demons here and they can't hurt you that way."

"Thank you for your warning."

"May God keep you safe," Simon added.

"May the Light guide you, as well," the man replied. It felt like a blessing.

With a faint smile, Simon headed down the stairs. Out of the corner of his eye he saw another figure to his left. When she turned and looked up at him, so much was written on that face—sadness, pain, worry.

Another lost soul.

"Are you Simon Adler?" the young woman asked, voice rough as if she was getting over a cold. Her black hair clung to her forehead in the heat. It was cut shorter on one side, a little longer on the other. A trapping bag sat at her feet next to a suitcase.

"I'm Simon. Are you Katia Breman?"

"Yes. Master Blackthorne said she left you a message about me. She had to go check on an injured trapper."

Ori knew exactly what Simon faced, and so did Riley. Had Heaven sent someone to help him, or was that just wishful thinking?

"I got her message. Did she tell you what I'm facing?" he asked, eyeing the young woman.

"Yes."

"That doesn't frighten you?" She shook her head. "It should. I don't need someone who is suicidal."

"I don't see you have much choice," was the curt reply.

That was brutally to the point. "Riley said you just arrived this morning."

"Yeah. I'm from Lawrence, Kansas. I was a problem child for the Guild there so they sent me here."

He couldn't hold back the laugh, rude though it was. "We're all problem children here, so you'll fit right in."

"Master Blackthorne said that after we talked, if you had time, she hoped you could take me to some grand master's house. He has a room for me. She said the guy is Scottish and that he's cool."

"That would be Grand Master Stewart, and he *is* cool. You'll be fine there."

Simon's phone buzzed again. Checking it, he sighed in relief at the text message. "The trapper who was hurt is going to be okay. Thank God," he said, then looked up to see the journeyman watching him closely. "Riley wanted us to know," he added.

"She was really worried. She felt bad leaving me here on my own, but that was okay. It worked out, and I got to pet the dog again."

Again? He decided not to ask about that as they started down the stairs. When he offered to take her suitcase, she shook her head.

"Katia. That's a different first name," he said.

"I was named after my grandmother. She was amazing."

Which suggested that others in Katia Breman's life had not been.

She frowned now. "You *really* wagered your soul with a demon?"

Simon winced. "I didn't intend that to happen, but the fiend was smarter than me. Now I have to make sure those kids get back home safe."

She thought on that. "Us."

"Pardon?"

"It's up to *us* to get those kids back home safe," she said, her voice stronger now.

There was steel in those words. Perhaps the Fallen was right and Katia Breman was the ally he so desperately needed.

I'll know soon enough.

†✷‡✷†

Ori's fingers tightened around the demon's neck as it flailed in vain. He'd found the fiend stalking an oblivious college student who'd had his head stuck in his phone as he texted his way to an early grave. Intent on its prey, the Grade Four demon had been equally oblivious until Ori had grabbed onto it and hauled it down a nearby alley.

"Answer me, Hellspawn!" he ordered.

"Azagar! It's Azagar!"

Now he had the name of the fiend who'd taken advantage of the exorcist's humanity, and that name rang a faint bell. He knew many of the stronger fiends in Lucifer's kingdom, but not all of them. Recently his informants had mentioned this Azagar who had been stirring up trouble down in the Pit.

"Does it have a demi-lord?"

The fiend flailed more frantically now. "I say no more or they will kill me."

"They won't get the chance," Ori said, scowling.

The Hellspawn's body vanished in a swirl of still smoldering ashes, destroyed by Ori's blade. A second later he felt the presence of another Divine, followed by the soft rustle of wings. He turned to study the newcomer, the sword still burning in his hand. For a moment he'd thought it might be one of Lucifer's executioners—but this one was from the Upper Realm.

It was a female, tall, covered in a stark white robe. Her hair was as strikingly blonde as the exorcist's, and it spiraled down in curls to well below her shoulders. The eyes were a deep crystal blue, and her wings were pure white.

"Ori the Fallen," she said, her voice lower and deeper than he'd expected.

"Obviously," he replied, letting his sword vanish. Until he knew her purpose there was no reason to antagonize her with a weapon. Words were another matter.

She frowned at him. "You are well shielded." Meaning she couldn't read his thoughts.

It went both ways, as her mind was as closed as his. "Some reason you're lurking in a dirty alley?"

"Divines do not lurk. At least *I* don't," she snapped.

"Nonsense. You *are* in an alley in the heart of what the mortals call Demon Central."

"I am here to observe you."

"Why? I have nothing to do with your realm."

"You don't, but you do. I know that makes little sense, but that's how it was explained to me," the angel replied. "Our Creator is why you're no longer on top of that tomb trapped inside a gargoyle. A fitting place for you, if it was my choice, but then I'm not in charge of those punishments."

Their Creator had bigger things to worry about than one Fallen angel, which meant someone else had sent her. Who had he annoyed recently? Hell, of course, but this one was from the other sphere. Of those in Heaven who despised him a single name always rose to the top.

"Michael sent you," he said.

"Why would you think the Archangel would bother with one such as you? Why would he care?"

"Because I refuse to bow to him. We have always disagreed about the mortals, which he dislikes because our Creator favors them over us."

"That doesn't bother you?" she asked. "The mortals, that is."

"At one time it did," he said. It had been one of the reasons he'd fled Heaven with the Prince. "Now it doesn't."

Now he knew what strength they held in their fragile bodies, the hopes they held deep in their hearts. The sacrifices they would make to save the world. How they could be incredibly full of love and then equally full of hate. He believed them to be the most complex of the Creator's designs. That thought alone would be considered sacrilege by the Archangel, and many of the other Divines.

"The mortals serve a purpose," Ori continued, "and though I don't know what that is, I trust it will eventually make sense. Michael would cast them aside because they insist on being themselves. What he cannot understand, he either subjugates, or destroys."

There was silence on the other side as the Divine thought that through. Then she shook her head as if to clear it. "I see now why the Adversary found you of value. You spin lies like a web weaver, Fallen."

"I speak the truth, which is why Michael wants my head separated from my body. Is that why he sent you? Are you to be my executioner?"

"No! I was told to observe and report your activities. That is all."

Ori could live with that, at least for the short term. It was curious that the Prince had sent his demon to tempt Simon Adler and now Michael the Archangel had ordered this Divine to follow Ori's every move. The stakes were higher than even he had imagined.

"Your name?" he asked.

"Serrah."

"Well then, Serrah the Observer, do try to keep up."

Ori promptly vanished. If he'd stayed a moment longer, he would have heard her tortured sigh, followed by an un-angelic curse.

FIVE

As the exorcist walked her to his car, Katia held her silence, taking that time to regroup. Her head still spun with all that had happened since she'd arrived at the bus station. As instructed, she'd called the number the National Guild had given her and someone named Jackson answered. He'd been surprisingly polite even though in the middle of a trapping run and had sent her to the coffee shop. With angelic help she'd found the right bus to take her downtown. Then she'd met *the* Riley Blackthorne.

The rumors within the Lawrence Guild claimed there was a lot that hadn't been reported in the news media. Despite all that, the online videos she'd watched proved that Riley Blackthorne was seriously badass. Nothing about her journey from apprentice to master had been easy, a trapper who had killed *three* Archfiends on her own. Meeting her should have been a total fangirl moment, but Katia'd been too tired and worried to react. Now it was all hitting home.

According to her former master, Blackthorne had been given credit for other trappers' efforts because Atlanta had no idea how to control her. When Katia had argued with him about that—there were those YouTube® videos after all—he'd decided it was time to ship her off to Georgia's capitol. A phone call to the national headquarters had set it all in motion. She'd bet Kelly told the Guild she wanted to make the move, not that he was forcing her to do so.

"You'll fit in fine with those Southern crazies," he'd said. "They'll just love you."

Katia didn't need love, she needed to trap demons. Nothing

else mattered—not even family, at least the few who still spoke to her after her brother's attack. Most still blamed her for his injuries. Now she was stuck with some guy named Simon who looked like he'd escaped from the 1950s with his white shirt, black slacks and that wooden cross. Could it get any weirder?

Once in the car, they immediately rolled down the windows to let the heat escape.

"Is it this hot in Kansas?" he asked, wincing as he snapped the metal seatbelt buckle into place, then blew on his fingers to cool them.

"Yeah. It's humid back home, but this is ridiculous. How do you stand this?" she asked as beads of sweat rolled down her face.

"You don't."

Once the car was moving, he rolled up the windows and turned on the air conditioning. Katia repositioned the vents on her side to aim directly at her, though at present it felt like a blow torch.

"How long have you been trapping?" he asked.

"A little over a year."

"Did you just become a journeyman?"

"Yeah, I passed the exam in February."

"Why'd you decide to become a trapper?" he asked.

This more personal question struck a nerve. "Why'd you become an exorcist?" she shot back.

He gave her a quick look, then turned a corner onto a busy four-lane street. "Sorry, I was just curious."

She noted he didn't answer her question. Increasingly chilly air poured out of the vents. Katia wanted to unbutton her shirt and pull it off, letting that air hit the sleeveless tee beneath, but then he'd see the scars. It'd been hard enough to reveal some of those to the masters.

She turned her attention to the city teeming with people. No matter where she looked there seemed to be no end to the skyscrapers. It wasn't that Lawrence didn't have their own, but Atlanta's seemed different.

As they passed a park, something caught her notice, something small and oddly shaped. She blinked, then turned to see exactly what it was, but there was nothing there. "Bus lag," she muttered, but luckily her driver didn't hear her.

Simon finally spoke a few minutes later. "I asked about why you became a trapper because I'm a journeyman, too."

What would make him change jobs? Katia wanted to ask, but then he'd expect her to talk about her life and that was a no-go.

The next lengthy, and increasingly awkward silence ended when her chauffeur pulled the car into a long driveway. The house in front of them was one of those stately Victorian mansions, done up in various shades of blue, with all those fiddly things they liked to put on those old places. This one even had a turret.

Her hometown had a few of these houses, and she remembered visiting one with her mom when she was a little kid. The high ceilings had seemed miles away when she was six. To her mother's horror, the walnut bannister had proved to be a fantastic slide when Katia had zipped down it from the second to the first floor. Luckily, she hadn't broken anything.

"Man, that's a big place," she said.

"It even has a ballroom. Riley had her wedding reception here," Simon announced as a genuine smile appeared. "It was a wonderful day."

Katia looked over at him. "She married a grand master, right?" When he nodded, she added, "I've heard about them, the grand masters, but I've never met one."

"You're about to. You'll like Grand Master Stewart. Everyone does. Well, unless you've gotten on his bad side then he'll put the fear of God in you. Come on, I'll introduce you."

Katia got out of the car, taking her trapping bag and her lone piece of luggage with her. "Why did Master Blackthorne send me here? Why not one of the bolt holes?"

That's how her last master would have handled it—stuck the newcomer in some sanctified place so the demons couldn't get to them until the trapper found a place to stay, however long that would take. He certainly wouldn't have gone to all this effort.

"You're here because Stewart is a good ally to have, his housekeeper is a great cook, and there will be fresh cookies on the counter in the kitchen."

The food especially sounded promising. "Always?"

"The cookies? No. Might be brownies or something else. The grand master has a sweet tooth." Simon paused. "Do you need some time to get settled?"

"Do we need to go somewhere?"

"Not until the demon starts sending fiends after me. I'm surprised it hasn't done that already."

He couldn't hide the worry, and she wasn't sure if that worry was about the Hellspawn, or her.

"I'd like a shower. I've been on a bus since forever and I feel yucky."

The front door opened even before they climbed the stairs and the man who met them was in his sixties, as best as Katia could guess. White hair, broad shoulders and a brace on one leg. His eyes seemed to sparkle in greeting.

"Grand Master Stewart," Simon said politely. "This is Journeyman Katia Breman."

"Lassie, welcome! Good ta see again, lad," the grand master replied, actually sounding like he meant it. "Come on in."

Stewart wasn't what she'd expected, but pretty much everything in Atlanta had been different from the moment she'd stepped off the bus. His big house was equally surprising. Pretty blue floral wallpaper greeted them in the entryway, along with dark oak wainscoting. To her right, a wooden staircase led to the next floor. The interior smelled of fresh lemons.

"Welcome ta my house," Stewart said, gesturing. He handed Katia a set of keys. "We have a room all ready for ya."

For a half a second, she was speechless, then her brain kicked in. "Thank you! Can I . . . I'd like to get a quick shower and change my clothes."

"Of course." Stewart pointed up the stairs. "Second floor, ta the right. It's the room with the yellow bedspread. There's a bathroom right next door. Should have all the towels and such ya need. When yer done, ya can find us in the kitchen. If ya get lost, just call out."

"Thank you, sir," she said and hustled up the stairs, her luggage in hand. Behind her, she heard Simon say he needed to talk about what was going on. Part of her wanted to be in on that conversation. Part of her knew it was best that she wasn't.

As they walked down the hall toward the kitchen, Stewart lowered his voice. "She's skittish. Riley said she has reason ta be."

"The Fallen claims she's here to help me."

"Ah, yes, the Fallen. Now there's one that's hard ta read. I will admit ta bein' damned pleased that Ori was given a second chance. From what I'm hearin' he's doin' serious damage ta the demon population, and not only in Atlanta. But he's choosy, doesn't kill every fiend he meets. I'm thinkin' he's bein' canny, buildin' himself a network of informers."

"For what purpose?" Simon asked.

As they entered the kitchen, the grand master grabbed onto a white ceramic plate loaded with lemon bars and set it on the table next to three glasses. Apparently, their host had told his housekeeper about his guests, but then Scottish hospitality was always first rate.

"That's what bothers me," the grand master continued. "Is Ori just stickin' it ta the Prince, or does he have some other plan? Like replacin' his old boss, maybe?"

"He says no."

"Ya asked him?" Stewart said, surprised.

"I did. I think it's a sore point for him."

"No doubt. It canna be an easy existence, neither part of Heaven nor Hell. Much like bein' a grand master, perhaps." He paused and then added, "There's a pitcher of iced tea in the refrigerator if ya'd be so good as ta fetch it."

Simon collected it and took a seat.

His host settled into a chair, moving his braced leg into a

more comfortable position. "So, what's goin' on with ya, lad?" the man asked after taking a long sip of the tea. Two lemon bars had already made the trip to his plate.

There were times Simon had kept certain subjects secret, but this wasn't one of them. He recounted precisely what had happened from the moment Ori had offered his assistance at the house, to the encounter with the demon, and then the so-called "bargain".

"Three boys, huh?" Stewart said, shaking his head. "Hell is uppin' the stakes on this one. That means they're either after ya, or the Fallen, and are usin' ya as bait."

"I think it's me. The demon went out of its way to ignore Ori."

"I wondered when this was gonna happen."

That confused him. "Why would they go to that kind of effort over me?"

The grand master shook his head. "Oh, lad, ya've no idea how much ya've annoyed them. Heaven made a special effort ta keep ya from dyin' from those demon wounds, so Hell retaliated by sendin' Sartael after ya. But ya didn't oblige them by losin' yer soul ta that Fallen. If that wasn't enough, ya became an exorcist, and a damned fine one at that. I'm not surprised yer on Hell's hit list."

"Well, at least I'm in good company," Simon muttered.

"That's for damned sure. Now what do ya wanna know because I'm thinkin'—"

The sound of steps in the hallway brought the conversation to a halt. Katia stopped at the kitchen door, her hair damp, clean clothes hanging from her thin frame. She looked at Simon first, then Stewart. Then her eyes came to rest on the plate in front of them.

"Ah, there ya are, lass. Come on, have some lemon bars. Mrs. Ayers is particularly good at those."

Katia joined them at the table, then took a bar and placed it carefully on a napkin as if it was a precious treasure.

Stewart raised an eyebrow. "Ya can't eat only one or I'll be havin' ta answer ta my housekeeper. She'll fret if there are any left when she gets back from the shoppin'."

Katia took two more bars.

"That's better." The grand master turned his attention back to Simon. "What are the parameters of this . . . deal ya have with the demon?"

"No help can come from Riley, Beck, any of the grand masters. Or the Fallen."

Stewart shifted his eyes to Katia. "But this lass isn't included in that list?" Simon shook his head. "Ya willin' ta watch his back?"

"If he watches mine," she said.

"As long as you don't do anything that compromises my exorcisms, I'll do my best to keep you safe," Simon replied.

She scrutinized him for a time, then nodded. It seemed that gesture had cost her in some way.

"Trust issues," Stewart said. "Always happens when ya first form a new partnership." He eyed Simon. "That demon will continue ta press ya, tryin' ta gain more concessions because it knows ya'll do anythin' ta keep those kids safe. Ya have power on yer side—it can't shake yer faith—but yer limited as ta what ya can do outside of an exorcism."

He looked over at Katia now. "This lass is yer wild card. She's not constrained by the bargain ya made, and that makes her a perfect weapon against the fiend. But at all times, ya must make sure she is safe from harm. Ya ken?"

Both of them nodded.

"Plan on Hell playin' dirty. Now's the time ta do the same, even though it will chafe yer sense of honor. It's not just three souls on the line. Remember that."

"I know," Simon murmured.

That was what frightened him more than dying at the hands of a demon. He knew what that felt like, and if Riley hadn't agreed to Heaven's bargain his family would be laying flowers on his grave every week, mourning for the loss of their son, their brother, their uncle.

This time he'd have to bend the Vatican's rules and it might cost him the job that eased his guilt and let him sleep at night. Now only those kids mattered. And his new partner, who Heaven, for whatever reason, had sent to help him. Simon's eyes met Katia's and hers immediately shifted away. There were mysteries there and he wasn't sure if he wanted to tackle them right now.

"What's yer next move?" Stewart asked.

"Not sure. The demon could be anywhere in the city and I have no idea where to find it." An admission that made his heart ache.

"It'll find ya, have no doubt. It thinks it's got ya on its leash and so it'll enjoy makin' ya sweat. They're hellishly good at that."

"It said it'd be sending other fiends my way. I . . . we have to deal with them and then we'll finally confront the big one."

He'd just finished his last bar when a guttural voice shouted in his head. He winced at the pain, and at the message.

"Are ya alright, lad?"

Simon nodded, trying to clear the roar in his head. "The demon said my first test begins now. It's told me where we need to be."

They all rose from the table.

"Let me know how it's goin'. I can't help directly, but there's a lot a grand master can do behind the scenes," Stewart offered.

"Will do."

Even as they headed for the front door, Simon couldn't help but notice that Katia had wrapped two more lemon bars in her napkin and stuck them in her trapping bag. There was a story there, and if they were lucky, he'd live long enough to hear it.

† * ‡ * †

Ori was known for being stealthy, a skill he'd needed to track and kill any Hellspawn his former master deemed a threat. Still, when he'd taunted Heaven's bloodhound about keeping up with him, he had meant just the opposite. The sooner he lost the other angel, the better.

Looking back, he should have realized something like this would happen after his unexpected resurrection from the dead. He knew that whole "Oh look, he's alive again!" surprise had infuriated the Prince because resurrection wasn't in Lucifer's skillset. Only their Creator had that power.

His former master had thought Ori out of the way forever, his essence, his very soul, trapped in that gargoyle on the top of the Blackthorne mausoleum. In the Prince's truly twisted fashion he'd made sure that statue faced the sunrise, because he knew that would torture the trapped soul within.

You could always count on Lucifer being a total bastard.

When Ori had found himself freed from his stone prison, naked, shaking, and furious at being alive again, he'd known that his Creator had returned him to the living for some purpose. It hadn't taken him long to figure it out: Heaven needed an executioner to kill a rogue angel, and who better than the Fallen who'd honed his deadly skills in the service of Hell?

Ori had always thought he'd die during his battle with The Destroyer, but for some reason he hadn't. He'd bet Heaven had thought the same, and now they had the problem of an unaligned Divine, one who had his own agenda. Because he'd be damned a second time before he joined up with either crew.

His demand for independence was why he now rated an Observer who was entirely too persistent. Only a few seconds after he appeared near what the mortals called Terminus Market, at the site where he'd once saved Riley Anora Blackthorne's life, his shadow appeared next to him. Ori eyed her, wondering how she was able to find him so easily. Of course, she was still clad in the same garment, her wings tucked up next to her body.

"Wearing a white robe here is not a good idea," he warned. "Especially not with your wings visible. The last angel who did that came to destroy the city. These mortals have long memories."

It took Serrah a moment to make the connection to The Destroyer. With a frown, the wings slowly melted away, as did the robe, leaving behind slacks, T-shirt and shoes. They were still stark white.

Ori rolled his eyes. "Can you be any more obvious?"

The angel scowled in response. "Can you?" she said, gesturing toward his solid black clothes.

"Let me help." He thought for a moment, and then with a swiping motion, lettering appeared on her T-shirt.

HEAVEN FOR CLIMATE
HELL FOR COMPANY

That earned him a deep frown. Apparently, she'd never heard of Mark Twain.

"That's the problem with the Upper Realm—you have no sense of humor," Ori muttered, then turned away. Neither had he until he'd spent time with the mortals.

"Why are we here?" she asked, still frowning.

"I'm trying to track a particular demon. He has tempted a righteous man and I want to ensure we do not lose the exorcist because of it."

"Simon Michael David Adler," she said, quietly.

Which told him she wasn't as clueless as she appeared.

"Are you here because of him as well?" he asked.

No reply.

"He did not intentionally make a bargain with the fiend, but Azagar will try to twist the situation to claim Simon's soul if he is not careful. I will not let that happen."

"You cannot interfere," the angel said.

Yes, it did appear this one knew a lot more than he'd thought.

"But you can."

"What? No, I dare not."

"Of course, you can. The fiend did not name you. In fact, I doubt Azagar even knows you are here in the city. That means you can help me keep Simon alive, and then he can save the three young mortals who are in the demon's claws."

"Why do you do this?"

"This?" he asked, puzzled.

"Track Hellspawn. You are Fallen."

"My mission is to do everything I can to ruin Lucifer's infernal plans." He glared at her. "This is personal now."

"All because he let you die?" Serrah asked.

"All because . . . " He hesitated, unable to admit the truth, even to himself. "It doesn't matter."

Ori heard the cry for help even before it had been vocalized. Swiveling, he looked into the distance, seeing the danger and knowing what it meant.

"Azagar has begun. Come, it's time to earn those wings of yours."

The two angels vanished at the same time.

SIX

After Simon had announced their destination was a daycare center, Katia's mind had conjured up bloody images of what they might find there. When she'd voiced her fears, he shook his head.

"It'll want me there before it hurts anyone."

To her relief, he'd been right. The Hellspawn was outside, near the playground, though that's where the good news ended. Just as they got out of the car, the demon, one of the ravenous Gastro-Fiends, trapped a group of tiny, terrified kids and a young woman against a tall fence. The only thing standing between them and a savage death was a young man, armed with a red plastic baseball bat. The mind-numbing terror on his face struck Katia like a body blow.

"That isn't the demon from this morning," Simon said. He clicked the remote to open the trunk. "Unless it's one of the higher fiends and it's mimicking a Three."

Katia concentrated on the Hellspawn, then shook her head. "No, I don't think that's the case. I can usually tell." Simon's eyebrow rose at this observation.

As the Three continued to howl, he grabbed his trapping bag, and one of the wire mesh bags they'd need to secure the fiend once it'd been trapped. The metal must have been hot as he held it by the leather straps at the top. He dropped it in front of the car as Katia joined him, her own trapping bag in hand.

"What's the plan?" she asked.

"Since I don't use chicken guts for my exorcisms, we'll need to distract this thing somehow." He handed her a Holy

Water sphere from his trapping bag. "I'll set a ward to keep the innocents safe. Can you buy me some time to get in place?"

"Sure. I'll play bait."

He gave her a quick frown. "Don't get hurt doing it, you hear me?"

His concern sounded genuine. "I'll be careful."

The playground was enclosed with a tall metal chain link fence designed to keep the children out of harm's way. Now it just hemmed them in with a monster who had no doubt clawed its way up the barrier and jumped inside.

Unless Katia did the same the only way in was through a gate. Careful not to spook the fiend, she moved to the entry. Once there, she dug for her folding knife, stuck it in her jeans pocket, then retrieved her steel pipe. If she could hit the fiend with the Holy Water sphere, it'd give Simon time to set the ward.

"I'm ready," he said from behind her. A quick glance showed the exorcist was armed with a pipe, as well. Something liquid glistened on his forehead.

The plan was immediately jeopardized by a numeric keypad, one strategically placed far above toddler height. Katia gave a test pull on the gate—no go. "Code! What's the code?" she shouted, hoping someone would help her. The result was the gate swinging open on its own accord.

"Thank you!" she called out, though she wasn't entirely sure who she was thanking. Stepping inside the enclosure, Katia moved away from a nearby picnic table, and then began to drag her steel pipe against the metal fence. As she'd hoped, the noise was loud, immediately gaining the fiend's attention. She'd seen Master Blackthorne use this tactic in a video, and it seemed to work now.

About four feet tall, this Three's fur was a mangy yellow and its stench fouled the air. It was an older one with the double rows of razor-sharp teeth. That meant it'd be faster and probably smarter.

"Hey, ugly. You know who I am?" she called out, continuing to make a racket with the pipe.

The fiend eyed her, and the drool increased at the corners of its mouth. "Foooood!" it cried.

"That's right." she said. "I'm nice and tasty. How's about you and I play?"

The Three took a step in her direction, then swung back toward the kids when one of them began to wail. The young man with the bat waved it back and forth, as if it were capable of stopping this killing machine. His companion stood in front of the kids, shielding them as best she could. Both would die unless Katia could get the demon to take the bait.

"Damn, damn, damn!" Katia jammed her pipe in the back of her jeans and then pulled the knife free. Popping the blade, she took a deep breath, sliced through the sleeve of her shirt, opening a slit on her left arm. Blood welled, running free. She wiped the knife on her jeans, collapsed it and then jammed it in her pocket as she waved her injured limb in the air.

"Smell that, demon? It's lunchtime! Come and get it!"

The fiend whirled back, its nose inhaling the enticing scent. Despite the crying child, her blood proved a stronger lure.

"Come on, you miserable bag of stench!" she called, shaking drops of blood from the wound.

"Chewwww your bones!" it shouted, and then charged straight toward her.

As the demon headed for Katia, Simon climbed over the fence behind the trapped children, his steel pipe tucked under an arm. Once he was on the ground, he sprinted in front of the captives. The guy with the bat was so startled by Simon's appearance, he swung at him. Fortunately, he missed.

"Get back with the kids!" Simon ordered. "Go!"

Even as he issued the order, he touched the Holy Water on his forehead, then bent down to touch the concrete, intoning a prayer as he raised a Holy Water ward, one larger than usual. To his relief, it immediately shimmered into existence around them, shielding not only the toddlers, but the two aides.

"What . . . what is that?" the woman called out.

"It's Holy Water. You're safe from the demon. Just stay inside the circle!"

Both adults nodded, then huddled with the kids as their frightened cries grew louder.

With a prayer on his lips, Simon carefully exited the circle, feeling the tug of its power as he did so. The moment he left the ward, he took off at a run toward the battling pair. The demon had already reached Katia, slashing at her, trying to get around the steel pipe to hook its claws into her skin and draw her to her death. Snarls filled the air as she ducked its wicked swipes and landed a few brutal blows of her own.

"Demon!" Simon shouted, raising his own pipe.

The thing whirled, belatedly realizing it had enemies on both sides now.

"Betrayer!" it bellowed in return, then slashed at him. Katia didn't hesitate, slamming her pipe into its skull from behind. As it tottered on its feet, Simon delivered the second blow, which spun the Three around and sent it into a heap on the ground.

Even as the thing rolled onto its back, Katia smashed a Holy Water sphere directly into its face. It flailed, then grew still, its chest rising and falling in jerks.

"Well done," a voice said.

Simon swung around to find Ori standing just beyond the fence. Next to him was a young woman clothed all in white.

"Great, another one," Katia muttered. At Simon's puzzled look, she pointed at Ori's companion. "That's an angel and she's way brighter than the other one, in case that matters."

How could she know that?

Katia eyed them. "Which of you opened the gate?"

Ori angled his head toward the other Divine. "I could not interfere."

The angel in white studied Katia now, almost as if she were weighing her mortal soul. Then her eyes went to Simon for the same assessment. Finally, her attention strayed to the children and the glowing circle. The gate swung open on its own again.

Then she joined the kids, walking right through the Holy Water barrier as if it didn't exist.

Kneeling in front of the children, the Divine held out her arms, murmuring something to them. One by one, they broke away from their guardians and ran to her. She encircled them, whispering quietly. The tears began to slow as little heads nodded at whatever she'd said to them.

"What is she doing?" Katia asked.

"Helping them forget the worst of this horror," Ori replied. "If not, they will have nightmares for years."

Nightmares.

Unbidden, memories returned: The screams of agony from that night at the Tabernacle when Simon had nearly died. The faces of the other trappers who had not survived. Ori's eyes met his now, as if he knew exactly what had paraded through his mind.

"Do you hate them as much as I do?" Simon asked quietly.

"Yes. And their master even more," was the solemn reply.

He nodded, then turned away, a hand going to his abdomen as if he could still feel those claws ripping into him, hear the ominous click of the fiend's fangs near his neck. Simon forced himself to look at the knot of toddlers. They'd stopped crying, their faces still wet with tears. A couple even had tentative smiles as the angel showed them a small blue bird where it rested on her palm. Where it'd come from, he had no idea, but their fear was slowly disappearing, one healing word after another.

"*This* is why you survived, Simon Michael David Adler, so the innocents would have someone to protect them," Ori said quietly. "Azagar cannot win this battle against you or much will be lost."

Azagar. That must be the Hellspawn who had trapped him in this nightmare. Now he had a name for his enemy.

"She is really good with them," he said, his eyes still on the angel and the children.

"Serrah is pure Light. Not like me."

Simon looked over at the Fallen. "You might not be pure

Light, but every time you help us, you shed more of your darkness."

Ori shook his head. "If only it was that easy."

Katia watched the female Divine, all white light and glowing wings. A glance at Simon told her he couldn't see any of that. Had he known the guy at the church was an angel? *Probably not.*

A quick glance down at the demon reminded her it wasn't smart to be distracted. She trotted back to the car and collected the wire mesh bag. Judging from the fiend's size there was going to be a lot of cramming involved, hopefully before the Holy Water wore off.

She'd just begun the process when there was the slam of car doors. Master Blackthorne and a thin, wiry man with a ponytail joined them.

"And we missed all the action." He didn't sound sad about that. As he approached her, he added, "You must be Journeyman Breman. I'm Master Jackson. We talked on the phone."

"Sir," she said politely.

He shook his head. "Oh, no, don't start that crap. I'm Jackson."

"Anyone hurt?" Riley asked. She spied the blood on Katia's arm. "Like you?"

"It's not from the Three so it doesn't need treated," Katia replied. She kept eyeing the demon and the bag. "We got a chunky one here. I'm going to need some help."

Jackson laughed. "Hold on. I got just the thing. Brand new. You're gonna love it." He took off at a jog back toward the parking lot.

As the angel rose from the children, the protective circle vanished. A moment later the side door to the daycare center opened and more staff rushed out. With cries of joy the kids were scooped up, hugged, kissed, then carried back inside. The Divine was speaking with the two aides now, and she could tell from their faces their own fears were beginning to ease.

Riley looked over at the Fallen. "Two of you now? Is there some special angel thing going on in town?"

"I have apparently rated an 'observer,'" Ori replied.

She smirked. "Lucky you."

His scowl said otherwise.

Jackson returned at that moment, carrying a piece of mesh. "Here you go—the latest in Grade Three Hellspawn containment. No stuffing or jamming required," he said, dropping the item at Katia's feet. "When we're done, I've got a First Aid kit for your arm."

"Thanks!"

There wasn't the tension she'd always felt between the trappers in Lawrence. If anything, these people acted as if they were friends. Good friends. Was this all an act for the newbie?

With some colorful running commentary, Jackson showed her how the piece of mesh worked. It was straightforward: Lay it on a flat surface, roll the demon onto it, then clip the two long sides together. The top and bottom portions flipped over, then snapped in place, securing the fiend completely.

"Those clips will hold?" she asked, dubious at something this easy.

"Have so far. They're enchanted by the witches so you have to know how to open them." He paused and tested all the connections anyway. "National sent us a few to give them a test run."

"This is sweet!" Katia said. "No more getting clawed when the thing wakes up before you've got them secured."

Jackson dragged the Three out the gate and into the parking lot, leaving it to lie in the sun. Which would do nothing for its epic stench.

Simon's stare remained locked on the demon as it began to stir in its mesh prison. He'd reacted instinctively, protecting the kids but not getting in her way. Like they'd been trapping together before.

"You okay?" she asked. Instead, he headed toward the daycare center entrance. *Apparently not.*

When she turned back toward the others, the two angels

were gone. Riley and Jackson were talking quietly to each other, glancing at her every now and then. The conversation ended when he waved her over. Sitting on top of the picnic table was the First Aid kit. Katia rolled up her sleeve, knowing he would see the other scars. The cut was about two inches long and still weeping blood.

Jackson carefully cleaned the wound, then applied a bandage.

"I wouldn't do that too often if I was you," he suggested. "We get enough scars from this job without adding our own. You know that as well as anyone."

"It just seemed the best way."

"It worked, that's for sure. Ori said you did exactly the right thing, and he's not known to hand out praise to anyone. Glad to have you onboard."

She blinked a few times. "My master in Kansas would disagree."

Jackson huffed. "Then your *former* master is a dumbshit. But then you already know that."

Laughter burst from Katia's lips, laughter she didn't even know she had in her. "You guys are the real deal, aren't you?"

"In all our very messy glory," Riley said. "Emphasis on the messy part."

"All I ever heard was rumors about you guys. And I watched all those videos."

Riley groaned. "Yeah, *those*. There are days I wish the internet hadn't been invented."

"Do you usually have angels just hanging around?"

The two masters traded looks.

"Off and on," Riley replied. "But certainly not one from Heaven tagging along with a Fallen. That's a new one."

"Any idea why that's happening?" Jackson asked as he shut the kit and snapped the lid closed.

"Since Ori's no longer working for Hell, I think that makes Heaven nervous. My guess is that the Angel in White is watching him so she can file a report with her boss. Or bosses. You never know what's going on upstairs," Riley said, pointing toward the blue sky. The other master nodded.

Simon had returned during this whole exchange. When he looked over at Katia, there was worry in his blue eyes.

"You okay?" he asked.

"I am." *Not so sure about you, though.*

"We can take the Three to Fireman Jack for you," Riley offered.

"That would be great. Thank you," Simon replied.

Fireman Jack? What kind of name was that?

Since Simon didn't look that inclined to chat at the moment, she filed that name away for later. After they collected their gear, they tucked everything away in his car. Katia noticed something stuck under one of the windshield wipers and a tug revealed a glossy postcard. Once inside the vehicle, she skimmed the info, then read it again in case she'd gotten it wrong.

> **Are you a fan of the Demon Trappers?**
> **The Demon Hunters?**
> **Or are you rooting for the Other Side?**
>
> *You'll find them all at Atlanta's first annual TrapperCon*
>
> **May 25-26th, 2019**
> **Spirit of Atlanta Hotel & Convention Center**
> **Visit our Website for more Details!**
> **www.TrapperCon.com**

This thing must be a big deal because Blaze, Jess Storm and Raphael Montoya, the leads from the hit TV show *Demonland*, were going to be there. They'd even be signing autographs.

Only in Atlanta. Katia smirked as she stashed the postcard inside her trapping bag. Except, now that she checked, only their car had one of these ads. Maybe Master Blackthorne had left it, just to mess with them. That had to be it.

As they drove away, it was clear her companion wasn't going to talk her to death, so she let that silence ride. Something was bothering him, and she hoped it had nothing to do with her.

It was a long time before Simon spoke. "Every fiend from

now until midnight has to be stopped for those kids to be freed."

It sounded like he was talking things through, trying to get a handle on the situation.

"If I don't do everything right, those kids are gone. Eternity in Hell," he continued.

"Then we do what we have to. If it's a trapping, we do it together. If it's an exorcism, I'll back you up. Between us, we're not going to give in to these monsters."

He looked over at her now, then delivered a thin smile. "You hungry?"

"Always," she said, caught off guard with his abrupt change of subject.

"My mom and my sisters are convinced I'm going to starve to death, so I have a refrigerator full of food. How's about we go to my place, eat some lasagna, and work out some sort of strategy?"

That sounded good. What she really needed was some sleep. Even a quick nap would help. It'd been impossible on the bus. She thought back to the creeper sitting next to her with his roaming hands. It'd taken her nearly breaking one of his fingers for him to leave her alone. When he'd switched seats, a chatty grandmother of seven delightful grandkids got on the bus in Des Moines and insisted on educating Katia about her precious darlings. The lengthy lecture had included cell phone images *and* videos for *every one of them.* It'd taken all of Katia's patience just to be polite. Somewhere in Heaven her own grandmother would be immensely proud.

"I'd like a nap. Is that possible?"

"You got it. Food, nap, strategy," Simon replied, then focused on his driving.

Her caution kicked in, again. She barely knew this guy and he was taking her to his house. She'd just have to trust that Master Blackthorne was right about him. If not, this would be the shortest job she'd ever had.

SEVEN

Serrah had journeyed to this place because Oakland Cemetery had its own Divine. From what she'd heard, Rahmiel had been sent here because she'd defied the Archangel Michael. Few dared make that transgression. Perhaps Rahmiel might know more about the feud between the Archangel and Ori the Fallen. At this point any information would be of value.

Serrah never understood the mortal need for graveyards for they housed the bodies of the dead even though the spirits of the deceased had long fled this realm. Perhaps it was because they gave grieving survivors a location to visit, a chance to place tokens of their affection on the graves of their loved ones. And yet, it still seemed odd when your lifespan encompassed millennia.

Most cemeteries were simple, while others were more elaborate. The one Serrah had come to was much the latter. Here, along with old gravestones, solid stone buildings housed the mortal remains, some from centuries before. There were tall statues and stone-lined pathways, fountains, and so many flowers. Which only increased her confusion. Perhaps this wasn't merely a place for bones, though it was set in the shadow of the mortals' great city.

As Serrah stood under one of the massive trees, the smell of its large white flowers scented the air. She inhaled deeply, savoring the perfume. It was almost . . . heavenly. Here the noise of the city was muted, and the vegetation bloomed with an exuberance she'd not expected. Even the heat didn't seem as oppressive as she walked along a tree-shaded path, not knowing exactly where she was headed.

A bell tinkled behind her, then a cyclist offered up a wave as he rode past. Without thinking, she returned the wave, then felt embarrassed. That was a mortal gesture, not one for Divines.

Serrah'd been warned that the longer you were among them, the more you became like them. That was often said in derision, but she could see the truth in it. Mortals had a certain way about them that was both charming, and naïve. The Fallen was at home here, as if he were more mortal than angelic, but then to successfully steal their souls he would have had to appear that way. From what she'd heard, Ori had been *very* successful. A curious mix of seducer and executioner, one of the Prince's most prized warriors. At least until he fell afoul of The Adversary.

Serrah's unhurried walk brought her to one of the mausoleums, as the mortals called them. The name on the front of the structure said her instincts had been correct as this was the final resting place of the bones of Riley Anora Blackthorne's ancestors. Serrah had heard the tale of Paul Arthur Blackthorne, how he'd lost his soul, then regained it. A tale that had begun, and ended, with Ori the Fallen.

She sent her gaze to the top of the building, then to the stone creatures at the four corners of the roof. *Gargoyles.* What would it have been like to roost up there, encased in stone, watching the sun rise each morning knowing you would never be part of this world again? Such had been the fate of the Fallen until he'd been brought back to life by their Creator.

"It was just petty revenge," a voice said.

The Divine who walked up the path toward her looked like a mortal, clad in the type of clothes the old might wear. Yet, there was power in this one, more than Serrah would have expected.

"Are you Rahmiel, she who guards this cemetery?

"I am," the angel answered. "The mortals call me Martha, though. You are Serrah, the one watching over the Fallen."

"How did you know that?"

"I hear things," was the reply. "I also know that Michael can be very single minded."

Such candor was unexpected, though perhaps this was common for her.

"It is," was the other angel's response, because once again she'd heard Serrah's thoughts as clearly as if she'd spoken them.

If that was the case . . . "Do you trust the Fallen?" Serrah asked.

The other Divine frowned as she used her shoe to nudge a dried leaf off the path that led to the mausoleum. "That is not a question that can be answered with a simple 'yes' or 'no'. We are a sum of our experiences. The Fallen has been in Heaven, then in Hell. He has seen the best and worst of both."

"There is *good* in Hell?" Serrah asked, confused.

"Not to hear some tell it. However, even evil things can have a small measure of good in them, though I will grant you there is little of the Light in the Pit or in those who dwell there."

"But do you trust him? Ori, that is."

There was further deep thought. "I have watched his journey from the moment he came to this city. How he claimed souls, how he came to hate his master. I watched as he gave his life to save others. I felt his agony at every sunrise when he was trapped here, first as a statue, then as a gargoyle. I felt his fear for Riley Anora Blackthorne." She paused. "Ori never said it, but I know he felt that Blackthorne's Daughter was his Light until he could reclaim his own."

"You think he has done so?"

A shrug returned. "We are all judged by our deeds, both mortal and Divine. We can speak of many things, and some may believe our words. It is our actions that reveal what dwells in our hearts."

Rahmiel walked to the steps that led to the mausoleum and took a seat.

"Ori the Fallen has undertaken a journey that few would survive. Now he fights for those who cannot save themselves. Is he 'for real', as the mortals would say? I do not know. What I do know is that he could remain alive, and free, after he slew The Destroyer." Rahmiel gave her a long look. "Who made that decision? I can tell you it was not the Archangel."

Serrah pondered on that. "What of you? How did you come to be in this place?"

Her fellow Divine grinned now. "I spoke the truth to one who did not want to hear it."

Michael. "Do you miss our realm?"

Rahmiel arched an eyebrow, a truly human gesture. "I miss others of my kind, but I am at my best here. Watching over this place is a task I love, one that shows reverence for the dead and concern for the living, both mortal and Divine."

Serrah turned away for a time, letting her thoughts roam even as her eyes did the same. Bright flowers, clean paths, birds on the wing. *Peace. So much peace here.*

"How do I walk this path between the Fallen and the Archangel and not be sent somewhere . . . less peaceful?"

"Truth is the only path worth walking," Rahmiel replied. "If you fail to cherish and protect it, you will fail to protect what truly matters. It took me a long time to learn that lesson. I pray *your* lesson will be easier."

After giving her a final sympathetic look, the angel vanished.

Serrah sighed. She had come here to find answers, but now she had even more questions. A mistake would cost her dearly, cost the mortals even more. That was the problem with the truth—not everyone wanted to hear it.

†✶‡✶†

Simon parked in the driveway of an older white house nestled in a quiet neighborhood. The lawn of the one-story residence was mowed, the windows clean. Still, it lacked any extra touches, like a bed of flowers around the large oak tree that sat in front, or a few comfortable chairs on the porch.

"This was my great uncle's house," Simon explained. "He'd already updated the kitchen, put in new windows and a new roof, so there wasn't much for me to do. He wanted to move to Phoenix, so he gave me a chance to buy it before it was listed with a realtor."

"Must be cool living in your own place."

"It is. Since I'm an exorcist, if I live in an apartment complex it puts others at risk from Hellspawn. Here it's just me." He smiled at the house like it held special memories. "It's a 1921 Craftsman bungalow. They built them solid back then."

Still trying to grasp a house that was almost a hundred years old, Katia followed him up the walk and across the broad porch. Simon unlocked the emerald green front door and dealt with the alarm. As she stepped inside the first thing that hit her, besides the refreshing chill of the air conditioning, was the lack of any particular scent, like the house had been empty for some time. She gave another quick sniff and found no hint of a recently cooked meal.

The living room sat to the right of the front door, with a polished hardwood floor and the walls a pale green. Straight ahead was a dining room and then further on, through an archway, a modern kitchen with granite countertops. The other side of the living room seemed to be a storage place for packing boxes, both large and small. A quick count told Katia there were more than twenty of them, all neatly stacked along one wall.

The side of the room that was furnished had a tufted pale gray sofa, a darker gray recliner, a wood coffee table, but no rugs on the floor nor any art on the walls.

"I just moved in," Simon said, sounding apologetic as he placed his exorcism kit on the floor, then shut the door behind them. "Well, two months ago. I haven't had time to put anything away yet."

"Your family didn't help you?"

He immediately shook his head. "Don't want them to. My sisters act like I'm still a kid. At least the oldest one does."

Katia sensed this was a familial landmine. Rather than detonate it, she asked what she hoped was a safe question. "How many brothers and sisters do you have?"

"Seven. Three brothers, four sisters. I'm the middle one—number four out of eight. I love them all, but they can drive me nuts. How about you?"

Oh God, she'd done this to herself. "One sister, she's getting married in a few months. Leah works at my dad's landscaping firm. I tried that and got bored. And I have a younger brother. He's . . . Kevin's just sixteen."

"Are your parents good with you being a trapper?"

No. "Ah, you promised me food, right?"

"Will the lasagna be okay?" he asked, not acting surprised she'd dodged another of his questions.

"Sounds great." It really did. "How can I help?"

"The lasagna's in the refrigerator. Can you put it in the oven while I take a shower?"

Katia nodded, if nothing more than to keep him from asking anything more about her family. After Simon headed down a hallway toward what she guessed was his bedroom, she heard a series of doors open and then close. Finally, there was the sound of running water.

On her way to the kitchen, she noted the round dining room table with only four chairs. What did he do if all his family came for a meal?

The kitchen was lovely, and Katia took a moment to admire it. White cabinets, dark gray countertops, and new stainless-steel appliances. A small table sat in the corner, this one with only two chairs.

The exorcist had done well for himself.

After retrieving the lasagna from the refrigerator, she turned on the oven. Snooping through the mostly empty cupboards, she located a square glass baking pan and moved the lasagna out of its aluminum foil wrapper and into it. Now it was a matter of waiting for the oven to heat.

While she did, she couldn't resist taking another look around the house. It was a lovely space, but there was a bleakness here she hadn't expected. Simon was a positive person, but somehow his home did not reflect that. There were no magazines, no books except for a Bible on the coffee table. It had a bookmark in place, but she resisted the urge to see precisely which passage he'd been reading.

No television, no stereo, no family pictures.

And yet Simon Adler had lots of siblings, ones that kept him fed, and appeared to love him. Why was he so isolated? So alone?

She knew the answer all too well.

The same family that loved you, would also hurt you.

EIGHT

Simon didn't rush his shower, needing time to think through all that had happened so far. When he finally entered the kitchen, he found the table set for two. Standing in front of the oven, Katia poked an electronic thermometer in the center of the bubbling pan of lasagna. He didn't even know he had one of those, but then he didn't know a lot of things nowadays.

The plates, silverware and glasses on the table, the smell of the food, all that domesticity drove home just how much his job had consumed him. He wouldn't tell his guest, but this was the first time that table had been used for anything more than a bowl of cereal. The food his family sent over was either still frozen, or eaten as he sat on the sofa in the living room while staring at the blank walls.

Katia looked up at him and smiled. If he had to guess, she didn't do that often. "It just needs to sit a few minutes and it'll be ready. It smells great."

Simon pulled himself out of his dark thoughts. "My mom is a really good cook. I didn't get that gene."

"I did, but I don't get a chance to use it much."

He had the sense there was more she wanted to say, but instead she held back yet another part of her history. Was it so awful she couldn't speak of it, or was it because she didn't trust him?

Katia pointed him toward the table, mostly to get him out of her way as she opened drawers, closed them, then opened others until she found what she was looking for. He knew he should help her, but he honestly had no idea where anything was. His older sister, Deanna, had insisted on unpacking all those boxes. At the time he'd just let her, but now he wondered why.

A few minutes later he had a plate full of lasagna, a few slices of garlic bread, and a mound of steamed peas with a pat of butter on top. A glass of water sat next to his plate, as well as a folded paper towel for a napkin.

It smelled wonderful. He bowed his head and offered a prayer of gratitude. When he looked up, he found Katia's eyes on him, and he received another cautious smile.

"It's the best meal I've had in . . . awhile. Thank you," he said. "I had no idea I had any peas, or the bread for that matter."

"They were in the freezer. And thank you for all this. I've been living on nothing for so long that—"

He could tell the moment she'd realized she revealed another secret. Though he desperately wanted to eat, he set his fork aside. "Katia," he began.

Her eyes rose to his and he could almost see her pleading for him not to go there. He had no choice: Demons exploited weaknesses and though she wasn't an exorcist, she was working with one. That made her a valuable target.

"Tell me more about yourself."

She didn't reply, a forkful of lasagna vanishing into her mouth.

"You have a sister and a brother and—"

The now empty fork dropped to her plate with a clatter. Then she began to choke. Simon rose and slapped her on the back until she signaled she was okay.

He returned to his chair and began to eat, giving her time to recover. The peas were done just right and the lasagna reminded him of boisterous family meals. While he ate, his companion stared at her plate. He'd clearly touched a nerve, but if he didn't push this, now, one or both of them might die.

"You know Hellspawn exploit our secrets," he said quietly. "If there's something I need to know about you, about your family, tell me. I won't judge you."

Katia's eyes snapped up, fiery now. "Judge me? You?"

Simon held his breath—she was about to explode, and that might be the only way he'd find out what was hiding inside her head.

"You can't judge me!" she snapped. "You live like a hermit. You haven't even unpacked your boxes and you've been here two months. *Two months!*"

"Closer to two and a half," he admitted.

"That's even worse. It's like you don't really live here. You're just phoning it in."

"Not when it comes to the demons," he protested.

"Yeah, I got that. You're 150% all over those bastards. But what about the rest of your life? It's like you don't expect to last until the end of the week and so you're saving your family the hassle of packing up your stuff after the funeral."

That hit hard. "I've been too busy," he said, his temper growing.

"So busy you couldn't even buy your own food or put your stuff away in your new home?" She leaned forward now, arms on both sides of her plate. "You love this place, but why are you here? I mean, *really* here?"

"I have to live somewhere." The excuse sounded lame, and he knew it.

With an angry shake of her head, Katia scooped up her plate and fork and left him behind, muttering under her breath as she headed to the living room.

Simon stared at her empty chair, astonished at her outburst. Once his anger lessened, he carefully replayed what had just been said, then winced. Yes, he'd been busy, the need for exorcisms increasing each week. But . . .

Had he really believed he was going to survive this job? In all honesty, no. He'd always figured he was just one exorcism away from death. Katia had seen right through him. He *had* been phoning in his personal life, living in the shadows between each exorcism. Why else had he not bothered to unpack his stuff? Why else had he turned down going out with friends, spending time with his family? Why else hadn't he taken the sabbatical that Father Rosetti constantly recommended?

Instead he'd taken his guilt and honed it into a weapon, not for wielding against Hell, but against himself. He'd been more effective at that than any of Lucifer's spawn.

There was the sound of a fork on china from the living room.

She was sent here for a reason. Perhaps it wasn't just about the demons.

Simon collected his plate and silverware. It was time to face Katia's anger and to tell his story. Maybe then she'd tell him hers.

Katia's irritation at the holier-than-thou guy in the kitchen had begun to fade once she'd put some space between them. She ate mechanically now, refusing to let him ruin this great meal. As she did, dust motes danced in the light coming in through the windows, illuminating the bareness of the room.

She shouldn't have said anything. She didn't know Simon, didn't know what he'd been through, and yet she had judged him. If it had been the other way around, she'd be really angry.

He quietly crossed to the coffee table, set down his plate and glass, and returned to the kitchen. Then he was back, placing her glass of water in front of her because she'd not bothered with it during her escape.

Settling on the other end of the sofa, he began to eat again. Only after his plate was empty did he finally speak.

"You're right. I've been living like every day is my last. I didn't see I was doing that, but you are completely right."

Katia wasn't used to guys admitting they were wrong, so she leaned back against the sofa cushions. He wasn't messing with her, his expression sincere. "Why do you do that?"

"Because I only see the great task set before me."

"Exorcising the fiends?" He nodded. "You're obsessed?" Another nod, more grudging now. "Why?"

His eyes darted away from her. If she kept pushing, he'd push back and then the truth would come out.

Maybe it should.

"I betrayed Riley to the Demon Hunters," he said. "We were dating, it was all going good, then I was gutted by a Three. Almost . . . literally." His eyes returned to hers now, but she didn't think he was seeing her.

"We held our meetings at the Tabernacle downtown. It was a de-sanctified church that they used for concerts. We always met inside a Holy Water circle to keep ourselves safe." He swallowed heavily. "The Holy Water was fake. The demons came—both Pyro-Fiends and Gastro-Fiends. They killed so many of us, burned some of them alive."

"God . . . that's how you were hurt?"

"Yes. A Gastro-Fiend took me down, ripping—" He exhaled slowly, his hand moving to his abdomen now, though she doubted he knew it. "Riley stopped it from killing me." He paused, then huffed. "With a folding chair, of all things."

Having met Master Blackthorne, that she could believe. "How did you betray her?"

"Riley agreed to owe Heaven a favor in trade for my life."

Katia blinked, confused. "But how—"

"An angel healed me. One minute I was dying, and then I wasn't. I still dream about that. So what did I do? Did I step back and think through all that had happened? Did I thank Riley for saving me at the Tabernacle?" He sucked in a breath. "No, not me. I was *so* damned smug I thought my faith was sufficient armor against *all* evil, and I'd never get hurt because I was so righteous. Instead, I listened to someone who spun lies about her. I told the Vatican about Riley and the Fallen, and they came after her. I betrayed my girlfriend, Katia. I betrayed the one who saved my life."

"Was the Fallen the one you call Ori?" she asked, still trying to process everything he'd just revealed.

"Yes. But I had my own Fallen whispering lies into my ear. His name was Sartael. He planned to overthrow the Prince, take control of Hell. He came damned close."

She put all the pieces together. "You believed a Fallen angel's lies and betrayed your girlfriend to Rome?"

"Yes," Simon said, his answer a mere whisper. "They might have executed her for what she'd done. Thank God they didn't."

"Has she forgiven you?" Katia asked, her eyes narrowing.

"Yes."

"Then why haven't you forgiven yourself?"

He jerked at the question. "I don't know." At that his eyes met hers. "What is it about your brother that makes you freak? I see it every time he's mentioned."

As she opened her mouth to tell him to shut the hell up, he pushed home. "What is your secret, Katia? I've told you mine. Now it's your turn."

Oh God. She took a long sip of water, then set the glass back on a coaster. Her hand shook, and, of course, Simon noticed it.

"I promise I won't judge you. I just need to know the truth."

He was right, he had to know. Hell would use anything they could against them, even her own brother.

"Because I was an apprentice, Kevin was fascinated with the trappers and wanted to join the Guild after he graduated from high school. My parents refused to consider it. Since they kept nagging at him, Kev started hanging with some guys who were into the supernatural. One night they got drunk and tried to summon a demon. The summoning worked."

This didn't seem to surprise Simon. "Is his soul still his own?"

"Yes. I had one of the trappers test him. Kev's been in a coma since that night. His buddies left him behind. It's lucky I found him before he died."

There was more. So much more. Did she dare tell him?

As if he somehow knew, he urged, "Go on. Tell me all of it."

"Right after Kevin was hurt, the first Three I trapped came with a message: If I gave Hell my soul, my brother would wake up from his coma."

She expected the next question. When it didn't come, she frowned.

Just ask me, dammit.

Instead, Simon went to where his black case sat by the front door. He unlatched it and removed a small metal vial, and when he returned, gestured toward her. *Holy Water.* A trapper was expected to undergo such a test whenever requested, even though she had just passed one this morning. If she refused, the exorcist would be required to report that refusal to Master Blackthorne.

Katia's heart hammered. Her soul was hers, but this had to be papal Holy Water. What if it was different somehow?

Simon murmured something under his breath and then allowed a drop of the liquid to fall on her palm. A tingling sensation spread up her arm, but there was no sign of Hell's mark.

"As I expected," he said, smiling.

What? "Then why did you test me?"

"Because sometimes we need to see the proof with our own eyes. You included. You blame yourself for what happened to your brother. Why?"

"Because I wanted to be a trapper. That's why he got so interested in all this."

"Ah," Simon replied. He carefully capped the Holy Water. "Kansas doesn't have any newspapers, television? No social media? He could only know about the demons and the trappers because of you?"

These were such elementary questions that she blanked for a moment. Then it hit her. "No. One of the kids at school almost died when a Three attacked him."

"Your brother knew the boy?"

"Yeah. They were good friends and . . . "

With a deep sigh, Simon looked to the ceiling, as if for guidance, then back at her. "Time for confession, I think. I've been stupid. I've have been paying penance for a sin that has already been forgiven. What about you?"

Just say it. "And I've been throwing myself at the demons, over and over, racking up the scars because I will not give up my soul to save my brother."

"You've been paying for his mistake. It was his to make, not yours."

Tears rolled down her cheeks before Katia could stop them. She blotted at them with her shirt sleeve, then nodded. "You're right. That's what I've been doing."

"There is only *one* Katia Breman in this world," Simon said softly. "The fiends know that and they'd love nothing more than to destroy you, even if they have to guilt you into doing it to yourself." He sighed. "Don't let them win. They're not worth it."

Through the tears she looked up at him. "It goes both ways. There's only one Simon Adler. You've paid for your mistake over and over because the demons never let you forget it." She took a deep breath. "Time to knock it off, dude."

He burst out in laughter, followed by a broad smile. "Ori was right, you are here for a reason."

"Prove you're moving on," Katia said, feeling the need to challenge him. She pointed. "Open one of those boxes."

Simon eyed the stack along the wall. "Okay." He crossed the room in a few strides, grabbed one off the pile, brought it back to the sofa and placed it on the coffee table. With little effort he ripped open the tape and opened the flaps. Then laughed again.

"Did I tell you how much my family drives me crazy?" As if to offer proof to that claim, he held up a very ragged dark brown teddy bear. It was about ten inches tall, one ear was gone and the other looked like it'd been chewed on, repeatedly.

"Yours?"

He nodded. "This is my mom's doing. She insisted that we each have our own bears. We shared clothes and toys because there were a bunch of us, but the bears were ours." He sighed, bouncing the creature on a knee. "This is her way of suggesting grandkids would be a good idea."

"Already?"

"Yes, Mom is an optimist. She loves kids. That's why there were so many of us." He dug further into the box and unearthed a series of books on topics ranging from geology to space exploration. Young Simon had been a very curious boy.

He gazed around. "Gonna have to buy a bookshelf."

"A bookshelf?" Katia said, slapping a hand to her chest. "Oh, the horror! Then it'll be a lamp and then some stereo equipment, maybe even a *television*. Who knows where it'll stop?"

He gave her a mock frown. "If I buy stuff, you have to help me assemble it. I can't have my family help me or it won't go well."

Her initial instinct was to refuse, but instead she said, "Sure."

With a pleased nod, Simon methodically emptied the box, tore it down and began putting the contents in various places in the apartment. The books went in a stack in a corner, but it was a start. As he reached for another box, Katia smiled to herself. Maybe this was a lesson for her, as well.

NINE

Simon was four boxes in, moving right along with his unpacking, when he winced, and then shook his head like he'd been hit by a brick.

"Do you have a headache?" Katia asked.

"No, a Hellish challenge." He shook his head once more, then made a call to someone. Then within minutes he and Katia were in the car heading deeper into the city.

"This one is an exorcism," he explained. "The Archdiocese received the request about five minutes before I heard the demonic summons. It surprised them that I knew about it."

"Bet so."

The traffic was literally bumper-to-bumper as they made their way up Peachtree Street, a major north-south road through the heart of Atlanta.

"Is it always this busy?"

"Yeah, it's a pain. The interstates are worse. Rush hour is insane."

She made a mental note to avoid the interstates, or at least once she could afford a car. *Apartment first, then wheels.*

Simon gave her a quick glance. "According to the possessed's wife, he's been acting increasingly strange over the last few days. Some of this behavior is apparently normal for him, but the fact he's leaving claw marks on the walls in his office was a clue something else was going on."

"Definitely a clue. Only one demon per possession?"

"There's usually only one inside the possessed, but there may be others around. Plan on more so you're not surprised."

Katia decided to stop asking questions because so far nothing she'd heard made her feel any better about this.

It took another twenty minutes before Simon pulled into a parking lot next to an apartment building. According to him they were in Midtown, whatever that meant.

He collected the black suitcase from the backseat, as well as his trapping bag. "Grab that metal box. Careful, it might be hot."

The box he'd pointed at was square, emblazoned with crosses and Latin phrases, the lid clamped firmly in place.

"And this is for?" she asked.

"Once the demon is exorcised, it'll go inside that container."

"Even a big demon?"

"Even a big demon," he replied.

This she had to see.

The apartment building in front of them was all glass and steel. Katia's eyes rose, floor by floor, counting them as she did. "This guy is on the twenty-eighth floor?"

Simon consulted his phone, then gave her a puzzled look. "How did you know?"

"It feels wrong there. I've always been more sensitive to weird stuff. I don't know why."

"Riley's a bit like that," he said diplomatically. At least he didn't tell her she was nuts.

Her sensitivity to the weird stuff had begun early when Katia had warned her kindergarten teacher that a woman waiting near the school was all wrapped up in gray and black, and she hadn't meant the lady's clothes. Of course, the teacher didn't understand, and still hadn't when that same woman had tried to kidnap one of Katia's classmates.

Rather than accepting that she was just wired differently, tales began to spread. Embarrassed, her parents told her to knock it off, convinced her imagination was the issue. If only that had been the case. To keep the peace, Katia stopped telling others what she saw. It was only when she'd become a trapper that she'd actively used her "sight" again. Her first master had been sorta okay with it, but the second one had complained she was into all the woo-woo crap. For her, it was as normal as breathing.

The building's lobby was impressive, the walls and floor wrapped in an abundance of pale gray marble. Gold Art Deco-style lamps were carefully positioned along those walls, each with a stained-glass shade. Whoever lived here had some bucks.

Their footsteps echoed as they crossed to the security guard's desk. The guard was a middle-aged Black woman with a "I've seen it all" expression and a name tag with *Nia* inscribed on it. This lady was the type who could easily hold off a band of armed robbers with a single frown.

"We are here to see Mrs. Russell," Simon said, offering his driver's license. Katia did the same. The guard gave her Kansas license a longer inspection—and then they signed in. Simon never stated their true purpose here, but something told her that the guard already knew there was Hellspawn in the building. Once they'd been cleared, they were pointed toward a bank of elevators, and then rising steadily toward their destination.

"This place has to be worth some serious cash," Katia said, eying the interior of the elevator. Smoked mirrors reflected her image, reminding her that more sleep was still needed. She pushed a stray chunk of hair off her face. Now that she had some money, a real haircut was in her future, one done by a pro, not a dead broke demon trapper.

"Definitely serious cash. That's part of the reason I bought a house—the rent in Atlanta can be off the charts. Not that house prices are low, either."

Which meant Katia might be staying at Master Stewart's longer than she'd expected, at least until she could scrape together a deposit and a few months' rent.

The hallway on the 28th floor felt unwelcoming even though its décor matched that of the lobby. The possessed's wife met them at the door to the apartment. A trim woman in her forties, Mrs. Russell wore exercise clothes that looked nothing like the one's Katia had once owned. They did have something in common: The dark bags under the lady's eyes suggested nights of little sleep.

"Come on in," she said.

Simon waited until the woman had closed the door, then handed her his official Vatican ID. "Journeyman Breman is assisting me today." The woman nodded and the ID was returned. "When did these problems begin, Mrs. Russell?"

"Three days ago. Henry's on deadline and he usually stays up all night anyway, so I didn't think anything of it."

"Deadline?" Katia asked.

"Henry's an author. He writes mysteries. He's been on the *New York Times* Bestseller list five times." Along with the deep worry was a touch of pride.

"A very talented author, then," Simon said politely. "What were the first signs that something was wrong?"

"He began to hiss. At first, I thought it was the cat, but she won't go near him, and has been hiding ever since. Then Henry started to howl at all hours. The neighbors have not been happy about that."

"That's a common symptom of possession," he said, his voice reassuring and calming. Something told Katia this was just him, not something he'd learned as an exorcist.

Simon spent the next few minutes covering how an exorcism was performed, and the potential liabilities involved. Unlike for a demon trapping, there was no paperwork the woman needed to sign.

"I'm going to . . . go out for a while, okay?" Mrs. Russell said, indicating a workout bag near the front door. "I don't think I want to be here when . . ."

"I understand." Simon traded phone numbers with her, along with a promise to notify her when the exorcism was completed. With a stifled sob, the woman fled the apartment.

As the door shut behind her, Katia gave her companion a puzzled look. "Is that normal? I mean, bailing like that?"

Simon nodded. "Usually by the time they call for an exorcist they're scared out of their minds. Honestly, I prefer them out of the way so they won't get hurt."

"Why no paperwork?" Trappers always had forms to be

signed, at least in most situations.

"We used to do it, but now we have an online agreement that the Archdiocese has the family sign before I arrive. Saves time, which sometimes I just don't have if things go bad in a hurry."

Simon headed for the kitchen, which should have been on the cover of a magazine, it was that incredible. Six burner gas range, massive stainless-steel refrigerator, two long countertops sporting the latest small appliances. A cook's dream come true.

After an envious sigh, Katia watched as her companion carefully set the suitcase on one of the marble countertops, then prepped for the exorcism. He started with a prayer, then the application of the liquid from the small vial she'd seen at his house.

Simon offered it to her now. "You've already been anointed with Holy Water once today so you should be good, though I usually do a prayer at the time of the anointing."

When she hesitated, he added, "Do you follow any particular faith?" It was a sensitive way of asking whether she was Christian, and she appreciated it.

"I was raised as a Methodist, but I'm mostly confused. I haven't been to church since I became a trapper. I'm still working it all out in my head."

"Then do what makes you most comfortable," he replied.

It seemed right, so she took the vial from him, carefully placed a small dot of the holy liquid on her forehead, while whispering a prayer that they be kept safe. That she not betray this man when he needed her most.

She handed back the vial. "Thank you."

He nodded. "How much Latin do you know?"

"Almost none. *Carpe diem. Tempus fugit. Sit vis nobiscum.*"

"*May the Force be with us?*" he asked, zeroing in on the last phrase.

She shrugged. "It's all I got. Sorry."

"Well, that's a start, I guess."

As they talked, the temperature in the apartment seemed to drop precipitously. By the time they reached the room in which

Mrs. Russell said they'd find her husband, goose bumps had sprung to life underneath Katia's long-sleeved shirt.

Simon entered first, then gaped. "What the . . . ?"

If this was the kind of office an author rated, Katia was about to change professions. Then it struck her. "It's an illusion!"

"A very impressive one." Simon murmured, peering around at the vast space. "The fiend must be powerful."

What had been an office was now a massive library, and the faint aroma of vanilla, the subtle perfume of old books, scented the air. A scarlet carpet runner extended the length of this room, leading into the one beyond. On either side of them were dark cabinets filled with rare volumes. A second level of those cabinets soared above the first, supported by carved wood columns, each column accented with gold leaf. On that second tier, curtained windows allowed in a little light, but it seemed dwarfed by the sheer size of the room. Katia swore she heard rustling behind the walls. Surely a mouse wouldn't dare to live in such a space.

Simon peered upward, eyes wide. "It's like St. Peter's Basilica in Rome." Following his gaze, she looked up and gasped.

The ceiling's artwork was a vividly colored and detailed painting of an elegant lady surrounded by multi-hued flowers and numerous cherubs. It was majestic, and unlike anything Katia had ever seen. She could spend hours here, and maybe that was the point. For all its beauty, this was a breathtaking illusion designed to distract their attention from the real threat.

"Simon," she said, nudging him.

He blinked, looked down at her, then frowned, apparently coming to the same conclusion. "Thank you."

"Not a problem. It is seriously unreal."

"Which means it has to exist somewhere in this world for it to be so detailed. Hellspawn are not that imaginative."

They walked on, their footsteps muted by the carpet. The desire to step off the crimson highway, to open one of the cabinets and immerse herself in the knowledge was almost overwhelming. Out of the corner of her eye she saw Simon touch the wooden cross on his chest.

Illusion. Illusion. Illusion.

The pull toward the cabinets lessened now.

"This reminds me of the library at Trinity College in Dublin. It's the same century, I think, probably located somewhere in Europe," Simon said. "What I don't understand is why it's important to the demon."

"Maybe it has something to do with Mr. Russell."

"That makes more sense. We'll find out soon enough."

One final room awaited them just beyond an arched doorway that had a golden crown at its peak. At the far end of that chamber was a large portrait, the subject definitely a royal. Above that painting, at the peak, was another golden crown. This library had *Built by the King* stamped all over it.

Beneath the portrait were two figures, one unnaturally tall and clad in an all-white robe, the other on its knees, head bowed. Simon continued down the main aisle, then halted some distance away from the pair. Once he was sure she had joined him, he touched the spot on his forehead, then the bare floor at his feet. A shiny white protective circle rose around them, shimmering in the dimly lit room.

Katia blinked in wonder. She hadn't seen him create the circle at the daycare center, too busy trying not to be sliced apart by the Three, so she made a mental note to ask how he'd pulled off this bit of holy magic.

"Stay inside this and you're safe," he said. "Otherwise, it can get ugly."

She nodded her understanding, then pulled her steel pipe from her trapping bag, pushing the latter out of her way with a foot. Her eyes slowly adjusted to the circle's brighter light which illuminated the two figures in front of them.

"Simon Michael David Adler," the one in the robe called out in a deep voice. Its face was pale, and it had deep blue eyes and faint blond hair that reached its shoulders. "Do you know who I am?"

"Should I?" Simon said, his tone anything but respectful.

"I am the Messenger," the form replied, its deep voice

resonating throughout the chamber.

"The Archangel Gabriel? So, then what's your message?"

"You will die this day."

Simon didn't seem disturbed by that prediction. "I see. Some reason you're *announcing* this rather than leaving it a surprise?"

"You will lose your soul this day, as well."

"God decided you just had to tell me this in person?"

"You mock the Messenger?" the voice demanded.

"Well, you *could* be an Archangel. You could also be a very clever Fallen, or a powerful Hypno-Fiend."

Fallen? That wasn't something she'd considered.

"Why would you doubt my word?" the figure asked.

"Because I'm not a fool. At least not anymore," he said, giving Katia a quick wink.

What was going on here? She concentrated on the kneeling figure and realized it was an illusion. Nothing there at all. Then she studied the alleged Archangel, pushing to get a sense of what it was, and cringed. Her stomach roiled as the inky darkness pushed back.

"It's not one of Heaven's Divines," she said.

"Didn't figure it was. I'm one of the good guys, but I don't rate an Archangel delivering a personal message from the boss, especially not Gabriel."

Katia Allyson Breman. Your soul shall be mine. Surrender it now!

The voice echoed in her skull, like someone shouting in an empty warehouse. It wasn't the same voice as the fiend in front of them, so it was probably the Four who'd forced Simon into this "bargain" in the first place. She'd wondered when she'd hear from it.

Before she could respond, Simon hefted the large wooden cross.

"Spawn of Hell! Yes, I *am* Simon Michael David Adler, child of God, believer in the Risen Lord, wielder of the Light. *You* are an Abomination and are not worthy of this realm! Reveal yourself for all to see!"

The figure wavered but did not drop the glamour that hid its true form.

"Reveal yourself!" Simon commanded.

This time a man appeared, one she guessed to be Mr. Russell. He was clad in a wrinkled blue shirt, jeans and seemed utterly confused. Before he could speak, his eyes blazed red and he straightened up, seemingly taller than before as the demon made its presence known.

"Simon the Betrayer!" the fiend called out. "Your sins are many. Your sins will never be forgiven. You are nothing compared to us."

Simon shook his head. "*You* are nothing, Fiend. The Power of God is Eternal. You are the Spawn of Lucifer, vermin of the Pit, the lowest of the low. You will depart this man's body and leave his soul untouched. You shall be cast out!"

The exorcist switched to Latin, and even though Katia knew almost nothing of the ancient language, the power behind the words stole her breath away. The phrases rolled off Simon's tongue, growing in intensity, as his body vibrated with the strength of the Light that flowed through him. Around them, the walls of the ancient library began to buckle and warp as the illusion failed. With a resounding crack, it returned to normal, just a cluttered home office with long scratches in the wood paneling.

As Mr. Russell crumpled to the floor, drawing himself into a fetal position, whimpering, Katia finally got a good look at the demon. Definitely a Hypno-Fiend, short in stature, about four feet tall. Its body was clad in light armor with arms that ended in hooked talons. A long sword appeared, and with a growl, the fiend launched itself at them, slashing at the protective circle. With each strike a near-deafening boom struck her ears, making her head pound.

Katia shifted her weight, tightening her grip on the pipe, though if she attacked it, it'd be like beating at a grizzly bear with a toothpick. To her relief, the circle continued to pulse with each blow, but it held. Simon's voice rose, the Latin coming faster now. His eyes seemed to be a brighter blue, as if the words were changing him from within.

The fiend's blows weakened, then it fell to its knees.

"By the power of the Almighty, the Creator of the Universe, I cast you into the prison from which there is no escape!" Simon cried.

With a terrified shriek, the fiend abruptly vanished in a puff of acrid smoke. There was noise now, the rattle of the metal box near Simon's feet as an unearthly howl came from within.

Katia's mouth dropped open in astonishment. Not only had he exorcised the demon *out* of Mr. Russell, he'd sent it into that metal box. A box that was *inside* the protective circle.

Holy . . . How did he do that?

She raised her eyes from the box to the exorcist who was bent over at the waist, sucking in air, and trembling.

That was badass.

As Simon gasped for air, a prayer of thanks came between those gasps. When he finally straightened up, he looked over at Katia, then laughed, the sound of deepest relief.

"As Riley would say: Exorcist 1, Fiend 0." he said, smiling. "It is a joyous thing when it all goes right."

She took a deep breath, then another, her heart still pounding.

"How did you do that?" she said, pointing toward the box. It kept thumping like the demon was hammering on the walls with its fists.

"Faith," he said. "If you think this was weird, wait until the walls ooze blood. That's particularly gross." He glanced up. "Though I really did like this illusion. Best one so far."

A groan issued from Mr. Russell, who was still curled up on the floor. Simon dismissed the circle to check on the recently dispossessed. It took some encouragement but finally Russell sat upright, his eyes riveted on the snarling box.

"I didn't do a thing! I didn't summon it, I didn't make a deal with any demon," he insisted. "They'll think I got on the bestseller's list because I sold my soul. No way. I'm not that stupid."

"Sometimes demons just pick random people to torment," Simon explained. "We'll anoint you with Holy Water before we leave and then you should have your priest come in and do a thorough blessing of your apartment."

"I will. I will. After I meet my deadline." Russell groaned again, his head in his hands.

It took Simon another ten minutes to convince him that having the priest come *today* was a smart move. To her relief, a dab of Holy Water proved the man's soul was still his own, though Russell was quite offended they'd felt the need to check. After Katia found his office chair, she helped him into it. His hair was mussed, his face in need of a shave and his shirt filthy. A shower, maybe two, were in his future.

"What am I going to do? I'm so behind. My editor will shoot me," the man complained. "She gets *very upset* if I'm late with my manuscript."

Katia traded a look with Simon, who shrugged.

"Don't worry, you'll catch up," she said. This guy had no clue how close he'd come to spending eternity missing deadlines in Hell.

"She's not going to believe me. No way."

"If your editor needs some sort of official report about what happened here, I can provide it," Simon offered. That seemed to settle Russell more than anything they'd said so far. "One question. That library we saw. Does it actually exist?"

The author thought for a time, then nodded as if a few more cobwebs had been swept out of his brain.

"It's the *Biblioteca Joanina*. In my story, my heroine finds a murdered priest there. The library is in Portugal, at the University of Coimbra. I visited it last summer. I have a book about it here somewhere," he said, looking around at the trashed office in bewilderment.

"That's our cue to go," Simon said quietly. He picked up the metal box holding the demon and headed for the door, Katia right behind him. "I'll send a message to your wife, so she knows you're okay."

"Huh? Oh. Thanks," the man said, rummaging around in the scorched pile of paper on the floor. "Where are my notes for chapter twenty-nine? I have to find those!"

More rummaging was followed by a curse. Apparently, that chapter was going to be delayed.

TEN

While they descended to the lobby, Simon called Mrs. Russell and relayed the good news. He also insisted that a priest bless the apartment as soon as possible. She promised to make that happen, no matter what her spouse said, and then began to cry.

Once the call ended, he explained, "Usually, I'd do the blessing myself, but not today. The blessing can take some time, and I don't want to get in the middle of one and have to leave for another exorcism."

When they approached the guard to sign out, Nia eyed the box with the yowling demon. "Oh good, you got it," she said.

"You don't seem surprised that's why we were here," Simon said.

"It's happened before in one of the other apartments. I keep telling the condo association they need to use Holy Water to secure the entrances, but they don't want to spend the money. Lobby full of marble and these guys are cheapskates," she said, shaking her head in despair.

"Which is why you get these fiends," he replied, hefting the box.

"Amen. Now if you ask me—"

A resounding plop made Katia pause as she signed them out. "What was that?"

The guard didn't reply. Instead, she pointed behind them.

In the middle of the lobby was a Hellspawn, but not one Katia had ever seen before. It was about six feet tall, and about as wide, with the kind of spindly legs a flamingo would envy. It reminded her of a lime green beach ball with feet. Branching out from the thing were six sets of tentacles, three to a side. Slitted amber eyes blinked at them. Then it cackled in a high-pitched voice like it was enjoying a good joke.

"What *the hell* is that?" she asked.

"Another demon," Simon replied.

She shot him a frown. "What. Kind. Of. Demon?"

"No clue. I've never seen one like that before. Lucifer can create new fiends anytime he likes. Looks like he just did."

"Great, just great." Katia swore under her breath.

There was another one of those infernal cackles, the kind that made your skin pebble and your heart skip beats.

"Nia, we'll need you to keep the residents out of the way," Simon said. "We have no idea what we're up against here."

Though still stunned by the sight of the bizarre Hellspawn in her lobby, Nia muttered, "Will do."

Katia Allyson Breman. The Betrayer will be mine. He will cower at my feet like a beaten dog. Give me your soul and you will live.

She grimaced at the power in that demand, even stronger than it had been upstairs with the writer. *No. Not happening.*

Then die, mortal!

The ball-shaped fiend promptly changed colors to a startling red, so red it almost glowed from within. Then it opened its mouth, which kept expanding until it was the entire width of the demon. It had no teeth, which wasn't usual for Hellspawn.

Something the color of a moldy lime plopped out of the thing's mouth, hitting the floor with a splat. About the size of an over-inflated basketball, it rolled a short distance and then unfolded to reveal a miniature version of the bigger fiend.

"Oh, great, it's having babies now," Katia grumbled.

"Just one of them. We can handle it."

Even before he finished speaking, two more fell onto the marble floor. Then it was an assembly line, as twelve hideous fiends launched themselves out of the big thing's mouth, one after another. Finally, it belched and stopped generating copies of itself.

Katia shot her companion a horrified look.

"At least they don't have teeth," he said.

The cackle came yet again, and in response the smaller Hellspawn began to wave their tentacles around, only to have them sprout rows and rows of needlepoint fangs. Katia swore she saw bits of flesh caught in some of them.

"Just had to mention the teeth thing, didn't you?" she snarled.

A mumbled "sorry" returned.

"No, Mrs. Horner! Go back outside!" the guard called out, then set off at a trot toward the front doors. A gray-haired lady had just entered, a pocket-sized puppy at her side on a sparkly leash. Totally engrossed in her phone conversation, she ignored the warning. At least until her dog spied the fiends and lost its little mind in a shrill series of frantic barks.

"Get out of here!" Nia shouted.

The woman finally acknowledged the threat, then calmly tucked the phone in her purse, gave a firm tug on the leash and headed back outside. The dog, not quite so mellow, kept up its racket until the doors closed behind it.

"Thank God," Simon whispered.

In the time it'd taken to get the tenant out the door, the largest demon had grown in size again, its skin revealing that infernal red glow. It appeared that even more baby fiends were keen to make their appearance.

There was only one way to stop this. "Can you clear me a path to that big one?" she asked.

"Maybe. What are you going to do?"

Something told Katia not to voice her plan. "Just trust me."

Her companion's worried eyes met hers. "You got it."

Then to Katia's astonishment, the exorcist tightened his grip on his steel pipe and marched straight into the mass of tentacles.

Even before Simon began batting the fiends aside, he'd been bitten, a sharp pain in the back of his left leg. Grabbing the offending monster, he tossed it away, then began a systematic sweep back and forth with his pipe. Thunk, a fiend went flying, thunk and another sailed away waving its tentacles in fury. Two more bit him, the wounds burning like they were bathed in acid.

Simon kept moving, knowing to slow down would only gain him more bites and ruin any chance of Katia's plan. Whatever that was. Only now did it occur to him that what he was doing was suicidal if she didn't back him up. Had Azagar already made his offer and she'd accepted it?

The Big Mouth demon swung a tentacle toward him, and he staggered back, stepping on one of the little fiends to avoid having his throat ripped out. Teetering for a moment, he barely regained his balance. He kept bashing the monsters, but there seemed to be no end of them. When one of the long tentacles came close again, he smacked it, hard, generating a throaty roar.

A blur flew past him—Katia—sliding through the tangle of Hellspawn, as she leapt up and slam-dunked the Holy Water sphere directly into the large fiend's gaping mouth. For a second nothing happened, then a burst of glass and liquid cut off the Hellspawn's strangled cry.

The rustling of the smaller fiends suddenly ceased, even as Katia twisted out of the reach of the big one's tentacles. She kicked her way through a knot of the lesser demons, breathing heavily.

"The Holy Water didn't work!"

At first, he thought she was right, but from where she stood, Katia couldn't see the fiend's eyes widen, its body beginning to swell, its skin pulling tighter and tighter, almost as if . . .

"Run!" Simon shouted.

He had almost made it back to the guard's desk when Lucifer's newest creation exploded. Like an egg in a microwave, bits of Hellspawn flew upward in a grisly fountain, body parts striking the walls, the lights and the bystanders. When it finally stopped raining demon guts, tentacles, and a single large eyeball, the lobby grew eerily silent.

Nia peered out from behind her desk. "Damn," the woman said, then grinned. "You killed them all!"

As Simon rose from the floor, he realized she was right. Not only was the big fiend so much sushi, all the little ones had melted like marshmallows over a hot bonfire.

"Man, that's gross," Katia said, slipping on the wet floor as she joined them. Every few steps something nasty would fall off her clothes.

"That was an impressive slam-dunk," he said.

Her smile was one of true pride. "Guess who was on the championship high school basketball team and scored the most points?" she asked, waggling her eyebrows.

"Katia from Kansas?" She nodded happily. "I was into track and field. Basketball was never my thing."

"So, between us we've got 'throwing stuff at demons and then running away' totally covered?"

Simon burst out laughing. "That's it exactly." He held up a hand and they high fived. "Good Guys 3, Hell 0."

"More like fifteen what with all those little bastards."

When he looked back at the carnage, he kept the groan to himself. No way could they leave this mess to some poor underpaid janitor.

"We need to clean this up ourselves in case these things have a way of regenerating," he said.

"They can do that?" Katia asked, her smile fading at the thought.

"They can do anything their master wants them to do."

"Ugh," she said. "Just ugh."

While Nia was walking around the edges of the mess, shaking her head, and doing a running commentary on what she was seeing, they treated their wounds with Holy Water, the papal variety. Simon would normally use the locally produced version, but it was vital that neither of them fell ill today. Still, he made sure not to waste any of the precious liquid.

Sitting in the guard's chair, Katia at his feet, he winced as she applied some to the vicious bite on his calf.

"It needs a bandage. Maybe stitches," was her professional opinion.

It probably did, but he was going to ignore it for the time being. Just as they finished, a strange crackling sound began, causing the two of them to turn back toward the fiendish splotches. Uneasy, Simon picked up his pipe from where it had fallen. The crackling continued, and then slowly faded away.

"Well, look at that," Nia said, pointing.

Katia walked up to the nearest pile of demon remains and nudged it with the toe of her shoe. What had been gelatinous liquid was now grains of glistening green sand. "Huh."

"Y'all going to need a broom. Or two," the guard said as she headed off. "I'll be right back."

Katia gave him a side eye. "This the usual thing for your city?"

"A new type of demon? No. We must be special."

The irritated huff that came his way told him what she thought of that. "Lucky us," she muttered, then headed in the direction Nia had gone.

As his bites burned and sweat broke out on his forehead, Simon began documenting the demonic remains, one cell phone image at a time. So far, they'd outfoxed Azagar. He wondered how long their luck would hold.

ELEVEN

It took time to sweep up all the demon remains and bag them, though Nia had helped them with the process. Then Simon insisted that they treat the lobby with the local Archdiocese's Holy Water, which was packaged in quart bottles, the kind the trappers used. That had required a trip to his car and more digging around in the trunk.

Katia had taken over that task as she could tell the wound on his leg was hurting him. He'd also insisted that a small amount of Holy Water be added to every trash bag "just in case." Then he'd made sure those bags went in his trunk because he didn't want to leave them behind. No one could complain about this guy not being thorough.

Simon was in the car now, in the driver's seat with his foot propped on the dashboard as he applied a bandage to his leg. At least the wound had stopped bleeding. Other than a few aches, Katia wasn't feeling many ill effects from the bites, so that was a blessing.

"I'll need to tell Master Blackthorne that there's a new demon," she said. "I should have got a picture of that monster, but I didn't."

"I have some."

She stared at him. "You actually took pictures during all that?"

"Sure," he said, as if everyone had the presence of mind to capture the moment when they faced a truly lethal horde of flesh-eating fiends. "Father Rosetti will want to warn the other exorcists. I'll send a copy of the pictures to you, at least if they turned out decent. Tell Riley how you killed it. That'll earn you big points."

"I only got close to it because of you," she argued. "They would have chewed me to bits if I'd tried that on my own."

Simon shrugged, as if his part had been no big deal.

This guy is unreal. When the box at her feet rattled again, Katia glared at it. She'd almost forgotten about the Four they'd exorcised from the illusionary library. "What do you do with this thing? Take it to a demon trafficker?"

"No, not this one. A demon who possesses a mortal may return to that person if it somehow gets free. This one goes somewhere else, where it will be dealt with."

"Dealt with as in . . . ?" She made a slicing motion across her neck.

He nodded. "It's about a forty-five-minute drive down to the monastery, depending on traffic, and usually another fifteen minutes or so at the site. Figure at least an hour and a half minimum. I'll dump the other fiends' ashes down there as well."

For some reason that explanation triggered a yawn, one she tried to conceal.

"Do you want to come with me to the monastery, or get some sleep?" he asked, which told her she'd failed at the "I'm not really yawning" coverup.

No matter how interesting the trip might be, she was toast. "I vote for Master Stewart's place. I need a nap."

"You got it."

The box kept shifting. "How do you get that big of a demon inside that small space?"

"Do you want the long and highly religious explanation, or should I just say it's a holy kind of magic?"

"I'll go with the 'it's a holy kind of magic TARDIS', then."

He chuckled at the Dr. Who reference. "That's what I do. Father Rosetti explained it during our training, but frankly I just accept that it happens. Works better that way."

"Can it hold more than one of them at a time?"

"I've been told it can, but I've never tested that."

When Simon pulled up in front of Stewart's house a while later, he delivered a weary smile. "I'll send you a text when I'm back in town."

"Sounds good. Thanks. I mean it."

Katia waved as he drove off, wishing Simon had a chance to rest, especially since that wound troubled him. An old red truck was parked in the driveway now. Its rear window had a Georgia state flag decal and the official Guild emblem, along with the words "Kicking Hell's Ass One Demon at a Time." Demon decals lined the truck's side panel indicating how many Gastro-Fiends its owner had trapped. She lost count at thirty some. Whoever this was, they were doing some serious damage to the Prince's pack of monsters.

Once inside she heard Grand Master Stewart talking to someone in the back of the house, probably the truck's owner. Not wanting to interrupt, she headed upstairs where she found a large, hot pink sticky note stuck to her bedroom door.

Katia,
Hello! If you have any laundry you need washed just put it in the bag and leave it hanging on the door. I'll have it back to you the next day. So glad you are staying with us!
Cheers, Mrs. Ayers

Katia pulled the large plastic bag free from the door handle, then read the note again. Clean laundry and she didn't have to do it herself? *Score.* The bed looked like pure heaven, the towels were the fluffy kind, and these people seemed to like her.

She owed Master Blackthorne bigtime.

†*‡*†

"Why are we here?" Serrah asked, unable to keep her annoyance hidden.

Without any discussion, the Fallen had taken them a place

in the city where all the signs of mortal life were present: rows of houses, small mortals on bikes, and more than one barking dog. Except the dwelling in front of them, which looked to be deserted. The religious symbol on the front door told her why.

"This morning Simon Adler and I were here," Ori said, "and this is where the fiend issued its challenge. I think I missed something during that exchange. Something important."

"Returning to this place will help you retrieve that memory?"

He frowned. "It might."

They walked to the front door, and with a wave of his hand it unlocked itself. Once inside, Ori waited until the door closed behind them, then concentrated on the house's interior. A nod of approval came next.

"Simon has cleansed the dwelling of the Darkness. He did a fine job."

A Fallen praising an exorcist? That had to be a first.

Serrah had been inside mortal homes in the past. As was often the case, there were framed images of various family members carefully arranged on one wall. A ball of brindle fur tumbled across the floor at her feet. A dog? Yes, there was such a creature in one of the images. The mortals looked so happy, and yet Hell had still come here.

They often thought only those who had evil intentions were plagued by fiends, but that was not the case. Hell disliked tranquility, hated anything that made their presence unwelcome. In retaliation, Hellspawn would search out such happy mortals with every intention of ruining their lives. The fact that they did the same to the morally challenged, or downright evil, proved the fiends lived to spread chaos. Lucifer's Eternal Revenge, as one of her fellow Divines had called it. In this house, that had most definitely been the case.

When Serrah turned to see what the Fallen was doing, he was gone, and with an irritated sigh she tracked him to a larger room beyond. As she had expected, it displayed the usual hallmarks of demonic possession: overturned and damaged possessions, as well as scorch marks high on the walls.

"They are an abomination," she muttered, pushing a shredded pillow aside with a foot. No reply. "What are you doing?"

Ori broke his concentration on the far wall. "I am looking into the past. At least I was until you distracted me."

Her frustration grew. "Then show me what you are seeing."

He thought about it for a moment, then closed his eyes and focused. Serrah did the same, hoping to view the morning's events with him.

"There were three fiends," Ori said. "The first attacked even before Simon could raise his circle of protection." In her mind's eye, Serrah saw that ambush, and how the Fallen had swiftly dealt with the Hellspawn. He truly was a warrior angel, his reaction to the threat nearly instantaneous.

"Then the strongest of them appeared," Ori continued. "Azagar is on the verge of shifting to an Archfiend. At least that's what the mortals call them."

Serrah now understood what had been bothering him. A fiend with that much power should have challenged the rogue Fallen immediately, if nothing more than to curry favor with the Prince. Especially a Fallen who had escaped Lucifer's shackles. Instead, Azagar had focused all his efforts on the exorcist, taunting him, then displaying the three young mortals whose lives now lie in Simon Michael David Adler's hands.

Why? Destroying the exorcist would count as a worthy offering to Lucifer, but Ori was a far bigger prize. The exorcist's superiors would just replace him, though the new one might not be as expert as Adler. If the fiend had captured a Fallen and thrown him at the Prince's feet in Hell? *Priceless.*

Ori ended their journey into the past, still frowning. "What am I not seeing?" he demanded.

"You really think there's something you missed?"

"My instincts say there is."

Once more they followed the scene as it played out. Sometimes Ori would pause the "replay" to pose questions she could not answer, to think something through. By the end, he seemed even more puzzled.

It was during the third time they observed the events that Serrah saw the shadow. She pushed harder at that part of the room, focused intently, then barely swallowed a gasp of surprise at what she'd seen.

Why were you here? And how could she explain this to the Fallen?

Fortunately, Ori didn't notice her reaction, too caught up in his own thoughts. He waved a hand and the past evaporated. Turning on a heel, the Divine was out of the house in a heartbeat, the front door slamming behind him. After a minute or so, she followed him only to find he wasn't waiting for her outside.

A shout made Serrah jump as a child on a bicycle zoomed by on the street, hair streaming behind her. Another one followed. *Mortals.* She never understood them, but then maybe that was the point.

Closing her eyes, she found the Fallen in the city's center, on the top of a tall building, staring at nothing. She would not join him, at least not yet. Serrah had her own dilemma—there had been another Divine in that house, someone who should not have been there. Someone shielded from the demons, the exorcist and the Fallen.

But not from her.

One of the children zipped by on the street again and that brought a brief smile, along with a bit of envy. Divines never had a chance to play, not even the cherubs. Serrah accepted that her life was an eternity of service. An eternity of following the rules. She'd always been good at that.

Until now.

†✷‡✷†

Rahmiel sat on a stone bench, feeding a baby squirrel perched on her lap, the delicate creature deftly nibbling on the seeds she presented, one by one. When it spied Serrah, it fled in a scurry of feet.

"Oh! I am sorry!" she said. "I didn't mean to frighten it."

"Don't worry, it'll come back. It loves the seeds too much

to remain a stranger." The other Divine waved her over. "Come, sit," she said, patting the open area next to her. "Did you know that this plot of ground has been sanctified for almost one hundred and seventy mortal years? In our sense of time, a mere moment, but not to them. Because their lives are so short, they understand things in ways we do not."

Serrah wasn't sure why the angel was telling her this, but no doubt Rahmiel had a purpose.

"Why do you think they were created?" she asked.

"I am not sure," Rahmiel admitted. "They are less than us, but more than us in many ways. One mortal suggested that we Divines were our Creator's prototype, and that the mortals were the improved, second version."

"That's impossible!"

"Why not?" the other angel replied, watching her closely. The small squirrel approached slowly, all its attention on Serrah, as if she might snatch it up and devour it if it wasn't wary. "Neither you or I will ever have a chance to quiz our Creator as to the reason of the mortals' existence, and if we did, I doubt we'd get an answer we'd understand."

This angel was as outrageous as Serrah had heard. "You can't mean that."

A soft smile came her way as the little beast crawled into Rahmiel's lap. After a few seeds were devoured, it ignored Serrah completely. "Maybe I don't mean it, still I like to question what I see and that doesn't always go well with certain of our fellow angels."

She meant Michael.

"You may not realize it, but this city no longer has a Divine guardian. It hasn't for some time. I do what I can, which isn't much since I have this holy site to watch over."

"You were assigned that task, to watch over the city whenever possible?"

"No, I took it on by myself."

She dared to take on a task without permission?

"Yes," Rahmiel replied. She could hear Serrah's thoughts,

though that ability didn't seem to be reciprocal. "The last guardian had lost interest in the city, and that had consequences. I hear he's been reassigned to another task much less demanding."

"Hmm." Serrah didn't understand Divine politics as well as she thought she did. "I have a problem."

"I figured, or you wouldn't have risked visiting an outcast like me *again*."

Serrah's eyes swept across the garden and gravestones in front of them. "Is it difficult being an outcast here?"

"It's absolutely horrible," the angel replied, followed by a mischievous wink. Even Serrah heard the falsehood. "Long hours of tedious work watching over the mortal remains of all these souls, and counseling those among the living who come my way."

"Who would come here?"

"Riley Anora Blackthorne. Ori the Fallen. Even the exorcist. Well, except for him I issued more of scolding than counseling. Simon Michael David Adler deserved it." Rahmiel set the squirrel down and dusted off her skirt. Spying a loose paving stone, she marched over and reset it so it rested evenly among its kin.

"I was here when Michael and Lucifer were so eager to go to war. I watched as Riley Anora Blackthorne argued with them, insisting they step back from the Last Battle. It was an unforgettable moment in my long existence."

Serrah couldn't imagine such a thing. "Simon the Exorcist? Do you know what he is facing?"

When Rahmiel shook her head, Serrah quickly explained, then added, "When the fiend challenged him to save the three mortals' lives, there was another Divine there, besides Ori the Fallen. He was hidden from all of them."

"One of the Prince's?"

"No, one of Michael's."

Rahmiel stopped fussing with a shrub and straightened up, her attention caught. "Which one?"

"Zareth."

"Ah yes, Zareth," she said, nodding as if that made sense.

"He's the one who reported my supposedly 'blasphemous' comments to Michael." Rahmiel thought for a moment, then added, "I might owe that fool a debt of gratitude for my exile, which is a depressing thought."

"But why would Zareth be there? Why did he not assist the exorcist and free those young mortals?"

"Perhaps he was told not to interfere," Rahmiel suggested.

Would the Archangel have done that? Serrah shook her head. "No, I think he was there to watch the Fallen even though Ori didn't sense his presence. That meant Michael was shielding him."

"Or Zareth may have hidden himself. He has enough power to do so. Which means you have a dilemma, don't you?"

Serrah rose and walked to a nearby gravestone, one dedicated to a mortal named Georgia Harris. It proclaimed her 'once a slave, and now free'.

It took some time before she could find the words. "I have a choice—I can keep Zareth's presence a secret, or I can reveal it to the Fallen. Zareth being present at that moment may mean nothing, or it may be the key to saving those mortals' lives."

Rahmiel nodded in agreement. "That is how I see it."

"What do I do?" she pleaded.

"*You* must make the decision, for no matter what happens, you will be judged for that, not I."

"But I have no idea which is right!"

"Then ask yourself what is more important—perhaps doing something opposite of what the Archangel wants, and paying penance for that insubordination, or saving three innocent mortal souls?"

That was the dilemma. "You had to make that decision, didn't you?"

"Something similar, yes."

"But mortals are not as important—"

"Are they not?" Rahmiel challenged, her hands on her hips now. "Or are they as integral to the Divine Plan as we are?"

Serrah sighed. "I do not know."

"Neither do I. I based my decision not on what I felt Michael might want, but what I felt our Creator would desire. As you can see," she said, gesturing around her, "this is my penance for that decision."

"I won't end up anywhere as nice as this."

"Always a possibility. The former guardian of Atlanta is currently on a tiny uninhabited island in charge of watching over the tortoises, the birds and the crabs. From what I hear, he actually likes it there because there are no mortals to annoy him."

Her fellow Divine took a deep breath and then slowly let it out. "Riley Anora Blackthorne often speaks of tests, the kind we face each day. Small ones and big ones, all designed to judge our minds and our hearts, to teach us lessons along the way. Perhaps this isn't about the Archangel, or Zareth, or even about the Fallen. Perhaps this particular test is for you alone."

That was what Serrah feared most. She slumped down on the bench, then felt Rahmiel's hand touch her arm.

"Trust your heart. It'll rarely lead you wrong." After a last reassuring squeeze, she announced, "Now I must find out why one particularly persistent mole insists on uprooting an iris bed despite my *repeated* warnings."

Serrah could not hold back the smile. "Thank you, Rahmiel."

"You're welcome. And if I were you, I'd trust the Fallen more than you'd think wise. He is honorable, and has paid for his ill-fated decision in ways even we cannot imagine."

With one last nod the angel of the cemetery vanished, off to scold a particularly pesky mammal. Serrah sat on that bench for some time, then rose to join the Fallen. Perhaps together they would find the answers they sought.

TWELVE

Ori came often to this high place to gaze down on the city, to observe the mortals in their daily pursuits. From here it was easier to spot the truly dangerous fiends, then to hunt and kill them.

When the other angel appeared, he did not look her way. Instead, he felt a wave of anxiety pouring off Serrah that even she couldn't hide.

"What is troubling you?" he asked, still not moving his focus from the city laid out in front of him like it was his kingdom. Perhaps, in some ways, it was.

"We need to speak . . . privately."

"About?"

She looked around, uneasy. "Not here."

He gestured. "Then lead us to where we *can* speak our minds."

In a blink of an eye, he stood along a shoreline with pale white sand, rolling foam-capped waves, and a golden-amber sun just above the horizon. It was a highly detailed and private illusion, one of Serrah's own making. He'd done the same with Paul Blackthorne's daughter, taking her on a picnic when he was trying to seduce her so he could claim her soul. The troubled expression on Serrah's face told him nothing like that was on her mind.

She didn't speak, but turned away and stared at the waves for some time. In so doing, she had exposed her back to him, a weakness he could exploit with one slash of his sword. Did she realize she had done that?

A movement along the shore caught his attention and he walked a short distance across the sand to a piece of driftwood. A yellow crab had gotten one of its claws stuck in a notch of the wood, and it struggled to free itself. Kneeling, he gently released it, then set it on the sand. It clacked its white claws at him in warning, because even the smallest creatures were not often that grateful, then headed toward the water.

"Why did you free it?" Serrah asked from behind him.

Ori rose. "I freed it because it was trapped. Helpless. I am surprised a gull did not make a meal of it."

Serrah pondered on that reply. "What would have the Archangel done?"

She meant Michael. "He probably would have let it perish. He would not have seen it as important."

The other angel nodded, then sighed. "The small gesture you just made to an insignificant creature, even one that does not truly exist, tells me you are more honorable than some in the Upper Realm."

"Is that why we're here?" he asked, perplexed.

"No. We're here because I am about to take a step across a line, as the mortals say. But before I do, what did you see at the house where the exorcist was given the challenge by the demon?"

That wasn't a question he'd expected. "I witnessed Simon Adler being forced into risking his very soul for those mortals."

"But nothing more?"

He frowned, not sure what she meant. A quick glance told him that the small crab had made it to the ocean now, hustling into the safety of the water. Had she set up that test on purpose?

"Yes, I did."

Serrah had heard his thoughts, something she'd not been able to do in the past. That wasn't necessarily a good thing.

"What did I miss at the house?" he asked.

"Another Divine, one who was hidden from you."

"Who?"

"Zareth."

Ori's mind reeled. "Why would Michael's . . . " he struggled for the proper mortal word, "toady be there? Why did he not intervene to save the captives?"

"You seem to sense things I don't, yet you did not know that Zareth was present. How did that happen? Why involve Simon Michael David Adler in this?"

Ori strode away from her now, angry at how blind he'd been. He'd known something was odd about that whole setup. Had it been a trap for him, or one for the exorcist?

He spun around to find Serrah had followed him. "What is your assignment in regard to me?"

"I was to observe Ori the Fallen and report back on his activities, in particular those in regard to the mortals."

"Michael gave you that assignment?"

She hesitated a moment. "Yes, but Zareth was there when I received the task. He seemed far too pleased that I was chosen for it."

"He has always been an ambitious one. Is he currying favor with the Archangel, or is there some other purpose for his involvement?"

"I honestly do not know."

Ori took a deep inhalation, letting the scent of crisp ocean air fill his lungs and calm his emotions. He could see why Serrah chose this illusion—it was restful. "You risk much telling me this."

A half shrug returned, though he could still feel her worry. "I will pay whatever penance is given for aiding a Fallen."

"Hopefully not," he said, still unsure. "Since you have been honest with me, I will tell you that there is unusual demonic movement in the city of Atlanta. I do not understand what that means. It may be related to the exorcist, it may not. If we are done here, I need to return to the top of that building to continue my surveillance."

After one last look at the waves, Serrah gestured and once again they were on top of the structure overlooking the sprawling city. Ori resumed his perch but made sure to allow room for her to join him. It took Serrah some time, but she finally did, carefully ensuring their bodies did not touch. Because no matter how much good he did in this life, he would always be Fallen.

Always.

† ✶ ‡ ✶ †

Riley felt the trapping had gone remarkably well for having two newbies along, but then Biblio-Fiends were not that dangerous unless you were Paul Blackthorne's daughter. She rolled her eyes at her own library disaster memory, ensuring the two apprentices didn't see it. Her history with the foul-mouthed, book-destroying Grade Ones was not pretty. Eventually these two would hear the tale of how she allowed a demon to trash a section of the law library, but that was for another time.

Now that her first trio of apprentices were mostly out from under her wings, she'd been assigned these two who were as different as humanly possible. Mickey Rivers was in his mid-twenties, dark-haired, dark-eyed and built like an NFL linebacker. She had no doubt, if given the chance, he could flip a car on its side with little effort. He was from Utah, and not inclined to take crap from anyone. Tim Darling was a local, shorter in stature, wore round glasses and had brown, curly hair. Sort of like a Harry Potter clone, though she wouldn't dare mention that. No major muscles except in his brain, which was far sharper than most apprentices.

There'd initially been friction between the two and Riley had allowed it to play out, hoping she didn't have to intervene. In the end, she was saved that step. The reconciliation had something to do with Tim fixing Mickey's 'bricked' cell phone and from that point on they'd been best buds. Now they joked back and forth about muscles vs. brains and which was better for a trapper. Soon enough they'd learn they needed both to remain alive.

As they walked back to her car, the apprentices replaying how the trapping had gone, Riley's phone buzzed. She smiled when she saw who it was.

"Hey, guy, how's it going?"

"Pretty good," Beck replied. "How about you?" His voice sounded off. "Something up?"

"I'm thinkin' so. You outside the library?"

"Yes. Why?"

"When you get to your car, let me know," he replied.

"You're being way too mysterious."

"I'm just seein' if my hunch is right. Remember that guy who called you about a month ago? The one who wanted us to go to that new convention here in town?"

Riley remembered it all too well. Atlanta was known for conventions, especially the science fiction, fantasy and multimedia variety. Some were small, others medium sized, and one was massive, clocking in at over eighty-five thousand attendees every year.

The conference call had been about a new event called TrapperCon and even though Riley was impressed someone had thought of the idea, she worried. The Prince loved any opportunity to wreak havoc so what could possibly go wrong at a convention dedicated to Demon Trappers and Hellspawn?

Absolutely everything.

The organizer had invited her and Beck to be on a panel and sign autographs. *Autographs.* Maybe even judge the costume contest.

When Riley had become speechless at that point, her mind reeling in horror, Beck had smoothly stepped in and taken over the conversation. He politely declined the offer, wished them a great convention, and hung up. Then listened to her fret about exactly how totally batshit crazy such a thing might be.

"What does this have to do with my car?" she asked, her eyes narrowing.

"Just check it out and call me back."

"Ohh . . . kay."

Riley ended the call and picked up the pace, her apprentices trailing behind. When she came to where she'd parked her car, she stalled in her tracks. Every inch of the vehicle, from front bumper to rear, was covered in rectangular squares of paper.

Even the tires.

"Cool," Tim said. "I love what you've done with your ride."

Riley shot him a frown, then marched up to the vehicle. The instant she grabbed one of the pieces of paper off the rear bumper, the faint tingle of magic nipped at her fingers. She flipped it over, suspecting what she'd find.

Bold graphics and a rather cool logo told her the rest.

"TrapperCon," she said, shaking her head. "How did they know this was my car?"

She dropped the rectangle and it floated back to the vehicle and re-attached itself.

"Guys, don't touch those things," she warned as her apprentices moved closer.

"Bad stuff?" Mickey asked.

"Not sure, so it's better to be cautious." She called her favorite grand master. "Hey. There's TrapperCon postcards all over my car. Hundreds of them. How did you know something was going on?"

"My truck was covered in them after that meetin' this mornin'. As soon as I began pullin' them off, they all disappeared. Well, except for one."

"I'm not liking this," she said.

"Yeah, same here. You checked in with Ori recently?" Beck asked. "He'd have a better idea if there's somethin' Hellish goin' on or not."

That made her raise an eyebrow. "I'll ask him, then."

"You know what this means."

"No. No. I'm not going to this . . . *thing*. No way."

There was a faint chuckle. "Uh huh. Just keep tellin' yerself that."

She frowned. "Don't you have someone else to harass, Grand Master?"

"Yeah, I do. I'll catch you later. Love you, Princess!"

Riley returned the love part, then pocketed the phone, still frowning. She pulled a few of the ads off, but they just flew right back to the car.

"You want to play that game? Okay, then." She motioned to her apprentices. "You two should stand back." Mickey and Tim immediately complied, whispering to each other as they did.

So far Riley had not performed any magic in front of them, but that was about to change. After a quick look around, she was pleased there wasn't anyone else nearby. Spying a security camera, a quick gesture changed what it would see. She followed that up with a pale flash of light and a brief dose of heat, just enough to turn all the ads on her car to fine ash, while being careful not to damage the paint. She swirled that ash around in the air and then dumped it down the nearest storm drain. If this were Hell's prank, they'd get the message.

Another gesture reinstated the security camera. She hoped whoever was watching the footage had enjoyed the brief interlude with the frolicking sea otters. Had to be better than watching a parking lot for eight hours at a time.

"Woooow," Tim said, his eyes wide.

"Yeah, what he said," Mickey added. "I'd heard you could do stuff like that, but man, that's wicked."

"Thank you," she said, executing a short bow. "Now let's get out of here."

If she was lucky, that'd be the end of it.

†✶‡✶†

The destruction of the exorcised Grade Four had gone smoothly, as it always did. The process still awed Simon, but then much of his job was like that. When he'd first began destroying the demons there'd been a monk to assist him, but that help was no longer needed. He knew the code to the building's keypad, knew exactly how to handle the fiend's remains after the fact, so it was a solo job now.

The structure itself was separate from the monastery, some distance away in the woods, and was sanctified as holy ground. It was pretty out here, peaceful, and it reminded him of the week he'd spent at Pluscarden Abbey in Scotland. Maybe it was time for another sabbatical, something Father Rosetti had been very tactfully suggesting for the last couple of months.

After placing the metal box into its proper place, he stepped just outside and waited. The Light always destroyed the Hellspawn, and did it quickly, turning it to ashes. It never failed, not with the walls and floor covered with crosses. Removing the box, he locked up the building. Once he'd dumped the ashes on the bare earth, along with the remains in the trash bags, his task was complete.

A few minutes later, after another deep breath of the country air, Simon headed for his car, the empty metal box and bundled up bags in hand. He'd purposely parked the vehicle under a shade tree to cut down on the scorching seatbelt problem.

As he neared, he found someone standing near it, someone he didn't know. The newcomer had short pale hair, a nondescript face, and equally unremarkable clothing, as if he was trying hard to blend in but not quite sure how to do that. No matter what, he was unable to hide the arrogance that seemed to flow off him in waves. Not one of the monks.

A demon? Possibly. This part of the monastery's grounds was not sanctified, only the building and the field where the ashes were dumped. Was this a Fallen? Maybe a witch or necromancer? The first was a possibility, the last two less likely.

"Simon Michael David Adler," the figure said, straightening up. As he did, the faint impression of white wings flared out behind him.

Simon halted a good distance away, his right hand automatically going to the wooden cross on his chest. "And you are?"

"Zareth. I serve Michael, the Archangel."

"I figured you were going to say you were the Archangel Gabriel."

"Why would I do that?"

"It's not important. Something you want to tell me?"

"I was sent to warn you about the treacherous Fallen."

"Any Fallen in particular?" Simon asked, though he suspected where this conversation was headed.

"Ori the Fallen," the newcomer replied, frowning as if he

were particularly dense.

"What has he done recently that's treacherous?"

From the glower, the Divine didn't appreciate the question. "That one serves the Prince."

"Not anymore, at least that's what I hear."

"He lies."

"That's possible. Why give me a warning? Why do I rate your Divine presence?"

"You are a very important mortal."

"Am I really," Simon replied flatly. "If I'm so important why didn't you warn me about Sartael when he was trying to claim my soul?"

"That was *not* important. The traitor Ori is."

"I see. So, keeping my soul safe and stopping Armageddon didn't matter? But now that it's all about Ori, I should heed your warning?"

"Yes."

"No." He shook his head. "Not buying it."

"You dare to argue with me?" the Divine asked. His wings were clearly visible now, the angelic equivalent of a threat display.

"No, I'm not arguing with you because that would be a waste of my time. What's the real agenda here, because it has jack to do with my soul?"

That got him another glower. "The Fallen will betray you. You must stop him from doing so. You must find a way to destroy him."

"If I do, what do I get in return?"

"Your soul will remain yours, and those of the mortals the fiend Azagar has taken."

There it was, the ultimate bribe. Play our game, destroy the rogue Fallen for us, and we'll do all sorts of good things for you because you're just such an awesome little exorcist. It sounded so much like something Sartael would have said.

"You guys use the same playbook, you know that?" Simon grumbled.

"I do not understand."

"No, you probably don't," he replied. He walked past the Divine, and then opened the car door. A wave of heat poured out, despite having the windows cracked.

Turning back to the being, he added, "I'll think about your offer."

"Do more than think about it," the angel insisted. "Do not trust the Fallen for he always lies."

"There's a lot of that going around."

"You dare to challenge me?"

"You have told me nothing worthy of my interest," Simon replied.

"I will tell you what I know—Katia Allyson Breman will betray you to the demon. If you fail to destroy the Fallen, you and those young mortals are lost. Doing as I demand will be your only chance of survival." At that, Heaven's most surly messenger promptly disappeared.

Simon ground his teeth. He'd have to report this to the Vatican, and he could just imagine Father Rosetti's thoughts about this conversation. The priest had once said that Simon's reports were always enlightening, which was a polite way of saying that they were always odd.

Riley had once said that the schemes of the Upper and Lower Realms were much like a multi-level chess tournament. You never knew what would happen next, and you would never be permitted to leave the game.

Simon had learned much at the hands of the liar, Sartael. Despite this latest angel's warning, he would judge Ori by the Fallen's actions. The same with Katia. If that risked his soul, so be it. It was already on the line anyway.

THIRTEEN

Katia sat on the front steps of Grand Master Stewart's house, waiting for Simon to arrive. He'd said he was about fifteen minutes away, depending on traffic. Being outside in the heat seemed to help clear her nap-fogged brain. It'd been an epic one brought on by sheer exhaustion and stress. She executed another yawn and more fog cleared. Maybe by the time Simon arrived, she'd be back in the game.

She was also procrastinating. A few times a week, Katia sent a text to her sister to check on Kevin's condition. The problem was that the answer was always the same: NO CHANGE. It was like a knife to her heart.

She turned as the door behind her opened, expecting it to be Grand Master Stewart. It wasn't. *Oh my God, it's him.* No wonder the truck in the driveway had so many demon decals.

Denver Beck was a legend among the trappers, just like his wife. He'd killed an Archangel, and though gravely wounded, he'd somehow survived. Now he was a grand master, one of the few in the world. And he'd just sat down on the same set of stairs as an insubordinate journeyman from Kansas.

Grand Master Beck was more handsome in person than in the videos, but then most of those had him fighting some fiend or another and that almost guaranteed you were covered in something disgusting. He was muscled, with blond hair and a striking set of brown eyes. Though a few years younger than her, those eyes told a story of death, grief and unexpected survival.

"Hi, I'm Beck. Yer Journeyman Breman, right?" he said. His Southern drawl came through, light and easy on the ears.

She nodded, unable to form any sensible words.

"Riley sent me pictures of those new demons. Damn, those mothers are ugly. You and Simon did good work there. Never easy when Hell starts screwin' around like that."

Katia gave another nod. He sounded like some guy you'd meet on the street. No ego, just another trapper.

"You need a ride somewhere?"

Her voice finally reappeared. "No, but thanks for asking. Simon's at the monastery getting rid of the fiend he exorcised. He's going to pick me up when he's done. Should be pretty soon."

"Good. Didn't want you stranded or nothin'." He paused. "You know, our guild isn't like any other place," he added.

"How so?"

"Well, some say we're misfits. We got Master Harper, one of the toughest SOBs on the planet. He's a hardass. But then you already know that."

"He's, well, scary."

Beck chuckled. "That's a polite way of puttin' it. We also have two grand masters in this town. Since there's only thirty of us in the whole damned world, that's a bit of overkill. Angus—Grand Master Stewart—is teachin' me the ropes. In time, he'll go back to Scotland and it'll just be me."

She had to ask. "You like being a grand master?"

To her surprise, he sighed.

"I like kickin' demon ass, and that's the God's honest truth. Every time I take one of those monsters down, I feel I'm evenin' the score, you know? Then I became a grand master, and I see it all differently now. I still like to take the things out, but I know they're not the root problem." He paused, then asked, "What do you think the world would be like if there were no demons and no Prince of Hell?"

It wasn't a question she'd ever considered. Her first response would be "Great!" But there was more here. Everything about this man said so.

"Not an easy question to answer, is it?" he said.

"No. It'd be simple to say that the reason everything is bad is because of the Prince. That he's the cause of all this evil stuff. But he isn't." She frowned, rubbing the scar on her left arm now.

He nodded. Beck's laidback smile told her why people liked him. Why Riley had married him.

"Yeah, got that right. Lucifer's one mean bastard, but he can't make everyone be evil all the time. That's our choice, right or wrong." He looked at the street, then back at her. "You got thrown in the middle of this thing with Simon. Riley says yer not that trustin' because of what happened to you in Kansas. From what I hear, that distrust is righteous."

There was more coming, she could feel it.

"Hell's lookin' to put the screws to you the first time they can. Am I right?"

Katia nodded. They already had. "I'm not sure I'm the one who should be watching the exorcist's back."

"The fact yer worryin' about that tells me yer a better choice than some. Also, the only Fallen angel I trust says yer here to help our friend Simon. I know I'm not supposed to trust a Fallen, but that one saved Riley's life. Gave her back her soul. Taught me how to kill angels." His eyes went back to her now. "So, I'm gonna trust him. Which means I'm gonna trust you. Don't mess this up, you hear?"

"I'll do my best."

"Good. Nice to meet you, Journeyman." He was three steps down when he turned around, his face pensive. "You like barbeque?"

The question was so out of the blue she answered without thinking. "Depends on what kind. Kansas City barbecue is the best in the world, and you won't convince me otherwise."

The grin that spread across the grand master's face said her challenge had been accepted. "When this is over, I will take you to Mama Z's. My treat. Then we'll find out who's is the best, and it won't be from Kansas, that I can promise."

She smiled back. "You're on, Grand Master."

After a thumbs up, he climbed into his truck and was gone.

Katia blinked a few times, then shook her head. *Two legends in one day.* Then she snorted. "You're going to lose that bet, dude. KC barbecue rocks."

After another minute or so processing that whole conversation, she glanced down at her phone, knowing she'd put it off too long: It was time to text her sister.

NO CHANGE had been the quick reply, and once again her heart hurt.

Their brother remained in his coma, hadn't done anything but act like no one was home inside his brain. His caregivers would exercise Kevin's muscles, feed him through a tube, keep him clean, but that was it.

Only rarely did he act like he was regaining consciousness, and the moment he did, Kevin went right back down into the blackness that held him hostage. Katia would do almost anything to see him chattering at them again, being the active kid he'd always been.

And Hell knew that.

At least her sister was still talking to her, although Katia hadn't told Leah she was no longer in Kansas. She also hadn't notified her parents because no way that would go well. They'd been furious when she'd refused to give up trapping when Kevin had been injured. They were convinced it was her fault that their only son was ill. In some ways, she felt the same.

"Lass? Ya doin' okay?"

Grand Master Stewart's voice made her jump, and then she felt stupid. He'd opened the door behind her, and she'd not heard him, so caught up in her own thoughts.

"Sir?" she replied, looking up at him. "I was texting with my sister to find out about my brother. Kevin's in a coma. He's in an extended care facility."

The grand master walked farther out onto the porch, then leaned against one of the carved posts. With his leg brace it would be difficult for him to sit on the steps.

"How'd that happen?"

Something about this man felt truly genuine, so she found

herself telling him how Kevin had been hurt, and how everything they'd tried to bring him back to consciousness had failed.

Stewart nodded. "First, ya have my sympathies. It's very hard ta watch someone ya love be so sick." It sounded as if he knew that personally. "But never give up hope. He may still come back ta ya."

"God, I hope so."

He straightened up. "It's also possible that Hell is usin' yer brother as leverage against ya which is why he's not awakened."

"I'm nobody," she said, shaking her head.

"Everyone is someone, lass. If yer brother remains in that condition, then Hell can always offer ya his complete recovery. Of course, there will be some sorta *debt* ya'll need ta pay. Not necessarily yer soul, not ta start with, but that's where they'll be headed."

A car drove by, followed by a convertible with its top down. The people inside it looked happy. She wasn't sure she could remember what that was like.

"I know how this goes," Stewart continued, "because when my wife was so terribly ill, an offer was made ta me: My soul in trade for her life. It would have been quite the thing—Hell would have owned a grand master."

"You didn't . . . ?"

"No, I didn't, and it ripped my heart out ta know my beautiful Lollie would die because I couldn't . . . I just couldn't." His eyes were shiny now, and he blinked frequently. "I told her of the offer, and my decision. She said she'd never loved me more."

"God, that had to be hard." Katia swallowed to ease the tightness in her throat. "My first master warned me that Hell would do that. That even if I agreed, Kevin still might die."

"His fate is in Heaven's hands, not yers, or Hell's."

"I know. It just hurts so much. I feel like I should be doing more."

He nodded. "Keep prayin', lass. Things may well change for the better."

A honk announced Simon's arrival as his car pulled into the

driveway. As she rose, slinging her pack over her shoulder, Katia smiled over at the grand master.

"Thank you for what you said. I needed to hear that."

"Thank ya for listenin'. Stay safe, lass."

"I will, sir."

Stewart waved at Simon, then returned inside the house.

The interior of the car was cool, and it felt good, but there was tension in the air.

"Did you get some sleep?" Simon asked.

"Yes. And another shower. I think I could take like ten of them and still feel dirty after those exploding demons."

She clicked her seatbelt in place, then remembered he hadn't had a chance to clean up. At least he hadn't been splattered with fiendish remains like she had. "Everything go okay?"

"It did. It's a very strange thing to watch, the power of good destroying evil," he said as he drove away from the house. "The next time I'll take you with me."

He sounded okay, but his voice was still more tense than usual, not like she'd expected if everything had gone well.

"What's happening now? Another exorcism?"

"No, a meeting. Riley called. She wants us to join her at Mort's house in a half an hour."

"Mort?"

"Oh, sorry. Mortimer Alexander is a necromancer. A powerful one."

She shuddered. "I've always thought them creepy. Necros, that is."

"They can be. I didn't trust them at first, but getting to know Mort has changed that."

"You think it's okay that they can summon the dead?" she challenged.

"No, I think the dead should be left alone, but that's not the way it is. Seeing how Mort handles that issue has taught me not to be as judgmental."

From anyone else that would have been a slap down, but Simon wasn't that way. She frowned out the side window.

"What's this meeting about?"

"Don't know, but from Riley's tone, something is up. Something not good."

"Like Hellish not good?"

"Is there any other kind?"

FOURTEEN

Simon drove them to an area of Atlanta he called Little Five Points and parked on a side street. It was an eclectic kind of neighborhood with unique little shops and kitschy restaurants.

"It feels different here than in downtown Atlanta," she said.

"There's a reason for that. I'll explain why in a bit."

After a few turns they reached a pedestrian-only street demarcated by a tall metal arch. An arch that seemed to vibrate on its own.

"Ah, Simon? What's going on here?" she asked. "That arch thing is, well, kinda moving. Well, not moving, but it seems like it is." Then she frowned because that sounded crazy.

He paused, then followed her eyes up to the metal structure. "There's a reason for that. This is the entrance to a street of magic users, mostly witches and summoners. If you're magic sensitive," he gave her a knowing look at this point, "you will feel something different than the rest of us."

"That's why I feel a lot of power here. Not the scary kind, but the 'you mess with us and your life will go bad in a heartbeat' kind."

"Exactly. If you're not comfortable—"

"No, no, I'm good." She frowned over at him. "We don't have this kind of thing in Lawrence. Well, at least we don't have a whole *street* full of it."

They continued down a passage with multi-colored flowers and deep green vines streaming along the stone walls. It had a European feel to it. Her parents had taken them to Italy one summer and this reminded her of the small town they'd visited.

A café sat on the right, patrons at various inside tables sipping coffee, then a store on the left. The name of the business—Bell, Book and Broomstick—was a dead giveaway who shopped there. A little further on a hand-lettered sign propped in a window proclaimed a bookstore would be opening soon.

Further on, as the passage split into two small alleys, the magical presence seemed to grow in intensity. Then there were the mailboxes.

"Those are . . . different," she said, being polite just in case any of the magical people were listening to them at this point. No reason to annoy them in their own backyard.

The mailboxes were arranged at various heights, composed of assorted colors, and each one decorated. One had a pinwheel, and another was painted to make it appear the mailbox was a dragon and the hinged door its mouth. She wondered if it belched fire if you tried to put bills in it.

"You should know that Mort might have a reanimate answering his door. He usually has one as his cook, and sometimes one as his housekeeper."

Katia pushed that bit of information around her brain and found it all kinds of unfathomable.

Her silence spurred Simon to explain. "He only reanimates with the family's approval, and he pays them really well for the service the reanimate performs. Then he ensures they have a dignified burial. Or reburial, I guess."

"Why would people do that?" she blurted.

"Usually, the families are poor or have major medical bills. Sometimes the reanimate made arrangements with a summoner before they die so the money is left to their family sooner, rather than later. It's sort of an insurance policy. It's non-taxable so the family receives all the money." To his credit, Simon winced at this point.

"It sounds awful."

"It can be if the necro isn't honest. Mort? No problem. He's friendly, polite, and yet can be downright lethal if you're a threat to anyone he cares about."

Katia inhaled deeply. "Then I shouldn't piss him off."

"Honestly, I doubt you could. He's very forgiving. But once you cross that line, God help you. I've seen him kill Archfiends with his magic, so I'm not exaggerating the kind of power he has."

Archfiends? Those were only a step down from a Fallen.

"Thank you for the warning. And the information."

"Not a problem," he said, then led her down the left passageway. They continued to a purple door with a shiny plaque on the wall next to it which announced that this was the home of the Summoner Advocate of Atlanta. It appeared that Mr. Mild Mannered Mort was also someone of importance in the necro world.

Simon knocked, and a short time later the door was opened by a young man. He was probably about twenty or so. His T-shirt was beige, and his jeans looked comfortably worn, like they were his favorite pair. His brown hair curled at the ends. What caught her notice was his eyes, light brown and expressive.

This guy did not look dead.

"Hey, Simon. Good to see you again," he said with a big smile.

"Alex. It's been a while. This is Katia Breman," he said, gesturing her way.

"Please tell me you're a female exorcist. I'd love it!"

"Nope, I'm a Journeyman Demon Trapper," she replied.

"You know, you couldn't pay me enough to do your job," he replied, shaking his head. He must have read Katia's expression and added, "No, I'm not a reanimate. Anya is in the kitchen working on a cake. I'm told it will be chocolate. That's all I needed to hear."

Katia nodded. You couldn't go wrong with a nod. Hopefully.

Alex waved them into the house. "My uncle is in the fountain room. Or the fireplace room depending on the season. Home decor is a lot easier when you can do magic."

He chattered along like they were family, and everything was completely normal. She still hadn't quite processed what was going on here, but if Simon was good with these folks, she'd trust his judgment. At this point, she had no other choice.

The house was pleasantly arranged, the occasional potted plant here and there, a few pictures on the walls. None of those were illusions. Maybe Mortimer Alexander was like anyone else, except that the Summoner Advocate could kill powerful Hellspawn with his hocus pocus.

The illusionary fountain burbled away in the room where Alex led them. The space was welcoming, with a large skylight allowing in just enough light, but none of the heat. Their host had been prepared for them as there were comfy chairs and a cedar table set with refreshments.

In one corner of the room, Riley sat next to a large man clad in slacks and a blue shirt. There was some sort of spellwork going on if the swirling air in front of them was any indication. They looked up and the magic immediately vanished.

"Hey, guys." Riley gestured, "Mort, this is Katia Breman, our newest trapper. She just arrived from Kansas."

"Welcome, Katia," the necromancer said, giving her a warm smile.

"Hi."

"You know, I think there are about," he scrunched up his face in thought, "twenty some summoners in that entire state, so I'm guessing you might not have met one of us before."

"Only one. He was . . ."

"Odd?" Mort suggested.

"He was *way* odd. I don't know if it's a thing for you guys, but he wore a robe with glow-in-the-dark plastic skulls sewn onto it. Scared the little old church ladies, that's for sure."

Mort chuckled. "His robe was pale gray?"

"How'd you know?"

"He was so new to the profession that he had little or no magic to speak of. Some try to compensate for that by looking scary."

"I thought the skulls made him look, well, stupid."

"I won't argue that," he replied as she and Simon chose

places to sit.

"A summoner's magical abilities are indicated by the color of robe they wear," Riley explained. "Beginners wear light gray, then proceed up to deepest black as they acquire more skills."

"Your master has attained a dark blue robe," Mort said with pride. He sent Riley a mock frown. "Would have gotten it sooner if she had focused on her levitation spells."

A groan returned. "Yes, I suck at levitation. You've known that since the first time I tried it."

"Just how badly *do you* suck at that?" Alex cut in. "I ask only for information."

"I levitate, and then I immediately flip upside down. And stay there. It's like my internal gyroscope is totally screwed up. I used to do that *every time*. Now it's one out of every five. Did I mention I suck at levitation?"

Alex barely held back the laughter.

"My nephew is studying to be a summoner, as well," Mort said.

Alex appeared pleased that had been mentioned.

"My folks are hoping I'll get bored. Fat chance of that. I want to become a forensic necromancer."

"What is that?" Katia asked.

"When there's a suspicious death, I would summon the deceased to find out how they died, and if they were murdered, who did it."

"Would that work? I mean, in court?" she asked, skeptical.

"No, evidence like that is not admissible in court, at least not yet. I'm hoping to change that."

Alex certainly wasn't aiming low for his new career. "I hope you can make that happen."

"Won't be easy, but then change never is," Mort added.

The doorbell sounded, and Alex left the room to welcome the new arrivals.

"These two rated an entirely new fiend today, courtesy of the Infernal Pest Himself." Riley accessed the photos on her phone and showed them to the necromancer. "It looks like a giant beachball with tentacles and spits out duplicates of itself like a demented photocopier."

Mort leaned closer, studying the image. "How'd you get rid those things?"

"Holy Water. Slam dunked the big one right in the mouth," Simon said. "It exploded and took out the rest of them." He angled his thumb toward at Katia. "She did it. I just ran interference."

"Well done!"

"I got lucky," Katia said.

"Then stay that way," her master replied. "You two are going to need it."

FIFTEEN

Voices came from the hallway, and then a pair of angels entered the room followed by a puzzled Alex. He was far enough into his magical training to know these two were something different, but not exactly what they were.

Mort rose in respect. "I bid you both welcome to my home," he said. "Ori, it is good to see you again. May I know the name of your companion?"

"I am Serrah, and I offer blessings upon your dwelling Mortimer Beaumont Alexander."

"We are honored to accept your hospitality," Ori added.

"Oh! You're Divines! Wow!" Alex blurted, then grimaced. "Sorry!" He glanced at his uncle. "That was rude."

"Your greeting is probably the most enthusiastic I've ever received, Alexander Rowan Greene," Ori said, clearly amused.

"No harm, Alex," Mort said, smiling.

"Yeah, well, I'm still sorry." The apology didn't keep him from staring at the latest guests with intense curiosity.

Riley checked her phone. "Okay, the grand master dude should be here in a couple minutes." Alex took that as an excuse to exit the room, his face still slightly red from embarrassment.

"Your nephew is studying with you?" Ori asked.

"Yes. He's smart, and he has a good heart. That's a solid basis upon which to build."

Serrah looked toward the door, then back. "He will do well."

"I am reassured to hear that, especially from you."

Beck arrived while Mort was ensuring everyone had something to eat or drink. The angels declined, which Riley found curious as Ori had dined in her home on more than one occasion. Was it because of Serrah? From what she could tell they were more comfortable in each other's presence now. What had happened to change that adversarial dynamic?

Riley made sure her spouse was introduced to Heaven's angel, and then to the new journeyman.

"We met when I was at Stewart's," he said, smiling over at Katia. "I was horrified to discover that she thinks that *Midwestern* barbecue is somehow *better* than ours. I will be showin' her she's wrong about that."

Katia shook her head. "Not a chance." Then added a quick, "Sir."

It was obvious the two had hit it off if Beck was already razzing the newcomer about his favorite food.

Once Alex found a chair, Riley began. "Does anyone have objection if I use the magical equivalent of soundproofing? We'll be talking about certain things that I don't want *others* to overhear."

There were no objections, so Riley executed the spell. "That good?" Mort nodded his approval.

"May I add to it?" Ori asked.

"Sure."

He didn't move, didn't close his eyes, but the room's acoustics changed somehow. The space now felt more like a sanctuary than a hollow bubble.

"Sweet! Is it the whole house?" Riley asked.

"Yes. It will likely attract attention since I'm involved, but what we discuss must not be overheard."

Riley looked over at Simon. "Please let the others know what's going on with you and those kids."

Her ex-boyfriend delivered a tight nod and then laid out what had happened during the exorcism earlier that day, as well as the stakes involved. Mort grimaced at the part where the demon had snared Simon in its unholy bargain. He gave Alex a pointed look—the teacher equivalent of "see how dangerous those things are?"—and his nephew nodded his understanding.

"Since you were there," Beck said, looking over at Ori now. "What's yer take on this?"

"There's a lot more going on than just these three mortals' souls."

"Because of . . . ?" Mort asked.

Ori traded a look with the angel next to him. "Serrah and I returned to the house where the exorcism took place. I created a means for her to witness the event as it occurred. She saw something I did not."

All eyes went to the other angel.

"There was another Divine there, one who serves the Archangel Michael. Zareth did nothing to stop what happened between the exorcist and Azagar."

Somehow that didn't surprise Riley. In her experience, Heaven's politics could often be just as cutthroat as Hell's.

"Michael's gopher didn't bother to help ya save those kids?" Beck asked, his voice as sharp as his anger.

"No. He made no attempt to indicate he was there," Ori replied.

"Did the demons know?"

"I don't think so. They weren't acting like it. Two Divines in the same room should have made them nervous, and they weren't. If anything, Azagar was too smug."

"Either they didn't know he was there, or the angel and the fiends have some sort of agreement in place," Riley said.

"Zareth is not to be trusted," Serrah admitted. "He is too ambitious. He seeks Michael's . . . position."

"How likely is that to happen?" Beck asked, folding his arms over his broad chest, a frown still in place.

"Not likely. Michael serves our Creator well, even if not all agree with his methods." She gave her fellow Divine a glance at this.

"I certainly wouldn't vote for him as Angel of the Year," Beck muttered.

A hint of a smile played on Ori's lips now.

"Zareth is cunning," Simon said. "When I was at the monastery today, he dropped by to make me an offer." He looked over at the Fallen. "If I betray you, then he will ensure that my soul, and those of the boys', are safe from Hell."

"Then I suggest you do just that. Your soul and those of the others are worth more than mine."

Simon shook his head even before the angel had finished. "No! Absolutely not! I know a lie when I hear it. Sartael taught me that much. Zareth sounds more like a Fallen then one of Heaven's crew."

"Well, damn. So, we have demons schemin' on one side, and a Divine schemin' on the other," Beck said, shaking his head.

"Situation normal, I'd say," Mort replied.

Riley snorted, then looked over at the exorcist. "How do we help you save these kids without violating your agreement with the fiend?"

"I don't know," Simon replied. "Azagar's kept me . . . " He glanced over at Katia now. "He's kept *us* busy most of the day, and I think he's just getting started. I have no idea where this final confrontation will happen."

Riley and Beck exchanged looks, but it was Ori who spoke.

"I think I do. It's my habit to watch how the fiends move about the city because they have certain patterns. For some of them, that pattern has altered today. The stronger ones are making their way toward the center of Atlanta. That is unusual."

"Downtown." Beck said. He sighed and looked over at Riley. "Ya know where they're goin'."

She issued a groan. "TrapperCon."

"What's that?" Simon asked.

Katia dug in her trapping bag where it sat at her feet.

"It's this," she said, handing him a postcard. "It was on your car at the daycare center. None of the other cars had one."

"'Atlanta's first annual multi-media convention celebrating the Demon Trappers, the Demon Hunters, and their archenemies from Hell,'" Simon read.

He looked up, stunned. "You've got to be kidding me. Don't they know what could happen there? You just don't tempt

Lucifer like that, especially not in *this* city."

"We pointed all that out to them, but the organizers insisted it'd be just fine," Beck said. "It's like throwin' a bunch of chicken guts in front of a Three and bein' surprised when it decides yer dessert."

"You couldn't make them cancel it?"

"No. They have the right to hold their convention," Beck grumbled. "Harper was gonna send down a couple trappers just to keep an eye out, but now with what Ori's seen, Riley and I will have to be there. Probably Jackson and a few others, too."

"Higher level demons live to create chaos. Azagar forcing Simon to face him at this event would be the kind of thing the Prince would dearly love," Ori said. "Nothing makes Lucifer happier than large numbers of terrified mortals."

"I agree," Serrah chimed in. "If there must be a confrontation it'll be at this gathering."

"Okay, so we need to be there, but not as ourselves," Riley said. "Beck and I will draw too much attention and that'll interfere with our jobs, at least until people need to know who we are." She looked over at Mort now. "Glamour?"

"That was my thought."

"The average person won't notice the magic," she explained. "Glamour for me is no biggie, but Beck will need some help because I might not always be close enough to hold his spell in place. We'll need something like you did for me when I was hiding from the Demon Hunters."

"You guys will need weapons, right?" Alex asked.

"Yeah. Swords, steel pipes, spheres, whatever works. Why?" Beck replied.

"Because the cons I've been to won't let you bring those in unless they're peace-bonded. It's their way of making sure people don't channel their inner stupid and hurt each other. They usually secure swords so they can't be drawn from their scabbard, that sort of thing."

"What if a weapon looked totally fake rather than like the real item?" Mort asked.

"No harm, no foul. They'll stick some tape on it to show they've checked it and you're good to go."

"Okay, amulets for the weapons as well," Mort said. "How many?"

A quick count was generated, plus a few extras.

"We will need no such assistance," Serrah said. "We shall be there as ourselves. Well, without our wings, at least."

Mort looked over at a clock on the far wall. "Give me a few hours and I'll have what you need. Alex can deliver them to you. He's going to be there anyway."

"Yeah. Don't want to miss this one," his nephew replied.

Riley gave the apprentice necromancer a frown. "Really?"

"It sounds like fun," the young man replied, grinning. "I'm dressing up as a summoner. Go figure."

"That will not help you score with the girls, trust me on this."

"She might be lyin' about that," Beck said. Riley's frown moved to him now, but he just gave her a wink.

Simon's phone rang and he excused himself to the far side of the room. There was a quick conversation, and once he was off the phone, Katia asked, "An exorcism?"

"No, my mother. She's worried I might forget about the church social on Monday. Because obviously nothing else is that important."

There were chuckles, at least from the mortals. "Is she still introducing you to Nice Catholic Girls?" Riley asked.

"Yeah. They like me right up until they find out I cast out Hellspawn for a living. Funny how that changes things." He sobered, then turned to the angels now. "Do you think I have a chance against Azagar?"

Ori took some time before he replied. "It depends on whether your faith, and your courage hold," he said. "You'd readily sacrifice yourself if need be, and I think that's exactly what Hell wants. This demon's goal is to push you into a corner where you have no other choice but to surrender your soul."

"Then we will do everythin' we can to clear a path for you," Beck said. "Without violatin' that infernal contract."

"I will do what I can," Ori said. "At least I can keep other Hellspawn from coming to Azagar's aid."

"I will do the same," Serrah said.

Ori frowned at that. "Such an act might have consequences for you."

"I know. I accept them."

"Okay then, I'll let all of you know when and where we're meeting once I figure out where that is," Riley said. "Anything else we need to discuss?"

There were head shakes all around.

Mort rose. "I'll get to work so you have those charms by later tonight." He grinned over at his nephew. "And guess who gets to assist me?"

Alex smiled back, which told Riley he had no idea the effort, or the headache, involved in creating those things. He'd learn soon enough.

Once they were outside walking toward the main street, Ori held back, allowing the others to go ahead of them.

"You need to be very careful tonight, Serrah," he said. "This may be as much a trap for you as it is for the exorcist and myself."

"I trust that I will know the right path when I see it."

"I once thought that myself. Learn from my mistakes, and for all that is holy, do not repeat them."

"I most certainly will not follow a lying Divine into exile."

"There are more ways to be deceived than by the Prince."

She looked as if she was going to argue, then shook her head.

"I shall take care, Fallen. As must you."

He issued a grim nod and fell silent.

SIXTEEN

NO CHANGE.

The text from Leah was the same as it'd been earlier that afternoon and the same message for months. Katia often wondered if her older sister just cut and pasted the two words because typing them over and over would break anyone's heart. Reading them certainly broke hers.

After they'd returned to Simon's house, she'd fallen asleep on the sofa while he'd taken another shower and then made them supper. It was more like breakfast, with bacon and fluffy eggs, wheat toast and orange juice. It tasted wonderful. Her host understood that her body needed fuel so he'd heaped the eggs on her plate, and kept the toast coming.

As they ate, Riley texted them the rendezvous time and location. Now that those had been established, Simon went to change his clothes to something more appropriate, he'd said. Katia remained on the couch, staring at the packing boxes. According to Ori, all sorts of demons were headed toward this convention thing. If it went as they thought, Simon would face the fiend that had issued the challenge.

The next time Azagar's offer would be about Kevin, likely delivered in the silkiest of tones: "We will make your brother well if you do whatever we ask." That *whatever we ask* would mean betraying Simon.

Her brother or the exorcist?

Please don't make me choose.

Simon returned from his bedroom clad in all black—a short-sleeved T-shirt, and jeans. The cross was still in place.

She wondered if he slept with it. His white shirt had been a bit baggy, but the T-shirt revealed that the exorcist must lift weights regularly. That she hadn't expected.

"All you need is a collar, and you could be a priest," Katia said. He shrugged, but she wondered if that was what he'd been thinking as well. "What's this convention going to be like?"

"Not sure. I did go to DragonCon® once. A girlfriend dragged me to it. It was ten bazillion people, most of them in costume, and it was Labor Day weekend."

She could just imagine how hot it was in September down here. "How did it go?"

"It was okay, but we broke up right after that. I wasn't much fun back then."

Ouch.

He sat on the sofa. "You know, my parents always thought I'd become a priest. It really surprised them when I became a trapper." He grew a soft smile now. "For some reason me becoming an exorcist *didn't* surprise them."

"I didn't even know there were lay exorcists until I came here."

"It's a new thing. There just aren't enough priests trained in exorcism to handle the load, especially in Atlanta."

"What made you decide to become one?" He didn't reply, which made her wonder if she'd asked one question too many. "Look, if you're not comfortable talking about it, I understand. I won't ask again."

"I think you need to know why because there has to be no secrets between us when we go after Azagar." He took a deep breath, then let it out. "After I was . . . after I nearly died, I was sure I'd lost my faith."

He huffed. "If Simon the Self-Righteous could almost die at the hands of a fiend, and believe the lies of a Fallen angel, what did my faith mean?"

He stared at the far wall for a time, then touched the wooden cross on his chest. "I almost lost it all, Katia," he said, the ache in his voice palpable.

"What did you do?"

"I went on a Sabbatical, traveled all over the world." He was still focused on the wall, not looking at her. "I did a lot of thinking, about myself, what being Catholic meant to me, about where I'd gone wrong. I talked to people of many different faiths, even with those who didn't believe in a god. You know what I realized?"

She shook her head.

"Pride really does go before a fall."

She could imagine what it took for him to admit that to her, someone he barely knew. "Yet you kept your faith."

"The truth is I have a different kind of faith now, one that is less rigid. I still believe in the basics, but now I see how the Light and Dark interact, more of what it all means. Which is why I became an exorcist."

Simon leaned back against the sofa. "The priest in charge of the Demon Hunters in Rome knew how to counsel someone who'd faced a test like mine. Father Rosetti said that perfection is not something we humans will ever attain, nor is it required among the faithful. We are fallible, no matter how religious we believe ourselves to be. He also said that the greatest error I could make was not examining my conscience and learning from my mistakes. Because if I walked away from the Light, Hell would win."

He cleared his throat. "After a lot more soul searching, and a lot of time on my knees, I got my heart and head in the right place."

"Has it helped you being an exorcist instead of a trapper?"

"Yes, and no. People have died during my exorcisms, and those deaths are so hard to accept. I will always wonder if I did enough to save them,"

Simon picked up his phone off the coffee table, searched through it, and then handed it to her.

"Whenever I am most troubled, I remember one little girl. Her name is Carrina. That's her picture."

The child was maybe six, if that. She was cuddling a calico

kitten and smiling as if the world was wonderful.

"Carrina is alive today because with God's help I exorcised a vicious demon from inside her. I was able to do that because of my faith, and also because Riley and Beck were there to watch my back."

"Faith and friends," Katia murmured. She returned the phone. "Why would a demon go after a little kid like that?"

"It was after her parents' souls. It failed."

"Thank God," she said.

"I do, every day. Carrina has put that bad time behind her. In fact, Riley says that little girl will probably be a Demon Hunter when she's older."

"I thought the hunters don't accept women."

"They don't right now, but all things change. Even stubborn self-righteous guys like me." He glanced down at his phone again. "It's almost seven-thirty. We should head downtown. I'm not sure how long it'll take to find a place to park."

"Thank you for telling me your story," she said. "I mean that."

"It felt good to share it."

"Everything here is so different," she said as she rose. "One day I'm in Lawrence, now I'm in Atlanta. I think I have the bus equivalent of jetlag."

Simon chuckled as he locked the door behind them. "Maybe you'll find a home here."

"I'm not sure yet," Katia replied. She didn't have anywhere else to go, but that thought was just as depressing.

"Make sure the job and the city are right for you. If you don't like it here, tell Riley and she'll find you somewhere that might fit you better." When Katia didn't reply, he added, "I'm serious. She will help you. That's what she does."

"I'll see," she said, filing that information away.

"Me? I'm hoping you'll stay," he said, then climbed into the car.

You won't if I sell you out to the demon.

†✶‡✶†

The downtown parking lot Riley had chosen as a meeting place was nearly full. Simon had managed to find an open space in the back row, and he carefully slotted the car in place. His passenger had fallen silent ever since they'd driven away from his house, and he let Katia have that respite because he needed it as well.

Tonight, he'd either save those kids, or lose it all. The grumbling he'd done about attending the various church functions over the years seemed so insignificant now. If he was alive on Monday, he'd be pleasant to all the church ladies, smile at their daughters, and thank God that none of them knew the horrors he witnessed in this job.

Riley, Beck and Master Jackson stood near the open tailgate of Beck's truck. As they joined the group, the grand master gave him an up-and-down glance. Probably making note of the fact he wasn't wearing his usual white shirt. Lying on the tailgate were trapping bags, various weapons, and an assortment of amulets. The summoners had delivered the goods.

"I have been informed that the angelic portion of this team will be making their own way to the convention," Riley announced. "Time to hide what we want to hide, and join them."

First were the amulets to disguise the weapons. It was fascinating to watch how Beck's short sword went from the real deal to one of those plastic kind kids tote around on Halloween. Worse, it was a screaming neon orange.

"Now that's just embarrassin'," he said, shaking his head.

When the other trappers' steel pipes turned into short, lime green pool noodles, Katia began to chuckle, then she lost it, breaking out in laughter.

"We appeared to have amused our newest trapper," Riley said, smiling.

"Sorry, it's just so silly. Which is point, I know, but . . ." Katia said, shaking her head. There were a couple more chuckles and then she regained control.

Riley picked up an amulet, checked its tag and then dropped

it over Beck's neck. He immediately winced. "Just breathe through it. It'll pull a little energy from you, but not too much," she advised.

At first there was the grand master, all muscles and brawn in his T-shirt and jeans, then the transformation began. Too quickly he became someone's idea of what Denver Beck might look like if he had lost most of his bulk, added forty pounds, and had a noticeable beer belly. A scraggly beard was just the right touch.

"Damn," Jackson said, shaking his head. "That's not a good look on you."

The grand master eyed the changes, touched the beard, and then glowered at his wife. "Really?"

"Yeah, really. They'll think you're trying to look like Beck but not quite making it. No one would guess it's actually you."

He took a deep breath, then nodded his agreement. "Yeah, yer right. What about you, Princess?"

Not needing an amulet, Riley's change went swiftly. She appeared taller now, her hair coal black and secured in a tight bun at the base of her neck. The Vatican's Demon Hunter uniform fit her perfectly. All business, much like the hunters themselves.

"That works!" Jackson said, nodding his approval.

Riley looked over at him. "You sure you want to be yourself? I've got an amulet if you need it."

"No, thanks. You'd put me in a tutu or something."

She laughed. "Yeah, I would. Simon?"

He shook his head. "No magic, not for me."

"I figured you'd say that."

There was a quiet moment between them, words left unsaid, then the master trapper turned her attention to Katia. "What about you?"

His companion chewed on her bottom lip. "I'd like something different. I just don't know what."

Riley picked up an amulet. "Mort didn't set any particular glamour on this one so whatever you think of will be what you become. There will be a bit of an energy drain, but you'll adjust to it." She walked over and placed the amulet over Katia's head.

"Just close your eyes and think of how you'd like to appear and it'll happen. Just be cautious what you choose."

Her forehead wrinkling in concentration, Katia did as ordered.

Simon watched in anticipation. What would she choose? For a few seconds nothing happened, then Katia began to transform.

"What in the . . . ?" Jackson began. "Oh man, that rocks!"

Gone was the skinny trapper, and in her place was a nun. But not like any holy sister Simon had ever seen.

Katia looked down at her costume and burst into a smile. She hadn't been sure her imagination was strong enough to create this particular glamour, but here it was. She'd seen a picture on the internet, thought it was incredibly cool, and now that's what she wore.

It began with a long, black nun's habit which had been shortened in the front to reveal a pair of flat soled, black knee-high boots. A traditional black veil and snow-white wimple covered her hair. There was even a silver cross, like the one her grandmother had given her when she was small. At her waist was a thick black belt to which she could attach her steel pipe, a quart bottle of Holy Water, one of the smaller spheres, and her folding knife.

She closed her eyes to deal with the sudden wave of weariness, but it quickly passed. Eyes open again, Katia did a quick turn to see how the costume moved, and was pleased it wouldn't get in her way if she had to bash on a demon. Then she remembered who she was working with tonight.

"You okay with this?" she asked.

As the others watched in uneasy silence, Simon examined the costume with a closed expression.

He hates it. Why did I think this would work? He probably has sisters who are nuns and I've just dissed them. Good move, Breman.

"Am I okay with this?" To her astonishment his smile broke

free. "This is *badass*, Katia! Seriously badass. This is *exactly* what we need tonight."

"Then it's all good?"

He studied her for moment, then winked. "Yes, it is."

They high fived.

"So why did she get the cool costume and I look like . . . this?" Beck asked, gesturing downward.

Riley smiled like she'd been waiting for that very question. "I'm sooo glad you asked. Remember that joke you pulled on me last month?"

Beck looked puzzled for a moment, then he went, "Oh, that one."

"Yeah, *that* one. Consider this payback, Grand Master."

"Ah. Got it. Could have been worse," he said.

"Way worse. So now we're even."

"Doubt it," he whispered, then acted like he hadn't said that.

"You going to share what the joke was about?" Jackson prodded.

"No," they said simultaneously.

"Well then, I'll just have to try to guess, won't I?"

"Good luck with that one," Riley said as she looped an amulet over the top of Katia's pipe and knife, then gave one to Simon for his weapon.

"The con guy gave us these ahead of time so you don't have to stand in line," Beck said, distributing the badges.

"They know you two are officially going to be at the convention?" Jackson asked, clipping his badge to his T-shirt.

"Beck called them today and said there was something going on that required us to attend. The con chair was ecstatic, to say the least. Oh, and for those of us using glamour the badge names are magically altered so they don't know who we really are," Riley replied. Hers said *Captain B. Thorne*.

Katia checked out the others. "Father Simon," she grinned at that. "Sister Badass." Then the grand master. "Denver Beck Wannabe."

That elicited more good-natured razzing, and to his credit,

Beck took it well.

"Are we done yet?" he asked, but Katia could tell he was trying to hold back the laughter.

"Yes, we are," Riley said, handing him a trapping bag and then closing the truck's tailgate. "Let's pray the demons are too spooked by Atlanta's finest nerds to hang around."

"The chances of that happening are . . . ?" Katia asked.

"Zip, zero, not a chance," Jackson replied, falling in step next to her as they headed down the sidewalk, the others trailing behind. "Still, miracles happen in this town so who knows?"

"Considering what I'm wearing, I'm all over those miracles." She hesitated and then asked the question that had been plaguing her. "Are you guys always this crazy?"

"Pretty much. Hell's Chief Asshole has made Atlanta his primary target, so we've learned how to enjoy each day. Mostly because tomorrow we might not be here. Comes with the territory. Not like that in Lawrence?"

"No. We had bad demons, but nothing nuts like this."

"Welcome to the Big Leagues, Sister Badass. Don't worry, you'll do fine. You didn't get those scars because you're a wimp."

No, she hadn't. She'd gotten them because of her brother, but tonight that might not matter. Tonight, there'd be a reckoning, one way or another.

SEVENTEEN

During the walk to the hotel the group shuffled around, and Katia ended up paired with Simon. He'd noticed her talking to Jackson, how much she was focusing on whatever the master had been saying. Hopefully, it was something that gave them a chance in this fight.

Now he was curious how she'd react to their trek through the heart of Atlanta. He caught her glancing up, then further up, at the skyscrapers, then turning and staring at something even as she continued by his side.

Though certainly not as crowded as during DragonCon, when it was tough to find a straight path on the sidewalks, the streets were busy nonetheless. There were the usual buskers here and there, a guy with a trombone, someone with a guitar. Whenever Simon encountered one, he'd drop some coins into whatever was serving as the busker's cash box, be it a hat or a guitar case. A glance over at Katia caught her smiling at him.

"Thanks for thinking of them. If I had some change, I'd do the same."

"I'll put in double from now on," he replied, and she nodded her appreciation, along with a wider smile.

The hotel finally came into view. There were more people now, and most were in costumes. Since this was Atlanta, a street preacher was exhorting his fellow mortals not to fall into Hell's hands by being part of this latest abomination.

"You must be wary! Demons walk among you!" he cried. "See them! See all of them!"

It didn't help his case that when he pointed at the nearest

fiend, the little girl giggled and tossed a handful of wrapped candies at him. But then that's what you'd expect a three-year-old to do.

"I love her hot pink tail," Katia said. "And the glitter on the pitchfork is way cute. Hell should get with the plan here. Their usual red, black and armor theme is out of date."

Caught up in the moment, Simon began throwing out ideas of his own. Soon they had devised an entire new wardrobe for Hellspawn, one that involved stilettos, corsets and garish blue wigs.

"You're being silly now," Katia said. "I didn't think you had it in you."

"Neither did I. You are ruining a perfectly somber exorcist, you know that?" he said.

A thumbs-up came his way, along with a mischievous grin. This was the real Katia, the one most people never saw. Unfortunately, the preacher regained his composure and began exhorting the masses again.

"He's not getting anywhere," Simon said, frowning over at the man. "You say something is forbidden and it's guaranteed someone will give it a try. Which is why he might actually be working for the other side."

Katia's eyebrows rose. "Hadn't thought about that. My first master told me there is nothing that is plain black and white."

"He was right."

The hotel's entrance was tucked behind a circular drive, which allowed guests to be deposited right at the front doors. It was certainly serving that function now as luggage carts rolled inside in a steady chain.

"Hey, guys!" a voice called out. A glance around found Alex tucked away from the main entrance, but still close enough to be visible. He was clad in a light gray robe, but this one had glowing silver stars woven into the fabric.

Riley eyed it as she walked closer. "I don't think this," she gestured at the stars "is going to catch on with the Summoner's Society."

"Not a chance," Alex said, grinning. "I didn't dare wear my real robe or my uncle would freak. This one he actually liked." The apprentice checked out their costumes. "You guys are great." His scrutiny paused on Beck. "Well, most of you."

The grand master's eyes slid over to his wife. "Ha ha."

She smirked, then turned back to Alex. "How's it looking here?"

"Well, we got lots of people. I figured it'd be about three hundred, now they're saying it'll be closer to the mid-four hundreds or even higher, probably because of the rumor that certain *famous Demon Trappers* are going to be here," he said, waggling his eyebrows. "The attendance bumped up a lot off that."

"Wonderful," Riley muttered, shaking her head. "The convention was supposed to keep our part quiet."

"Riiight."

"The bad news is that TrapperCon isn't the only event here this weekend. There's the Ferguson wedding reception, and some church is having a revival."

"Oh great," Beck said. "More civilians to worry about."

Jackson angled his head toward someone about thirty feet away. "Looks like at least one demon is here. The *real* kind."

Grade Fours usually had a talent for blending in, except in this case. The Mezmer felt that the long black dress and the black pointed hat were perfect for this crowd. The deep green skin, hooked nose and strategically placed wart let you know exactly what it was trying to mimic. It even carried an old-fashioned broom just in case it decided it wanted to fly.

Riley whistled under her breath. "Talk about a stereotype. That thing better hope none of Atlanta's real witches see it, or it's going to get nailed."

"Too late," Beck said. A pair of genuine witches, both scowling, fell in behind the fiend as it entered the hotel.

"Do they need any help?" Jackson asked.

"No. I know them. They've got more power than that thing, and it's about to learn that the hard way."

"Well, that's one fiend off our plate," Jackson replied. "I'll go wandering around and see if there's any others we need to worry about. I'll let you know if I find anything."

"We'll do the same," Beck said. He looked over at Simon and Katia. "You two want to stick with us?"

Simon shook his head. "It's best we're on our own so Hell doesn't think you're helping me."

"Got it. Stay safe. Give a yell if something goes wrong," Riley said, and then they headed off into the crowd.

By his side, Katia fiddled with her wimple, then adjusted the belt on her hips. Finally, she fanned her face with a hand.

"Hot?"

She nodded. "I know it's only glamour, but it feels real."

"Mort knows his magic."

Simon looked at the entrance, then at his phone. It was just after eight-thirty. The deal with the demon had to be settled by midnight. Had they guessed right, and this is where the final confrontation would be? They'd learn soon enough.

"*Facilis descensus Averni,*" he whispered to himself.

The descent into Hell is always easy.

Once inside the hotel Katia and Simon were immediately shifted to the right by a series of signs and roped stanchions, where they joined a line to have their badges checked and their weapons inspected. Ahead of them were two Merlin lookalikes and right behind them was the Grim Reaper, complete with a fake scythe. Katia shivered at the sight, especially when the reaper winked at her and licked his lips.

The noise level steadily increased as they kept shuffling forward, foot by foot. Someone in a hotel uniform rolled a cart crammed with luggage past the line. The lobby was full, almost everyone in costume. Katia found herself checking out each one, looking for signs of a glamour spell in case someone was hiding their appearance. To her relief, she didn't see anything suspicious.

"I heard they're going to be here!" one girl said. "I can't wait to see her!"

She wore ripped and stained jeans and held a small glass ball. Her wig was shoulder-length brown, close to Riley's hair color, and dirt was smeared on one cheek. When she turned around to call out to a friend, the back of her T-shirt said *Girl Trappers Rock!*

"I know a certain master trapper who is going to scream if she sees that," Katia murmured. "Look at all the work they put into these costumes. Like that Three over there," she said, pointing. "It even has dirt embedded in its fur, just like the real thing."

"I'm not sure how I feel about this," Simon replied, shaking his head.

"Yeah, I know what you mean."

Finally, they reached a member of convention security who checked their badges, eyed their magically obscured weapons, stuck pieces of tape on each, and then waved them on. Once they were cleared for entrance, Simon immediately cut back toward the lobby.

"This hotel is big and spread out. Downstairs is where most of the exhibit halls are, this floor has the hotel registration, and one floor up is the bar area and more conference rooms. There is a connecting skywalk to some of the other hotels."

Lots of space to play hide and seek with a fiend. "If you were a big, bad demon where would you be?"

Simon stopped so abruptly she almost ran into him. "I have no clue." He hesitated, then admitted, "I have no damned clue if I can do this, Katia. I'm—"

"Ohhh! Wow! Look!" a young woman said, pointing at Katia. Dressed as a fairy, a few bits of strategically placed greenery barely making the costume PG, she fumbled with her smartphone. "That's soooo cool! Can I take your picture?"

"Sure!" Katia said, earning a frown from her companion. "Blend in," she whispered. "We can't have people think we're for real. Just go with it."

He grudgingly nodded, then took a deep breath.

As the fairy backed up to get a good shot, barely dodging people as she did, Katia added, "Smile, okay?" Then it occurred to her that maybe he was nervous for another reason. "Are you worried what the Vatican might think?"

Her companion shook his head. "At this point they're the least of my worries."

"Then smile, Father Simon, because she thinks we're awesome."

Katia pulled out her pool noodle/pipe and acted as if Hell's worst fiend was right in front of them. Simon just looked saintly. It wasn't a stretch.

After the fairy was done gushing about the costumes, more would-be photographers took her place. This was fun. How long had it been since she'd actually enjoyed doing something other than trapping?

Not since Kevin's injury. And she'd bitched at Simon about not having a life? Oh, the irony.

Once the initial flurry of photos was over, she and Simon wandered through the crowd, then up the escalator to another level. There were even more people here and they joined them with no particular idea where they were going.

Somehow, they'd moved into an area with various rooms, each with a placard denoting exactly what panel was happening inside. As they wandered, they encountered angels, demons, trappers, hunters, just about any costume you could think of. Another Grim Reaper, this one all in red, someone dressed as a nun, the more conventional version, two priests and finally a small band of elves.

"Oh look," she said, pointing. "A Magpie!"

The Grade One Fiend was a puppet creatively tucked into a small bag of loot that rested in a trapper's hand. The thing was well made and moved exactly like a Klepto-Fiend. It was evident the puppeteer had met one somewhere along the line.

"That's really cute, in a bizarre sort of way," Katia murmured.

"It is," Simon replied. "Not quite like Lawrence, right?"

The way he said it irritated her, though she suspected he

wasn't dissing her hometown. "Well, no, but we're not hicks, though everyone likes to think so. My hometown has a center dedicated to the study of science fiction. It's a part of the university."

"And I thought Kansas was just tornadoes, witches and cowardly lions."

She delivered a frown, then saw the glimmer of mischief in his eyes. "You like messing with me, don't you?"

"It goes both ways, Journeyman Breman."

Yes, it does. She noticed a sign near the closest door, and pointed. "They're showing movies. Let's check it out."

Curious, they stepped inside the room and quickly realized these weren't movies, but videos. The room was packed, and every eye was on the screen at the front.

"Riley really hates these things," Simon whispered.

Katia had watched most of these, some over and over. The current video was from the Demon Trappers' channel, one especially created to share Master Riley Blackthorne's exploits, as well as those of the other trappers. This one had Riley, Beck and a third trapper taking on a Grade Five demon, a Geo-Fiend. The room's occupants ooh'd and ahh'd as the debris swirled around the fiend and buildings toppled. Then Beck managed to roll one of the grounding spheres under the fiend and sent it back to Hell, twisting and bellowing as dirt fountained around it.

An enthusiastic cheer went up, along with equally enthusiastic clapping.

"Trapper Scores," Simon said, looking over at her. "Ever taken on a Five?"

"No. We had one last year, but I didn't see it. Don't want to, either."

"They're as bad as they look," he said. "Worse, actually."

They watched a few more videos, cheering along with the others when the trappers captured a demon. Katia particularly liked the one that showed Simon killing an Archfiend.

"Dude!" she said, amazed. "Now who's badass?"

Simon shrugged. "I got lucky." Then he abruptly rose and

headed out of the room.

She caught up with him in the hallway. "You okay?"

He nodded. "I didn't want to watch the part when Beck killed Sartael. He was so badly wounded. He almost died."

His tone told her to let the subject drop.

They continued down the hall, passing a room full of merchandise—the dealer's room—where you could buy pretty much anything related to the trappers, Heaven or Hell. Apparently, people wanted their own set of fake Holy Water spheres or a lighted set of demon horns. Those, in particular, made Katia cringe.

The room just beyond pulled at her for some reason, so she stuck her nose in. Then swore. Popping back outside, she tugged Simon away from the door.

"There's a Mezmer there. The whole room is hooked into it. It's telling them how wonderful Hell is."

Simon nodded, then typed out a text message, along with the room's location. A ping came back almost immediately. "Jackson will handle it."

Katia reluctantly moved on, and as she passed a table strewn with papers, she dug around until she found a pocket schedule for the convention. A quick glance at her phone gave her the time, and then she ran her finger down the programming grid.

"Okay, we've got some panel options coming up. *Angel Spotting in Real Life, Demon Trapper Tours: Crass or Cool, What's a Soul Worth?* Oh, we just missed the *Dressing for the Apocalypse: Clothing for the End Times* one."

Simon's eyes widened. "You're kidding, right?"

"Nope. They're all on the schedule," Then she couldn't resist. "Look, there's an *Exorcism for Dummies* panel, too."

"What?" He snatched the schedule out of her hand and began to hunt for that one. "Do they have any idea how dangerous that would be?"

Time to confess. "I'm joking, Simon. Really, honestly, joking about that last one. I figured you might need to lighten up a bit."

For a moment, he seemed mad at her, then the exorcist heaved a sigh of relief. "I should have guessed you were screwing with my head. I'm a little too wired to think straight."

"I never would have guessed."

Simon handed the schedule back, then pointed down the hall. "Bio break. I'll be back in a bit."

As he headed to the restroom, Katia leaned against a wall and people watched. There were so many happy ones here, laughing and joking with each other. Not at all like her own life, at least until she came to Atlanta. In the short span of a half a day she'd had more interesting conversations with her fellow trappers than in the last six months.

The gentle whir of a robot made her grin as R2D2 rolled by. Just about anything you could think of was here. Maybe this city was where she belonged.

The enticing tang of woods, moss and rain invaded Katia's nose now. A light tap came to her shoulder, and when she turned, she found the source.

It was a female of about her height, clothed all in white, with auburn hair piled loosely on top of her head. Streaks of white and silver were interwoven around the strands, as well as flowers and small ferns. Her skin was alabaster, her eyes a translucent blue, and her lips a deep blood red.

This certainly wasn't a costume. "What are you?" Katia asked.

Amusement shown in the figure's eyes. "I am what others do not see." Then she raised a single finger to her lips, and winked, as if they had shared some special secret. Floating down the hall, feet never touching the carpet beneath her long dress, she vanished into a solid wall. No one else seemed to notice her exit.

Katia blinked a couple times, then shook her head. The figure had been real, not an illusion or a glamour spell. And it certainly hadn't been an angel or a demon.

Did she dare ask Simon what that was? *No.* His expertise was Heaven and Hell and now was not the time to give him anything else to worry about. Besides, would he even believe her?

She filed the encounter away and resumed people-watching,

still on edge. A minute or so later Simon exited the restroom. He had just suggested they move on when a sharp tug on Katia's belt made her turn. It took her a moment to register what had happened.

"Hey, he's got my phone!" she shouted, and charged after the thief.

EIGHTEEN

As Serrah hadn't spent as much time with mortals, Ori found himself explaining them to her. In some ways that was good, he thought. The more Divines who comprehended these confusing creatures, the better.

"I do not understand them," Serrah said, taking care that those same mortals did not hear her. They were in a large, open area of the hotel filled with them. Some wore exotic costumes; others were only here to watch the show, take photographs, and then share those images. This latter effort seemed to involve the use of a myriad of electronic devices.

"They do know how to entertain themselves," Ori observed as a group came together for a photo. These mortals were dressed like the little fiends, the ones who hated books, though these versions were much, much larger.

"I do like the angels, though," his companion added as a pair of them walked by, all clad in white. Their wings were made of countless real feathers and their hair long and golden. "How do they—"

"Greetings, you two," Riley said as she and Beck joined them. "Anything we should know about?"

Ori looked over at Serrah, figuring she might as well give the report.

"We've found thirteen fiends so far. They range from the small ones to the kind you call a . . . Five?"

"Four, I think you mean. If we have one of those big mothers here, we're in deep shit," Beck replied.

"Katia found a Mezmer and Jackson took care of it," Riley

announced. "None of the people were hurt, just tired, so they'll be okay."

"This place is perfect for them. They can wander around, suck on someone's energy for a bit, and then wander off," Beck added.

"Growing stronger with each little meal," Riley muttered, her attention elsewhere. She frowned. "That's Katia. Something's up."

"Come back here!" Katia shouted, pelting through the crowd. The way the guy was moving it felt like he was leading her somewhere rather than trying to escape. When he skidded to a halt, and waited for her, she knew her instincts had been correct. Rather than race into a trap, she slowed as well, allowing Simon to catch up with her. Her senses told her the thief was Hellspawn, though it looked human. A lower grade Four, she guessed. As they grew closer, the fiend tossed the phone toward her. With a cry, Katia barely caught it, then heaved a sigh that it hadn't been damaged.

Why had it led them here? This part of the hotel was huge, the room's ceiling many, many floors above them. The balconies on each floor were attached to the main elevator shaft like ribs off a spine. Multiple elevators rose and descended in the center of the space, like something out of a science fiction movie. There were so many con goers here, most of which were gathered into distinct groups. A cluster of Star Wars storm troopers were hanging together, as well as a zombie ballerina, a tall cowboy in hot pink, and a man dressed as the pope. Nearly anything her imagination could conjure up was here.

To their left was a portable stage, currently empty. Someone dressed as a Gastro-Fiend kept flailing around near it, the costume hampering their movements. The fake fiend seemed silly, not dangerous. Maybe that was the point—taking one's fears and making them laughable in some absurd way.

Near the bar, people in business suits sipped drinks with

Captain America while Wonder Woman played catch with two small kids. A bride and groom formed their own universe, surrounded by smiling family members. The pair kissed amid cheers from well-wishers. Most out of place were the group of church ladies, dressed in their finest, watching their surroundings with a variety of expressions that ranged from curiosity to outright shock. One or two looked like they really wanted to join in the fun, but group pressure held them in check. To the right of them, on one wall, a giant video screen flashed up announcements, then switched back to YouTube videos of the local Demon Trappers.

Why here? Was it because this was one of the busiest areas of the convention? If that was the case, where were Azagar and the boys?

Katia's phone buzzed, and out of habit she checked the screen. It was lit with an incoming message and what she saw chilled her blood: her brother, Kevin, lying in his bed at the care center, oblivious. A picture she'd never taken.

The thief laughed now, and she could hear it over all the other noise. This was a warning—she played by Hell's rules, or Kevin paid for her defiance. She glowered over at the demon, but it didn't care. Instead, it grinned, displaying an unholy number of sharpened teeth, and a second later it was gone, weaving through the crowd, its task complete.

Hell's message had been delivered.

As he watched Katia and the demon who had taken her phone, there was no warning before the scars across Simon's stomach flamed red hot, causing him gasp in pain. Only one thing could bring on agony that strong.

"This is it," he said, lowering his bag to the floor, grimacing. The agony vanished as quickly as it had arrived. Retrieving his vial of papal Holy Water, he uttered a quick prayer and anointed himself. When he offered it to Katia, she did the same, then returned the vial.

He'd just put it back into his jeans pocket when shouts erupted and people around them began to point. In the nearly fifty-story atrium a figure slowly descended without the benefit of an elevator. It was the kind of grandstanding you'd expect from a Fallen, not one of Lucifer's Hellspawn.

Ori's voice filled Simon's mind. *Azagar is arrogant. Use that to your advantage. Good hunting, Exorcist.*

"Thank you for everything you'd done," he whispered.

I hope it will be enough.

The crowd's reactions to the demon varied—some were frightened, others thought this was part of the convention's entertainment and clapped in anticipation.

"This is awesome!" someone called out. "How'd they do that?"

"Yeah, just great," Riley said as she joined them. "If anything comes after the crowd, we'll nail it. We can't do anything else or that thing will say we cheated."

"I'm bettin' on you guys," Beck said, sounding as if he believed it. "Teach that bastard a hard lesson, you hear?"

Riley leaned close to Simon now, touching his arm, deep worry in her eyes. "No demon in Hell is stronger than you. *None of them.* Never doubt that."

He nodded in response, taking courage from her words.

She smiled over at Katia. "Trust your instincts, Journeyman Breman. And please watch our friend's back."

"I'll do my best," the trapper replied, then looked away.

Simon knew why. He'd caught a glimpse of her phone screen, though she'd tried to hide it from him. Given the trapper's stunned reaction, he knew that image had been her brother. Hell was already playing with her head, stacking the deck against them.

If you fight fair, you will lose.

He wasn't sure whose voice that had been, but he agreed. Whatever it took, the three boys were going home to their families tonight, their souls intact.

Simon picked up his trapping bag and walked a short distance away, closer to where the fiend would land. It was at the tenth floor now, still descending at a leisurely pace.

"I'm going to create the circle now," he warned. Katia nodded, her eyes on the menace above them.

Simon touched the carpet, then visualized the sphere of protection, how it encircled them and then flowed upward. Gasps came from those nearby. When he opened his eyes, he saw why—the circle glowed bright white, brighter than ever before, a perfect sphere protecting both him and his companion.

Azagar landed on the stage with a pronounced thud and immediately batted aside the microphone stand. Since just this morning the fiend's body had sprouted a thicker layer of armor. He was taller somehow, though the arrogant grin on his face hadn't changed.

"Simon the Betrayer!" he bellowed, the rough voice echoing throughout the atrium. The crowd noise continued for a few moments, then ramped down. Cell phones were recording this, and to Simon's dismay, the video screen began to broadcast their confrontation for all to see. Nothing he could do about that, so he returned his full attention to the Hellspawn.

"Azagar, minion of Lucifer, spawn of Hell," he called out. "In the name of the Almighty, the Creator, bring forth the three you hold hostage and release them to me."

As if on command the boys appeared on the stage, smoke swirling around them. They were on their knees to the right of the Hellspawn, tear-stained faces pleading with Simon to save them. He could not imagine what horrors they'd witnessed while in Azagar's possession.

The crowd swiftly went silent now. Even they knew that this wasn't some inventive cosplay.

"God, I hate demons," Beck said from somewhere behind them.

Azagar began to laugh, each intake of breath whistling past his sharp teeth. Flaming red eyes narrowed on Simon. "Exorcist! You show all here how weak you are! For I am Azagar, the most powerful demon in Hell!"

At this point Simon would usually begin the exorcism ritual, but something held him back. *If I fight fair, I will lose.* Then this time he wouldn't play by the rules. Maybe he'd live long enough to earn a stern lecture from the Vatican. That would be infinitely better than endless torture in the Pit.

"You?" Simon chided, loading his voice with derision. "*You* claim to be the most powerful demon in all of Hell? The cowardly fiend who hides behind three children? You have no notion of power, fiend."

"I *am* the most powerful of all in Hell!" the demon repeated.

"The *most* powerful?" he replied, egging him on. "Of all those in Hell? You dare make that boast? You are nothing but a Four, a Mezmer, one of Lucifer's slaves. Only a puppet who does whatever his master commands."

"You dare challenge me, Simon Michael David Adler? I, Azagar, am *the* most powerful of all in Hell!" the fiend repeated, banging his fist against his breastplate, generating orange sparks with each impact.

Simon held his breath. Maybe he'd been wrong . . .

A different voice answered, cold and sharp, like the slick of a blade from a scabbard. "You dare claim to be the most powerful in *my kingdom*? Then you must prove it, Azagar. Your challenge is accepted!"

Simon knew that voice, he had heard it during the battle at the cemetery. He grabbed Katia's hand, causing her to yelp in surprise just as the scene around them wavered, turned gray, then went pitch black. Her hand shook in his and he heard her whimper. When his vision cleared, he knew his rash gamble had worked.

Gouts of sulfurous flame assaulted the walls of their holy sanctuary, seeking a way in. Beneath the protective circle, as if it were an island suspended in midair, hellfire raged. Demons encircled them, shouting and stomping in triumph as they waved their weapons and gnashed their teeth.

They were in Hell.

NINETEEN

"Simon?" Katia whispered, her eyes wide in terror.

Before he could speak, another voice cut in. "Simon Michael David Adler. Welcome to my kingdom. I have been anticipating your arrival."

The flames parted in front of them. Clad in black armor, with a sword lying across his thighs, Lucifer sat on an ebony throne some thirty feet away. On each side of him was a Geo-Fiend, massive demons with curved horns and flaming eyes. Both were armed with scimitars.

Lucifer the Warlord.

One late night, Riley had told him of her time in Hell when she and Ori had been forced to answer the Prince's summons. How they had stood in front of this very throne while the Fallen angel Sartael was tortured, even as they watched. She'd spoken of how truly terrified she'd been that night.

Now it's our turn. Simon looked over at Katia, felt her rising panic as he released her hand.

"Stay *inside* this circle. You hear me? You break it, and we're both dead." *Or worse.*

The trapper's shivering continued for a few seconds, then she suddenly jerked in a quick breath. That seemed to steady her, and with a glare, she pulled out her steel pipe. "Inside the circle. Got it." Katia shifted her attention to the distant figure. "That's . . . *Him,* isn't it?"

"Yes."

"Oh my God."

The smoke and flames had cleared away to reveal a massive

space, one that made the hotel's atrium seem like a child's playhouse. The walls flickered with flames, which blew outward at random intervals. Steam rose upward, vented somewhere above. There was no ceiling that he could see. When he looked closer, Simon found the faces in the walls that Beck had spoken of, those trapped here until their sins had been purged. Their eyes focused on him, pleaded with him to save them. Begging him to trade places with them.

Somehow, Simon had always known it would come to this. He took a deep breath, grateful that the stench of raw brimstone couldn't penetrate their holy shield. His body might be in Hell, but his heart certainly wasn't.

"Almighty God, He Who Reigns in Heaven. Protect Us. Guide Us. Help us save these three innocent souls," Simon murmured.

When he made the sign of the cross in this most foul place the demons hissed in anger. Some banged their fists against their breastplates as a fresh wave of brimstone wove around the circle.

Katia met his eyes, then murmured a prayer of her own. Then she frowned. "Where's that big assed demon? Shouldn't he be here too?"

"*That* is an excellent question, Katia Allyson Breman," Lucifer replied. "Where *has* the mighty Azagar gone, I wonder? The self-proclaimed *most powerful* in all of Hell."

In that instant the fiend appeared. He seemed even bigger here. For a second, Simon thought he saw fear in the Four's eyes, but it rapidly vanished. Azagar shot a concerned look at the Prince, then turned back to them, arrogance filling his face once again.

"Welcome to Hell, Simon the Betrayer," the demon said, as if he was the master of this realm, and not the Fallen who sat nearby. "You are in my realm now. You will die here."

This thing has a death wish. Azagar hadn't bothered to pay obeisance to Lucifer, hadn't even acknowledged his master. And the "my realm" thing? That put a big bullseye on his back.

"You sure you want to do this in front of your master?"

Simon called out. "Here, in front of all the other Hellspawn?"

"I am superior to any mortal. I am superior to all demons. I am Azagar."

Through all those boasts Lucifer sat motionless like a statue, yet his midnight-blue eyes tracked every move.

Curiously, the three boys hadn't arrived with the demon, and Simon knew better than to ask about them. He'd never heard of any other exorcist being brought to Hell like this, unless he'd lost his soul. Simon's was still his, and he assumed the same of Katia's. Something else was going on here, something other than the fate of those three young mortals.

Challenge accepted, Lucifer had said.

The Chief of the Fallen was ruthless, frequently culling out the strongest of his fiends, the ones that threatened him. Or the ones that were just too arrogant to live. Was that what this was about?

The Prince's right eyebrow raised. Of course, he'd heard Simon's thoughts, they were in his kingdom, after all. Yet Azagar hadn't.

Around them Hellspawn shifted uneasily, sensing the increasing tension. There were the ones that every demon trapper knew, and some he'd never seen before. A few were tiny, others the size of a large dog, and some so big they almost dwarfed the Geo-Fiends standing guard over their master. Their appearances varied: Some had leathered skin, others were clothed in flames or were clouds of muddy vapor.

Lucifer's servants in all their unholy glory.

Azagar began to parade back and forth in front of their circle now. "You violated our agreement! You brought a trapper to aid you," he crowed, pointing at Katia.

"No, I have honored my word. *This* trapper wasn't in our agreement. None of those you excluded are here." Simon frowned. "How about you, fiend? Is cheating the only way you can win? Are you truly that weak?"

Katia whistled under her breath. Was he pushing too hard?

In response, the demon swore in Hellspeak, then puffed up

and spat at them. The spittle hit the sacred circle and bounced off. When it struck a nearby fiend, that creature burst into flame, then turned into a pillar of ash.

"So much for dental hygiene," Katia said, shaking her head.

Simon had to fight not to laugh, though he'd heard her voice quaver when she'd said it.

"I do not need to cheat! *I* am the most powerful in Hell."

Before Simon could reply, Katia called out, "Stronger than the Prince? Because I'm not seeing it. You're just a puffed up Four. Better armor, but fewer brains."

That caused the fiend to shift its gaze to her. "Katia Allyson Bremen."

When Azagar said nothing further, Simon knew a warning was being passed: Either side with the fiend, or her brother would suffer.

Katia's smirk withered. "Yeah, I know."

The look she gave Simon was heartbreaking. Had she given in? Would she break the circle? Wouldn't he do the same if it had been one of his brothers or sisters?

With a swear word she turned back toward their tormentor. "No, I don't sell out other people. You're outta luck, asshole."

"Your brother will die!" Azagar promised.

She glared at him and then shook her head, tears forming now. "If you're truly the strongest in this hellhole, you have to win this battle on your own. I will not help you, fiend."

"You love Kevin Damian Breman so little?"

"No, I love him so much."

"And yet you would let him die." With a chilling laugh, Azagar issued a command and a lesser fiend vanished in a puff of black smoke, no doubt sent on a killing mission to Lawrence, Kansas.

Tears ran openly down Katia's cheeks now. "I love you, Kevin!" she shouted, as if somehow he could hear her. "I will always love you." Then she began to sob.

†✺‡✺†

"Where'd they go?" Jackson said, staring at where the pair had vanished. Around them, the crowd grew agitated, everyone talking at once.

"That was Lucifer's voice," Beck said. Riley nodded in agreement.

"They are in Hell now. He summoned them," Ori said.

"Why?" Jackson asked, puzzled.

"Azagar challenged the Prince," the Fallen replied. "The fiend didn't realize he was being maneuvered into that . . . mistake. Now he will face off against Simon and the trapper *in front* of his master."

"So, the bastard can't lose or he's dead," Beck said.

"Correct."

"Then why are the mortal boys still here?" Serrah asked, gesturing at the trio. "Why are they not with the fiend?"

"I have no idea," Ori admitted, shaking his head.

"Then let's move them somewhere else in case the fiend does pull this off. Put them inside a circle so he can't get to them. There's too many people out here who could get hurt if Azagar decides to throw a tantrum," Beck said.

"If the Four returns, that means Simon is dead," Riley said, looking at Ori now.

"If the trapper betrays him—" Ori paused, then frowned as if something had occurred to him. He abruptly disappeared.

"Please tell me he didn't go to Hell," Riley said. "He'll die there."

Serrah concentrated, then shook her head. "He did not. He went somewhere . . . unexpected."

When she didn't explain, Beck gestured at the boys. "Then let's get these kids tucked away. If we lose Simon and the trapper, I swear to God I will send that demonic bastard back to Hell in pieces."

"You're going to have to stand in line for that honor," Riley replied.

†✵‡✵†

To Simon, it felt as if all the fiends in the Pit were holding their breath, eager to see how this played out. Azagar was probably demi-lord to a few of them, drawing strength from those who served him. Hell's alliances shifted frequently, depending on who was at the top of the heap at the moment. Right now, it was the fiend in front of them.

Though the large wooden cross was still in the bag at his feet, Simon raised his own fire-scorched one, for it had survived the massacre at the Tabernacle. Riley had found it in the rubble and kept it for him until he was ready to accept it once again, the visible symbol of his unbreakable faith in the Light. It was only fitting that he would use it here, in this place of Darkness.

"I am Simon. Michael. David. Adler," he said, his voice ricocheting around the massive cavern, each word a weapon of its own. Even Lucifer sat up now. "I am a child of God and follower of the Risen Savior. I am of the Light. You, Azagar, are Hellspawn, defiler of all that is good and sacred."

"Oh, wise exorcist, tell me how great you are," Azagar sneered. The demons around them laughed, pointing and making rude gestures.

"I am of the Light," Simon repeated. "By the power that Light, I *command* you to release the captives."

Azagar roared, causing many of the lesser ones to fall to their knees, covering their heads in terror. "They are mine and will remain mine for eternity." His expression turned sly. "Does she know what you did, exorcist? Does she know you betrayed one of your own? Does she—"

"Shut up and stop interrupting him!" Katia said. The tears on her cheeks had begun to dry and her anger felt as incandescent as the hell around them.

Azagar concentrated and with a groan Katya fell to her knees, her steel pipe dropping from her hand, rolling perilously close to the glowing circle. She cradled her head, as if it were exploding from within.

"Fight him!" Simon called out. "Don't let him win."

"Hurts . . . so much," she groaned.

"You can do it," he urged, touching her shoulder. "Remember who you're fighting for."

Cursing, Katia forced herself back to her feet, her whole body shaking. A thin stream of blood trickled from her nose, and she wiped it away.

Heaven was right. You are stronger than you believe.

She snatched the pipe off the ground and glowered at the demon.

"I am Katia. Allyson. Breman," she shouted. "I am Kansas born and bred, and damned proud of it! I *will not* bow to you. I will not bow to anyone, so just fuck off!"

An amused laugh came from the throne. "Even the trapper has more spine than you, Azagar. Is this how you deal with our enemies, you talk them to death? You claim to be a warrior and yet you cannot break their insignificant magical bubble," the Prince taunted. "No wonder you are one of the weakest in my realm."

The fiend growled as the fires of hate flamed in his goat-slit eyes. "I am Azagar," he shouted, pounding his chest.

"So you've said. Repeatedly."

If Simon defeated this abomination, he was playing Lucifer's game. If he didn't, the three boys were lost to Hell. There was no choice: The souls must remain free.

He took a deep breath. "You demanded that I meet your challenge and we have done so. We have defeated each of the fiends you sent to us today. It is time for you to fall."

Another deep breath as he raised his cross. "All Power is in the Hands of God, and I wield that immeasurable force against you, Fiend! You will be broken, and those innocent souls freed from your grasp! In the name of the Almighty, the Creator of the Universe, the Source of all Light, release them to me!"

Simon spoke in Latin now, his voice strong and resolute though he stood in the very heart of Hell. When Katia's voice joined with his, reciting the prayer along with him, Lucifer's face broadened into a cunning smile.

With a vehement curse, Azagar gestured at the circle, trying to break it. When nothing happened, he threw himself against the barrier, then fell away, his armor scorched in many places. As the words continued to hammer against the fiend, the other demons retreated, some climbing over others to escape the power of the sacramental. Through it all, the Prince sat on his throne, doing nothing to stop the exorcism.

As Simon reached the final portion of the prayer, his voice rose, gaining even more strength, as if the entire Universe spoke through him. His body vibrating and his mind ablaze, he sent the sacred words against their enemy. Smaller demons perished around them, their death cries filling the chamber.

And still, the Prince did nothing to stop him.

"Come to me, the three mortals!" Azagar ordered.

"They are free of you. They are safe now!" Simon called out. God, he prayed that was the case.

When the boys didn't instantly appear in chains at his feet, the demon bellowed again as more Hellspawn fled the chamber. "COME. TO. ME!"

Sweat flowed down Simon's face now, his fingers gripping his cross so tight they ached. It was as if only his strength of will was keeping the boys safe.

With a furious bellow, Azagar leapt at the circle once again, his sword blazing in an attempt to destroy it. The instant he hit the sacred space his arm burst into bright blue flames, the armor and flesh melting away at the heat. The fiend staggered backward, screaming in agony, beating at the fire.

"I will kill you!" he cried.

"You will try," Simon replied evenly.

Once the flames were extinguished Azagar pointed at the circle. "Destroy it." The fiends nearest them, the ones who owed him allegiance, backed away. "I order you to destroy it!" None of them obeyed.

"Dude, your leadership skills suck," Katia said, shaking her head.

Lucifer agreed. "Enough," he said. "This is pathetic. You are the best of *my* realm? I have seen worms more powerful than you."

With one final ear-splitting bellow, Azagar leapt at the circle, only to have it catapult him across the chamber where he landed in a burned heap.

"Bring him to me."

Two of the biggest demons took hold of the Four, dragging him across the cavern floor to the feet of his master. Lucifer looked down at Azagar as if observing an insignificant insect. "*You* are the strongest in my realm?" The fiend whimpered in response. "Those you command have fled, they have abandoned you. They see you are nothing, Azagar, as do I."

Spitting black blood, the fiend struggled to his feet, clutching his flame-ravaged arm to his chest. "I will defeat them all. I cannot fail!"

"Of course, you'll fail. You never had a chance. Your hubris was mightier than your cunning. That was your first mistake, the first of many. Be off with you." The Four abruptly disappeared.

Now that the exorcism had ended, smaller Hellspawn began to creep out of niches and from under rocks. Some glowered or hissed at the intruders, others seemed pleased that Azagar was gone. There were even a few cheers.

That celebration abruptly ended when the Prince rose from his throne, sword in hand. His expression gave no hint of what would happen next as he slowly walked toward the circle.

"Simon? What do we do?" Katia whispered, moving closer to him now.

"Nothing. It is no longer in our hands." As it had been since the moment they'd arrived in Hell.

Lucifer paused at roughly the same spot where Azagar had once stood, close enough for Simon to study him. He might be considered handsome if you didn't know him and his reign of terror. The Fallen's black hair held some silver. Those dark blue, bottomless eyes were impossible to ignore. One of Heaven's Divines until he wasn't. What kind of angel decided to rebel against the Almighty? And why him, of all of God's creations?

"Because I was the only one willing to risk it all," Lucifer replied.

Once again, he'd heard Simon's thoughts. "Yet other Divines followed you into exile."

"They did, and in so doing they learned what that meant once they were here. And now you are here as well." Lucifer studied him thoughtfully. "I have watched you for many years, Simon Michael David Adler. You do not cower in fear even though you are in my realm." He cocked his head. "Why is that?"

"You may rule in Hell, but I am of the Light." He looked over at Katia. "*We* are of the Light. We have no place in your world."

Lucifer walked around the perimeter of their sacred circle, assessing it. "No, you don't, at least not yet. Someday, perhaps you will."

"We have won against Azagar. The boys' souls are free."

"Azagar was stupid and you exploited that weakness."

"And yet, we still defeated him."

The Prince sighed. "So, you did." A furious growl came from inside Simon's trapping bag, signaling that Azagar was now imprisoned inside the metal box.

"The fiend is your problem, not mine. Ensure that he troubles me no more or I *will* collect those three mortals' souls as payment for your failure, and both of your souls as well. Do you understand?"

"I will not bargain with you," Simon replied. That was what had gotten them here in the first place. "Azagar failed. Those souls are free no matter what."

Lucifer sent him a searing glare, one that almost made him fall to his knees and beg for his life. Such was the power of the Prince.

"You have bargained with me for a lot longer than you know. The demon must be destroyed *by you*, do you understand?"

"Simon . . . " Katia began in warning.

If they wanted to leave this place alive, he had no choice but to agree, though it grated against his very soul. "I will destroy the fiend."

"Then depart, for I have no further time to waste on this matter."

With a dismissive wave of the Prince's hand, and a legion of demons shouting their derisive farewell, the blackness descended once again.

TWENTY

The furious howling continued. Where they still in Hell? Would they be able to find their way out?

"Simon?"

Riley's voice seemed to come from a great distance. Was she down there with them? *No.*

The spawn of Hell kept up their complaints as Simon slowly became aware of something fuzzy touching his nose. Something fuzzy with brown and cream stripes. His eyes were taking their time to focus properly, so he blinked to help them along.

Carpet? Hell's was molten lava, so he was nose deep in some place that wasn't Lucifer's living room. That perverse thought made him chuckle.

The effort it took to raise his head felt nearly impossible, but he did it. Katia was by his side, on her knees, staring at him in complete bewilderment, the tracks of her dried tears still visible. Riley paced outside the protective circle, which had miraculously remained in force during their trip to the Pit, and back.

"The boys . . . " he began. Then he saw them, all three, huddled near Serrah the angel inside their own circle of protection.

"You did it?" Riley asked.

Simon slowly nodded, as sheer astonishment flooded him.

"They did it!" she called out, a broad smile blooming. "They really did it!"

Beck hooted and shot a fist in the air. "Way to go!"

"Hot damn, do you guys rock or what?" Jackson said from somewhere behind them.

A menacing growl came from the trapping bag. *Azagar.* Simon ignored it. Instead, he pushed himself up to his knees, took a deep breath, and then whispered, "All Glory to God." He crossed himself and added, "Thank you for Your mercy."

Katia. He turned to her. "Your brother—"

Tears rolled down her cheeks, falling onto her shirt. Her hair was tangled and her body hunched.

"He's gone. I could have done what that damned fiend wanted, but Kevin still would have died. It's, it's not—oh God."

Tears began to fall harder now, and Simon reached out to hold her as her body heaved in grief. He had no idea what to say, how to comfort her. She had chosen him, and the boys, over her own brother. As she wept, something vibrated between them, followed by a ringing sound. It took him a moment to realize what it was.

"Is that your phone?"

Blinking away tears, she pulled away from him to check, then removed it from her belt. After a swipe, an image appeared on the screen. She stared at it for a few seconds, then her mouth dropped open.

Shoving the phone at Simon, she cried, "He's alive! He's awake!"

The image was of the same young man he'd seen earlier, except this time Kevin's eyes were open. It was who was standing next to him that caused Simon to laugh in sheer joy, a figure with wings and a stern expression.

While they'd been in Hell, Ori had gone to Kansas to protect Katia's brother.

She reclaimed the phone, hugging it like it was the most priceless thing in the whole world. When tears fell on the screen, she wiped them away. "My brother is alive. He's alive!"

Outside their circle, the other trappers celebrated Katia's good news with big smiles and cheers. The only one who wasn't in on that celebration was Serrah as she continued to talk to the boys. Simon swore he could feel her healing energy from across the room.

Katia blinked over at him, then wiped away more tears. "If I had to go to Hell with someone, I'm thankful it was with you. But only once. No more of that crap, you understand?"

"Only once," he replied, praying that was the case. "You were incredible, Katia. You stood up to that fiend and you recited the prayers right along with me. You know a lot more Latin than you said. Why didn't you tell me?"

She shook her head. "No, I don't."

"You did down there." He hesitated, then for some reason his eyes moved to Serrah again. She nodded at both of them before turning back to the boys.

"It was her, wasn't it?" Katia asked in a near whisper.

Looks like it. Heaven watched over all of us."

Behind them, Azagar growled again, reminding Simon of just how much he hated the damned thing. It was a visceral hate, one that could have easily seen him killing the fiend now, rather than hauling it all the way to the monastery. The anger didn't surface that often, but when it did it was hard to control. He'd never been that way before that night at the Tabernacle.

"Leave the demon inside the circle for now." Katia gave him a puzzled look but didn't argue.

Once they were free of the glowing space, Simon received a fierce hug from Riley and a solid back slap from Beck. Katia got hugs from both. The snarls he'd heard came not only from Azagar, but from two bait boxes along the far wall, the trappers' low-tech way to secure Grade Four demons. Once they were inside, the special witchy charms attached to the boxes kept the Hellspawn imprisoned.

"You guys had some trouble?" he asked.

Riley nodded. "I put the boys inside a circle in case . . ."

In case neither he nor Katia survived. Though still pale and frightened, the teens seemed to be responding to the angel. Jackson was on his phone, and as he spoke, he gestured toward one of the boys, then nodded.

"They were camping out this weekend, just the three of them. One minute they're roasting hot dogs and swapping stories and then this big demon carries them off," Riley said. "Jackson's calling the parents. The families were freaking because the kids' phones were all going to voicemail."

Simon nodded, then glanced back at the bag inside the circle. Azagar had fallen silent again, but he could still feel the demon's presence. Riley gave him a smile and then headed toward Katia.

"You know, if I was you," Beck began, "I'd be a whole lot happier about survivin' Hell than yer actin'. That tells me you think somethin' isn't right. Care to share what that might be?"

Fortunately, Riley had gone over to talk to Katia at this point. "You sound just like Stewart, you know that? Well, except you don't have a Scottish accent."

"My lovely wife would agree with you."

Beck waited him out.

"The circle held while we were down there." To anyone else Simon might need to explain what Hell was like, but not to this man. "Azagar threw himself against it a few times, but couldn't get through. He ordered his lesser fiends to attack us—didn't work—and he tried a few mind games." Simon shook his head at the memory. "Lucifer just sat on his throne and did nothing."

"I thought the Mezmer was more powerful than that."

"Me too. We were surrounded by hundreds, maybe thousands of demons, and we should have had to fight our way out of there. Even if he couldn't break it, Lucifer could have trapped us in that circle for eternity. It's not like someone was going to deliver us a pizza when we got hungry. But none of that happened."

"You think somethin' else is goin' on?"

Simon reluctantly nodded. "Maybe I'm just paranoid, but before we were sent back here Lucifer insisted that *I* had to destroy Azagar, and if *I* didn't then all our souls are his, the kids' too. I honestly think the fiend was just a part of something way bigger."

The grand master rubbed a hand across his face. "You want me to go with you to the monastery? Ride shotgun?"

He really appreciated the offer, but Simon shook his head. "No, we'll do it. I don't want the Prince to claim we didn't honor his infernal bargain. I had no choice but to agree or we wouldn't have been allowed to leave Hell."

"He really is a total bastard," Beck said, shaking his head in dismay. "Okay, then let us know when you get the deed done so we can stop worryin'. Because have no doubt, we'll be doin' just that."

"I will. God, I just want this night to be over."

"Same here." Beck gave him a less aggressive pat on the back and went to join Jackson.

Simon looked back at his trapping bag and the outline of the box within. Once again, the Prince had maneuvered them into playing his infernal game.

As Simon talked to Grand Master Beck, Katia's phone rang. The area code was from and her heart double beat. "Hello?"

"Kat? It's . . . it's . . . Kev," a gravelly voice said.

"Kevin!" she cried, then nearly choked on all the emotions tearing through her. She'd prayed for this day and now it was here.

"The angel said . . . " There was a lengthy pause while he cleared his throat. "I can't mess . . . with demons . . . anymore."

"You listen to that angel. He's really wise, okay?"

"I will. You come . . . see me?"

Her heart broke. He had no idea she'd left town.

"I'm not in Lawrence, bro. I'm in Atlanta now. Mom and Dad, well, *Mom* was really angry about what happened to you. She thought it was because I was a trapper."

"Not your fault," her brother said, his voice remarkably strong for someone who'd been in a coma for so long. Was that because of Ori?

"They needed someone to blame."

"Then blame . . . me." He cleared his throat again which led to a very long yawn. "Call me . . . tomorrow?"

"I will. Love you, Kev. Welcome back!"

There was a muttered "Love you" in return. She spent the

next few minutes talking to a night nurse who wasn't buying her brother's claim that an angel had woken him.

"Probably a dream," the woman suggested.

"Yeah, probably a dream."

One named Ori. *A Fallen.* It hadn't been one of Heaven's angels who had saved her brother, and she would remember that until she drew her last breath.

TWENTY-ONE

Back home, Katia's masters always handed Hellspawn over to a demon trafficker. In her opinion, that was the best part of the job: Grab up the fiend, drop it off, and that was that. It was even better if she actually got paid for that fiend.

That same process also happened in Atlanta, unless the Hellspawn had been exorcised. Which meant, despite his obvious exhaustion, and still suffering from the wound on his calf, Simon insisted on driving to the monastery where Azagar would be destroyed. He claimed that traffic wouldn't be bad, and since it was nearing midnight, he was right. Once in the car, Katia had reluctantly removed the amulet and the Badass Nun was no more. Maybe Mort would let her keep it.

The metal box holding the Four had sat at Katia's feet for the entire journey. Sort of like having a live hand grenade that did a lot of snarling and rattling of its prison.

"What keeps that thing in there?" she finally asked because her mind kept screaming that very question.

"The power of the crosses on the side of the box, as well as the prayers laid into the metalwork."

"Ever have one get out?"

"No. I was told they can't escape no matter what."

Then why did she feel on edge? "Simon?"

"Yeah?"

"Why didn't the Prince just toast Azagar while we were in Hell? You know, to teach them all a lesson about dissing the boss? Why use us as the executioners?"

His hands gripped the steering wheel tighter than necessary.

"I don't know."

The demon at her feet switched from growls to persuasion mode now.

Katia Allyson Bremen. I can reward you beyond your imagination. Set me free and we will destroy the Prince together.

She glowered at the box, barely resisting the temptation to give it a kick. "You sent a fiend to kill my brother. Did you forget that?"

A mistake. The Prince made me angry. You can have anything you desire. You wish revenge on your master in Kansas? You shall have it. Set me free and we will rule in Hell—

"No. Now shut up. This is the end of this conversation, asshole."

A vicious snarl was the reply, along with more rattling and hissing.

"He's tempting you?" Simon asked.

"Yeah. It's the 'Hey, babe, let's go kill the Prince and then we can rule in Hell for-evah.' Pretty lame, you know?"

Simon laughed. "Probably the best offer you'll get tonight. I was just going to buy you breakfast on the way back to town."

"Some place is actually open this time of night?"

"A Waffle House will be. You have them in Lawrence, right?"

She shook her head. "Gotta go to Bonner Springs or Kansas City for those. But we have *Perkins*. Their pies are incredibly excellent."

That set her reminiscing about her hometown, and when Simon encouraged her to share, she painted him a picture what life was like in Kansas. That it wasn't all *Wizard of Oz* and tornadoes, though there were a lot of the latter. Despite all that happened there, she missed her home, and missed her family. Especially her brother. She'd have to save up some money to go back to Lawrence to see him. *Sometime soon.*

"You think your parents will be better about your trapping work now?" Simon asked.

"Not sure. My folks are stubborn, so that would require them to admit they screwed up and that they should apologize. Not sure if that will happen."

"Tell them about Ori. Well, not that he's a Fallen, but what actually happened and why your brother is awake."

"They won't believe it."

"Show them that picture on your phone."

Katia retrieved it and hunted through the images. "And now Kevin's in the photo, but Ori's not, as if he'd never been there at all."

"Hmm. I wonder if that's his doing, or Heaven's?" Simon mused.

At her feet Azagar cursed, shaking the box. Apparently mentioning the other address wasn't appreciated.

"There's another person I should notify, but I'm not sure he's going to be happy to hear from me," she admitted.

"Your former master?"

"Former boyfriend. Noah sided with my parents, which is why he is now an ex."

"Ouch," Simon said, passing a truck and then pulling back into the proper lane. "How long had you been together?"

"Almost a year. He didn't like me being a trapper, but once Kevin was hurt, he decided I just had to quit, or we were history."

"His loss. If you hadn't remained a trapper there is no guarantee those boys would have survived. Or me, for that matter. You know that, right?"

Katia reluctantly nodded. As far as she saw it, he'd done all the hard work while she'd just bad-mouthed a demon. "If you hadn't become a lay exorcist, those guys might not be going home to their parents tonight." She let him chew on that for a while, then added, "Next time we'll do breakfast at Waffle House."

"You're on."

By the time they drew close to the monastery, Katia had learned that he loved fried chicken and banana cream pie. He wasn't fond of peaches, which might be considered heresy in the peach-growing state of Georgia, so he didn't tell anyone. She'd admitted to being addicted to apple pie and vanilla ice cream. During the entire conversation the demon had continued to rumble at her feet like a feral dog.

After he'd turned off the main highway, Simon sent them down a series of back roads, then executed a right turn onto the monastery grounds. More driving past the actual monastery itself, then further and further into the dark woods. He finally pulled into a gravel parking lot near a metal building where they would dispose of the Four. A single security light on a tall pole illuminated the area as much as possible. It was good she trusted him because they were in the middle of nowhere.

As Katia stepped out of the car, she pulled her trapping bag onto her shoulder. When Simon noticed, he nodded more to himself than her.

"Usually, I'd be feeling safe by now, but I'm not tonight."

"We can't be, not with the Chief Dickhead's warning," she said.

"I notice you didn't call him that while we were down there."

"I was so tempted. Lucifer is one scary SOB. When I first became a trapper, I'd tried to picture him in my head, but I was nowhere close. Same thing with Hell."

"Riley says Hell is different for each of us, so what we saw was probably a combination of your worst fears and mine."

"Sure did the trick," she admitted.

Simon popped the trunk, moved some items from his exorcism kit to his trapping bag while Katia retrieved the box from the car. Curiously, the fiend had fallen silent.

Simon keyed the code into the electronic lock, slid the heavy metal door to one side, and then waited for his companion's reaction to the radiance that naturally filled the inside of the building.

"Okay, that's cool," Katia said as she stood at the doorway, her face bathed in the white and pale blue glow. "What kind of lights are they using?" A pause and then "Oh!" She turned to him, eyes wide. "That's . . . *the Light*, isn't it?

"Yes, it is." Her child-like wonder reminded him of why he faced Hellspawn day after day. The Light was more than just a religious concept, but a true force in this world.

He made his way to a bank of switches inside, pushing them upward to illuminate the rest of the interior with more traditional lighting. No matter how many times he came here, each visit still awed him.

Huge crosses had been painted in gold on all four walls, with more on the floor, and the ceiling. In the very center of the structure was a dais made of marble, and resting on top of that was an ornate metal cage which also had crosses and Latin prayers carved into it.

The process was straightforward: Simon would place the box containing the Hellspawn inside the cage, and since this building was holy ground, that power would destroy the fiend. Once the demon was dead, he discarded the ashes in a sanctified field a short distance away.

Katia remained just outside the door, still staring. "Does it have to be crosses?"

It was a question he'd asked himself. "To no one's surprise, the Vatican's official position is 'yes', it must be crosses."

"And your opinion is . . . ?"

"Well, if you'd asked me before I almost died, I would have insisted that only crosses would work, and been offended you'd suggested otherwise."

"And now?"

"Now I believe the Light reaches people in different ways. If that's true, using a Star of David or Islam's Crescent and Star would work just as well. So would other religious symbols. They're all part of the Light. But, that's my personal opinion. If you ask Simon Adler, Lay Exorcist, it's crosses all the way."

"I now have blackmail material," she said, waggling her eyebrows.

Just as Katia began to enter the building, the metal box containing the fiend jerked in her hand, dragging her backward. When she fell, it kept pulling her along, like she was at the end of a leash. Finally, the box wrenched free and sailed some thirty feet beyond into a grassy meadow. When it struck the ground, it rolled over and over.

"What the hell was that?" she said, climbing to her feet, her jeans dirty and grass stained.

"Wait, I'll get it." Katia was already heading for the box, and he reacted on instinct. "No! Come back!"

"Why? I'll just—"

The top of the container flew open and Azagar erupted from his prison in a single explosive blast. The shock wave of that eruption rolled across the trapper, knocking her down again, then hit Simon, whistling around him like a windstorm as he gripped the metal doorway to stay upright.

As the wind diminished, he sprinted to Katia and helped her up. Hobbling over, she picked up her trapping bag where it had fallen, right before another gust of wind swept them off their feet. When he rose, Simon touched his forehead where the papal Holy Water had been applied, then did the same to the ground at their feet. Would it work? He'd never waited this long between the application and an attempt to call up a circle.

To his immense relief, the circle bloomed around them, encasing them even as Azagar shouted his joy at being free, then stomped in their direction, his sword blazing in the night. His arm was healed, his armor intact. How had that happened?

"What's happening here? Isn't this holy ground?" Katia demanded.

"The building is on holy ground, but not where he is. We never figured one of these things would get loose."

They never had, until tonight. Simon swore he could hear Lucifer's chilling laughter.

TWENTY-TWO

Simon gritted his teeth. "We never covered this in Exorcism class," he complained, watching as Azagar stomped around, spouting oaths. Most were in Hellspeak and aimed at his former master. In time, his focus would center on the two of them. Even worse, sooner or later one of the monks would come to investigate all the noise, and that unlucky soul would die.

"We'll just have to make it up as we go."

He huffed. "Any suggestions?"

"Can you get him inside a circle like this one? Lock him in?"

"Not unless one of us wants to be in there with it."

"Ah, no thanks," Katia replied. "How about getting him back in the box like you did the first time around?"

He gestured at the tattered remains of the demon's prison in the distance. "Not an option."

"Damn. Do you think Lucifer did this?"

"Maybe, but I don't think he could open the box." Which meant someone else had helped the fiend.

Azagar finally ended his rant and squared up with his closest opponents.

"Simon Michael David Adler! You thought you defeated me and yet I will carry your broken body to my master and throw your corpse at his feet. I will do the same with the trapper bitch. Then the Prince will accept me once more."

"Not a chance. The *Prince of Lies* doesn't trust you, which should tell you something," Simon called back.

The reply was a gout of fire that blasted the circle, curving around it, trying to find a way in. The grass around them smoldered. If they remained in the circle Azagar would grow tired of this and vanish. Lucifer would claim their souls, and those of the teens, and there would be nothing Simon could do to stop him.

The fiend had to die. But how?

When Simon didn't respond to the taunts, the Four rained more fire against the barrier. His anger growing, he charged up and then threw himself against the shield. The pain had to be immense, which only maddened Azagar further. Another strike, then another.

"Man, is this thing stubborn. You'd think he'd know that wouldn't work," Katia said. "At least I hope that's the case."

Except a thin flicker had begun to show at the top of the shield, about seven feet up. It was something Simon had never seen before. That area began to expand, as if someone was poking their finger into a water bubble, trying to make it burst.

"What's that?" she asked, following his gaze.

"Bad news," Simon replied. Their only other sanctuary was behind them, if they could reach it.

"I have an idea." She leaned close and whispered it into his ear.

"No." It was much too risky.

"You have something better?"

"No!"

"Well, sorry, but it's my way or nothing. Are you going to stand there or work with me on this?" she demanded.

What she was proposing was insane, but he knew they had no other choice, and that made him angry. Lucifer had let them escape Hell, only to ensure they died here.

"Simon?"

Bam! Another hit from Azagar who picked himself up, arms on fire, and bellowed into the night. "You are mine! I will destroy you, Simon the Betrayer! I will pull your heart from your chest and devour it!"

The weakened area on the circle began to widen, inching down the side of the barrier. If it reached the ground, he feared the protection would collapse.

"Dude, we've got no choice," she said quietly. "You're the one who was into track and field."

"Okay, but for God's sake, be careful."

While they'd argued, Azagar had backed up to where he'd first broken free of the box, preparing himself for a final run, no doubt intending to throw his entire weight at the weakest point in the circle. He dug his clawed feet into the ground, tossing turf behind him like an enraged bull.

Simon murmured a prayer and heard Katia's faint "Amen."

With a final bellow, the Four took off at a trot, eyes ablaze, sword in hand. Thirty feet, twenty-five, then twenty. All Simon could see were those wicked teeth and the blade that would carve them to pieces.

"Now!" Katia yelled.

Simon broke the circle and sprinted toward the building, the trapper right behind him. The demon thundered on, gaining on them, closer with each footfall.

Katia's panicked breaths mirrored his own. A glance over his shoulder saw the demon speed up. Fifteen feet, ten, then abruptly Katia dropped to the ground, tucking into a ball, covering her head. Azagar was so close, the fiend stumbled over her body. Off balance now, his tremendous momentum carried him on toward the building.

Just as the demon reached for him, Simon whirled out of range. Azagar kept moving forward, even as he tried not to, the claws on his feet sparking on the concrete ramp that led to the building's interior.

With an oath, Simon kicked out, driving a foot deep into Azagar's armored back, sending the monster careening inside. The moment the Hellspawn's feet touched Holy ground, steam began to rise, along with a terrified shriek of agony. Rolling the big door closed with a bang, Simon wedged himself against it.

"May the Light cleanse the Darkness within!" he called out. "May this fiend perish and with him all that is evil. May the Almighty make it so!"

The shrieks grew in intensity, the door shuddering as Azagar hammered against it in panic. Offers flew into Simon's mind—untold wealth, immense power, everything a mortal might want if he would only release the Mezmer.

"No," Simon said simply. "Die, you bastard. Just die."

A final heart-rending scream tore through the night, and then . . . silence. Simon's ears rang, and he shook his head to clear them.

The mound that was his companion was not moving. "Kat?" No reply. "Katia!"

"Yeah, yeah, I hear you," she said, unfolding. She leveraged herself up on an elbow, then flopped over on her back. "They don't die quietly, do they? That sounded awful."

"It would have been." It almost made him feel sorry for the fiends, but then he always remembered those they'd killed. Like his fellow trappers, or the young pregnant woman who hadn't survived her exorcism.

With more sustained effort Katia made it to her feet and limped over to him, her clothes covered in dirt. Wincing, she touched her back. She sighed as she parked herself on the ground and leaned up against the building. Tempted as he was to open the door, Simon did the same, his butt hitting the dirt. As a reminder of his own mortality, his calf throbbed in time with his heartbeat. He hadn't realized just how tired he was until this moment.

"You hurt?" he asked, watching her closely.

It was some time before an answer came his way. "One of his claws got me. It'll be okay if you treat it for me."

"I'll do it before we leave. Anything else?"

"I think my ankle is way pissed. Other than that, I'm good." She nodded to herself. "Yeah, I'm not dead, and I'm not serving brimstone cocktails in Hell's sleaziest dive bar. For eternity. With no tips, *ever*." She grinned over at him, drunk on the high that came with survival. "No, it's all good, Simon. It's *all* good."

"Brimstone cocktails?" he asked, trying to picture them.

"You know, the ones that come in a hollowed-out skull, with

the little flaming pitchforks and a slice of rotting lemon? I'm sure they're a big hit down there. Probably sell a ton of them during Unholy Hour. And don't get me started about the bar snacks they'd serve."

The horror and the fear gave way to genuine laughter, and he let it consume him. God, it felt good. How long had it been since he'd truly savored being alive?

Too long. Much too long.

Once the laughter ended, he looked heavenward. Above them the night sky sparkled with stars. Infinity. Life and death. Light and Dark. The concepts humans found so hard to comprehend until they had to face them head on.

"The boys are safe now," he said. He could hardly believe it. "Your plan worked great. You are badass, Katia Allyson Breman."

"*We* were badass, Simon David Michael Adler." she said, smiling over at him.

"We are," he admitted. "And its Michael David, not the other way around."

"Sorry. Why do you rate *two* middle names?"

"No clue," he replied. "The David is from one of my uncles. He lives in Sarasota now. He keeps hermit crabs as pets, of all things. The Michael is from the Archangel, and Simon was an apostle."

"Impressive. I was named after my grandmother. She was impressive too."

She'd mentioned that before, so it must be really important to her. "Your grand mother would be damned proud of you right now."

"I'd like to think so." Then she sobered. "That thing with the circle coming undone. Is that normal?"

"No, not at all." He'd been enjoying the sheer joy of surviving this entire horrible night, but some things needed to be addressed. "How did a demon escape from a warded box? There's no way it should have done that."

"I'll go find what's left of the thing. Maybe you can see how it got opened," she said, rising to her feet. Katia wavered a bit, then took a few steps. "More good news—the ankle isn't as pissed as I thought."

She headed off into the night, using the screen of her cell phone as a makeshift flashlight to aid in her search. He could see a rip in the back of her shirt and the blood that had soaked into it.

Simon made it to his feet, his calf still complaining, then gingerly pushed open the door. A large pile of ash on the floor was all that remained of the once mighty Azagar.

"*Deo omnis Gloria,*" he said, making the sign of the cross. *Glory to God.*

Katia returned with the remnants of the container, which looked as if someone had torn it apart with a crowbar. Parts of it were scorched, the crosses blackened. But what she held in her other hand was worse.

Simon took hold of the long white feather.

"It was near the box. That's not from a bird," she said. The pause went for some time. "So, which angel tried to get us killed? Was it the Prince?"

"No, it wasn't," a voice said.

Two Divines stood a short distance away. Neither Simon nor his companion had heard their arrival, so focused on what Katia had found.

"Fallen," Simon said, his eyes narrowing.

Ori nodded in his direction. "Exorcist. I am pleased to see that you and Katia Allyson Breman survived this night."

"Are you?"

"You believe I did this?" he said, gesturing at the shattered box.

Did he? Simon immediately shook his head. "No. Well, I did for a second or two, then I realized how stupid that was. You've done nothing but guard us from harm. If you wanted us dead, you would have done it yourself, not using Hellspawn. That would have only benefited your former master and you would never do that."

Ori nodded again. "Someone wanted you to perish. Someone

Divine."

With an oath that only the other angel was likely to understand, Serrah began to pace back and forth. The words issuing from her mouth made no sense to Simon, but apparently they did to Ori, who immediately created some sort of shield bubble around them. It was like the one he'd made at Mort's house, ensuring that no one outside of it could hear their conversation.

Only then did Ori answer her. The argument grew heated, with him gesturing and Serrah pointing a finger at him and arguing back.

"Azagar offered me anything I wanted in this world," Simon said as the two Divines continued their agitated discussion.

"Like having all the peaches in the world suddenly disappear?" Katia asked.

He grinned at that possibility. "Tempting. No, he offered to make me pope. Like it works that way."

"You'd look awesome in all white," she said. The argument continued inside the bubble. "You know, it's never pretty when Mom and Dad fight."

"Do you think they even remember we're here?"

Both angels turned toward them now.

"I'd make that a 'yes'," Katia replied.

"Who does this feather belong to?" Simon asked, though he had his suspicions.

Upon Ori's agitated gesture, the bubble expanded to include both of them.

"You already know," Serrah replied.

"I do, but I want to hear it from you two."

"Zareth," the angels said in unison.

"The one who wanted you to betray Ori?" Katia asked, looking back and forth between him and the Divines.

"Yes. One of Heaven's *own* tried to kill us," Simon said, his voice rising. "Zareth risked all our souls." His fists clenched. "Why?"

Ori looked over at the other angel. "He's right. Why?"

"I don't know," Serrah replied, anger blazing in her brilliant blue eyes. "I don't know, but I will find out." She gestured toward the feather. "I need that."

Simon's anger slowly deflated. It wasn't like he could speed dial the Archangel Michael and put in a complaint about one of his employees.

"But I can," Serrah said, reading his mind.

He handed over the feather. When Serrah gave the Fallen a pointed look, Ori removed the shield around them, and then she abruptly vanished, evidence in hand.

After a deep breath, Simon asked, "If she challenges Michael, is that going to get her in trouble?"

"I'm not sure. If he is feeling threatened, it could go hard on her. It's one of the reasons I don't miss being part of Heaven."

"So, you came down to hang with us mortals because that would be easier?" Katia asked.

The angel winced. "Good point."

"Is my brother still safe?"

"Yes, he is. I might have encouraged a certain master to put a demon trapper in the room with your brother, at least until Azagar was dead."

Katia's eyes narrowed. "That wouldn't be Master Kelly, would it?"

"The very one."

She broke out in laughter. "Oh my God, that had to be great. I can just guess what it was like having an angel in his face telling him what to do."

"I can be *very persuasive*," Ori replied. "I believe my flaming sword settled the argument. Not that he'll remember that part, of course." He frowned. "I would have been here immediately when Azagar escaped, but I was kept busy in Atlanta, on purpose it would seem. We came as soon as possible."

"Azagar was a pawn, used to get us here. Once Zareth released him, Katia and I would lose our souls. Or was it more than that? What else is at stake?" Simon pressed.

Ori didn't reply, his frown deepening.

Katia gave the Fallen a long look. "I expect Hell to screw

me over, but not Heaven. Makes me wonder why I risk my life day after day."

"I cannot explain why this has happened," Ori said, "but you are right: Lucifer has a grander goal in mind. Perhaps we will learn what that is." The Fallen looked back toward the city now. "I must go. There are more fiends that need my attention, as is always the case."

Simon stuck out his hand, and to his surprise, the angel shook it. "I owe you so much. If you ever need my help, let me know. I mean it."

"Same here," Katia added.

"I am honored," Ori replied. "Truly, I am. We must trust that Serrah will find a way to settle this issue with Heaven's traitor."

The Fallen walked a short distance away, bent his knees and shot into the air. A few seconds later they could barely see his wings in the moonlight as he flew toward the capitol.

"Go to Atlanta, they said. It'll be fun, they said," Katia murmured. "Riley was right—it sure as hell isn't boring."

"Well, it better get that way. I need to write a long, and incredibly detailed report to my superior in Rome. Father Rosetti is not going to believe this one."

"Yeah, I have to write this all up, too. I can just imagine some clerk at the National Guild making sense of this mess."

Maybe now was the best time to ask about the future. "Would you be okay working with me from now on? I mean, offering backup for my exorcisms?"

She didn't answer right off and that made Simon's heart sink. Why had he thought she'd agree? He was the reason she'd ended up in the Pit. What possible benefit would she gain from being his assistant?

"Work with you, huh?" Katia looked at the building, then back at him. "Would this be like what we've just been through?"

"Hopefully not, but it's certainly not a safe job. The Prince will always remember we got the best of him."

She seemed pleased by his honesty. "Okay, let's do this exorcism thing together, Simon *Michael David* Adler. I'd like that a lot."

His spirits immediately rose. "So, would I, Katia Kickass Breman."

Her laughter lit up the night. He and the lady trapper were still alive, their souls intact. There was so much to be thankful for, even if a visit to Waffle House wasn't in their future.

TWENTY-THREE

"You ready for this?" Riley asked, giving Beck a concerned look.

Now that Azagar was headed to his brutal end at the monastery, and the teens were reunited with their parents, it was time for the other big event of the evening—their panel with the *Demonland* crew. She hadn't wanted to do this, but in the end, she realized it had to happen.

They were still glamoured, waiting a decent distance from the meeting room where the panel was to be held. From the long line of people queued up, the room was going to be packed. And from the hopeful faces, they'd better make sure this went well.

Beck still hadn't answered her question.

"I'm sort of ready. How about you?" She received a huff in response.

Riley had finally convinced the usually fearless grand master that they needed to be on the panel, and that decision had required a long and testy discussion. In the end, he'd reluctantly agreed she was right.

It had always been Riley who'd visited the high schools to do the Demon Trapper 101 presentations, as she called them. The first few had freaked her out, but now they were just part of the job. Beck's job, now that he was a grand master, was to attend the endless meetings that the city, the state, and the federal government seemed to demand. The first few had freaked him out as well, but now he was more confident. Still, Beck felt out of his element here, and she could tell it was worrying him.

It didn't happen as often as in the past, but every now and then the young man from South Georgia, the one who never thought he'd amount to anything, surfaced. His body language told her this was one of those times.

"What's this gonna be like?" Beck asked, adjusting the strap of his trapping bag on his shoulder for the third time. That was uncharacteristic fidgeting.

"According to Alex, a moderator will ask us questions, and when that's all done, the audience gets to do the same. Blaze is a cool lady so no hassles with her. Her real name is Susan. Jess Storm is a bit self-absorbed, but you're used to dealing with those types. I don't know much about Raphael, except that he's cute."

That earned her a frown, which had been her aim to get his mind off his worries. "Cute huh?" She nodded. "That's all we have to do?"

Time to reveal the other event. "Then we're going to sign some autographs."

The frown turned darker, one that would have made anyone else whimper, which was why she hadn't mentioned that part until now. "After the panel we are signing with the *Demonland* actors. It's for charity. Well, at least our part is."

Beck's frown faded a few notches: Charities were his soft spot.

"The Orphan's Fund?" She nodded. "Okay. Then let's get this done."

Riley popped up on her toes, dropped a kiss on his stubbled cheek. Then, ignoring the line, she walked them up to the staff member checking badges at the door. The moment she removed her glamour the guy smiled, recognizing her. Beck pulled off his amulet, and the staff member's smile grew wider.

"Look! It's the trappers!" someone called out. "Riley Blackthorne is really here!"

"Holy Water's in place," Beck said. She glanced down to see a damp line on the carpet just inside the door.

"Jackson said he and Remmers would make sure the room is secure." Hell might be done for the night, or it might just be getting started. Until they heard from Simon, she'd assume it was the latter.

As expected, the room was jammed, almost every seat occupied in a space that would accommodate about two hundred people. The attendees milled around, and every one of them looked jazzed to be here. There was a strategically placed video camera, and someone messing with it, so apparently the panel would be broadcast to those outside the room as well. Then posted on the internet because everything ended up there eventually.

Riley had never been comfortable when the trappers had somehow shifted from everyday people to celebrities. Not because they wanted to be, but because the public nature of their work, the constant danger involved in capturing demons, elevated their efforts to something special in the minds of the public. Add in the major battles the city had witnessed between Lucifer's forces and the trappers, and it all took on mythic proportions. As Angus had said, "Myths have a life of their own." She and Beck were now part of that myth, and there was no way they would ever be free of it. It was a truly sobering realization.

The elevated stage at the far end of the room had five chairs behind a long cloth draped table. The *Demonland* actors were on one side, while she and Beck would be on the other. The buzz of conversations and the occasional flash of a phone camera followed them all the way to the stage.

"Sweet Jesus," Beck muttered under his breath, looking out at the room full of eager faces. She watched as he called up that inner reserve of strength that made him so incredible as a grand master, and a human being. Then his tension fell away as he shifted his gaze to a young boy in the front of the room in a wheelchair, his right leg in a cast that extended above the knee.

"Dude!" he called out. "Look at you!" He shot him a thumbs up. "Thanks for comin' tonight."

The kid beamed, enthusiastically returning the gesture, his whole day made because of this one moment.

Grand Master Beck was in the building.

Riley let her own smile loose as she headed for the empty

chairs. Susan, aka Blaze, jumped up, gave a squeal and headed toward her for a hug. Her long blonde hair was in loose curls and she wore a tight black tank top and even tighter jeans. But she also had on a red leather sleeveless vest, something that she'd adopted as Blaze became more of a fighter, and less of a sex object. The Vatican still didn't want anything to do with the television series, but Riley had heard that even Father Rosetti would watch an episode every now and then. He just wouldn't admit it.

"Riley!" Susan called out, her embrace intense and genuine. She'd been at the battle when Sartael had tried to claim the city, and helped save a number of innocent lives. For that alone, Riley would always admire this woman.

"You're looking great!" Riley said.

"Same for you." She eyed Beck and waggled her eyebrows. "Man, your husband is a hottie," she said. "You go, girl!"

Riley grinned. "He sure is." She smiled over at the other two actors, said hello, and then took her seat next to Susan. Beck sat to her right.

As a staff member delivered bottled water to all the participants, Riley searched the room until she spied Remmers and Jackson, each guarding a door just in case Hell made it across the Holy Water barriers. She received nods from both of them.

A ping from Beck's phone made him check the display, then he smiled. He tapped out a reply, then handed it over to her. It was from Simon.

AZAGAR IS DEAD. WILL TELL YOU MORE TOMORROW.

"Thank God."

Beck nodded, stashing away his phone. "Somethin' must have happened out there. Simon thought that might be the case."

Before Riley could reply, the moderator came on stage. A slim young man, he looked as wired, and tired, as she felt. The moment he picked up the mic, he smiled at the five members of the panel. Clearing his throat, he began, looking out at the crowd.

"Welcome!" he said, then waited for the noise to recede.

"Welcome to the first ever TrapperCon. Have you guys been having fun?"

A throaty cheer echoed through the room, along with a significant number of fist pumps.

"Good deal! Tonight we have two special events. First up is this panel: *Demonland: Reality or Make Believe?* Our panelists are Susan Dempsey, Jeff Campbell, and António Fontes, but you know them as Blaze, Jess and Raphael in the series." He waited until the cheers, wolf whistles and applause ended. "On the reality side of the panel we have Atlanta's own Master Riley Blackthorne and Grand Master Denver Beck."

More cheers and applause, along with more wolf whistles.

"Those are for you," Riley said quietly, shooting her husband a glance.

"Not a chance, Princess."

"After the panel, these five panelists will be signing autographs in the main lobby. Blaze, Jess and Raphael will be charging for photographs and autographs to help cover their expenses for attending this new con." He paused and added, "Help them out, will you? They were so awesome to be here tonight, let's send them home knowing Atlanta is *the* place for conventions. Our favorite trappers will not be charging for autographs, however a donation to the Demon Trappers Orphan Fund would be *very much* appreciated."

He looked down the row. "Now let's get started."

Riley leaned back in her chair, wishing her dad were here. What would Paul Blackthorne think of an event like this? Knowing him, he'd like the idea. Anything that helped people understand more about the war between Heaven and Hell was a plus, even if it required costumes and a little too much alcohol to get the job done.

After a quick introduction of each of them, the moderator began.

"First question: What is the *one* thing Hollywood does in *Demonland* that drives you trappers nuts?"

She looked over at Beck and winked. A wink came right

back at her.

The grand master raised an eyebrow now, leaning toward the mic so all could hear him. "Y'all really wanna go there?" he said, playing up his Southern roots. There were laughs now.

"We do!" someone called out from the crowd.

And so they went there.

TWENTY-FOUR

Once they'd swept up the remains of Azagar and tossed his not-so-arrogant ashes on sanctified ground, they returned to Simon's car, weary. After he treated the claw marks on her back, offering his sincere apologies as he did so, and she'd done the same to his leg, they headed back to town. The only reason Katia remained awake was because the fiery burn of her wounds.

Simon yawned, not bothering to cover his mouth. "I'm so tired."

"Right there with you. Even if we had gone to Waffle House, I wouldn't have stayed awake long enough to eat," she admitted. Since she had the appetite of a termite nowadays, that was saying something.

It wasn't until they were several miles down the road that Katia asked the question that had been on her mind ever since she'd arrived. If anyone would tell her, it'd be Simon. Now maybe she could get the truth.

"What really happened in Atlanta?"

"Which time?"

Apparently, she was would have to be more specific. "Last April."

Simon shot her a quick look and then returned his eyes to the road. "You mean the Fallen angel that came to destroy the city?"

"Nope, I'm not buying that. Not when there were other cities destroyed. Why would a Fallen bother? It's not their style."

"The real story is far scarier," he added. "You sure you want to hear it?"

"Yes, I do. I'm here now, so I need to know what happened.

Why it seemed like such a big deal, but the Guild kept playing it down."

"Okay, then. You asked."

As they headed toward Stewart's house, Simon told her the tale of how the Angel of Death had come to Atlanta. How it had been responsible for other decimated cities around the world.

"*The* Angel of Death?" she sputtered. "You mean the one that killed the first born of Egypt? *That* Angel of Death?"

"Yes. Ori killed it," he said.

"Get out! Really?" He nodded. "Wow. No wonder Heaven is pissed at him."

"He actually did them a favor because The Destroyer had lost its mind. Centuries of killing people finally made it snap."

"Huh. I'll be damned."

"Not tonight, at least," he said, then grinned. "You might think you're weird because you can see angels and such, but you're in a city full of weird. Remember that."

Katia would. She would also wait to talk to Master Blackthorne about the strange fae-like creature who had vanished into a wall at the convention. But not yet. There was no reason to push her luck, not when she might have finally found a home.

†*‡*†

It was close to two in the morning when they finally reached Atlanta. Simon dropped his companion at Stewart's house and waited until she was safely inside. A light eventually came on in a room two stories up, and then he saw her at the window. She gave him a wave and he returned it.

Katia Allyson Breman was a blessing. She had destroyed the Big Mouth demon, and her plan to trip Azagar so he'd tumble onto Holy ground had worked perfectly. She was strong of mind and spirit, and she had held her own in Hell. Even more, she was fun. Her former master was an idiot. As Ori had said, she was heaven sent, and Simon would be sure to offer his thanks the next time he went to Mass.

After he'd arrived home, Simon powered up his computer

and started writing his report, even before he'd taken a shower. A sensible person would do this in the morning when he wasn't so exhausted, but he felt driven to get it out of the way. Even though it was now the Sabbath and Father Rosetti wouldn't likely see it until Monday.

He added details, deleted them, added and erased paragraphs, put some of those back in, but finally close to four in the morning he had the final draft, complete with pictures of the new Hellspawn from the apartment building. He made sure to describe Azagar's escape in detail, and state who he felt was behind it, a shocking indictment that would ricochet around the Vatican. It might also come back to nail him, but at least he'd told them the truth.

Simon wrote a quick email to Father Rosetti and attached the report. Not the usual procedure, but this was an unusual exorcism. He hit the Send button, then crossed himself. It was out of his hands now.

When he finally climbed out of the shower and re-bandaged his leg, he was surprised to find a text from Rosetti, though it was early in the day in Rome. Simon headed to his bed, fearing that his superior might call into question his ability to perform this sacred task. How many exorcists met the Prince or visited Hell? None that he knew of. He took a deep breath and began to read the message, his heart in his throat.

> *Simon,*
> *You were mightily tested, my son. You kept strong in your faith and prevailed, saving the lives of three young men, as well as yours and the demon trapper's. Few would have survived such a dangerous situation.*
>
> *As you indicated, you will need the Atlanta Archdiocese to verify that you are still in possession of your soul. We both know that is the case, but others may have doubts given your most remarkable encounter*

with the Enemy, and the accusation you have made against one of Heaven's Divines. We'll discuss the "particulars" later today. Well done. Now rest.

Fr. Mateo Rosetti

"Amen," Simon murmured. He placed the phone on its charger, clicked off the lamp on his nightstand, and was asleep within minutes.

†✱‡✱†

To Beck, the line never seemed to end. He realized right off it wouldn't be polite to just autograph something without trading a few words, or have his picture taken with someone's cute little kid, giggling teenager, or the entire family. Those who'd come to see them truly loved everything to do with the trappers. Some had even come from out of state. Others wore T-shirts honoring the men lost in the Tabernacle massacre. Those really made his chest clench. Almost all of the people in line had dropped a donation into the box sitting between him and Riley, whatever they could afford.

He'd signed convention program books, pictures, T-shirts, you name it. He'd been especially happy to autograph the cast of the young boy who'd been in the front row at the panel. It was mind blowing.

There had been a few awkward moments, like when members of the *Demons Have Rights* group had gone through the line. Beck nodded to them, taken their pamphlets, and then they'd moved on. They had a right to their opinion, even if he thought it was complete bullshit.

By the time they reached the last few people in line—the convention staff—it was well after three in the morning. The box for the donations had been emptied regularly into a canvas bag that one of the con's security guys kept hold of for the entire time. The dude was big, serious, and likely to bust heads if anyone tried to steal it. What he didn't know is that Riley had put a spell on it to keep it safe.

"And that's a wrap!" Susan called out, rising from her seat. She looked a lot less tired than he and Riley.

"That was really fun," Jess said, then yawned, barely covering his mouth. "Did really well, too."

"Enough for that new refrigerator and mattress you've been jonesing for?" Raphael asked.

"Definitely. Or it'll cover a couple months' rent. Always a good thing."

It appeared that the Hollywood folks didn't get paid any better than trappers.

"How'd we do?" Riley asked, followed by her own yawn that had been triggered by Jess's.

"No clue, but it's a damned big pile of cash, that's for sure." Beck stood, stretched, felt something pop in his back. Once the tightness was gone, he felt better.

"Group photo," one of the con staff announced and so they all got together, in a line, and smiled for the photographer, including the big dude with the bag of cash. The staff member said the photo would go up on the con's website, along with the total of the donations received. Which meant someone, probably Beck, would need to count it all. And he would, grateful for every dollar they'd been given.

Once he had his gear packed, he claimed the bag of loot from the security dude and added in the remaining wad of bills and coins that were still in the box.

"Thanks for watchin' over this. We appreciate it."

"Happy to help," the guy said. "My brother-in-law's a trapper in Memphis. You guys did him proud."

They high fived, and then after promises to email the others he and his missus headed for the hotel's front entrance. Right behind them was the burly security guy who informed them he was escorting them to their car. Beck didn't have the heart to tell the guy that the most dangerous one in this trio was his very pretty, and very tired, wife.

TWENTY-FIVE

There was much to be thankful for on this sunny May morning, Katia's second in Atlanta. The boys—Adrian, Paulo and Scott—were home with their families. They had sworn off camping, for life. Their friendship was even stronger now because how many of your buds could claim to have been kidnapped by a demon? Holy Water had confirmed their souls were still their own, and time spent with Serrah had helped mitigate the horror of their captivity.

There were three more things to be thankful for—her own brother had already texted her twice, despite the time difference. They were due for a phone call later in the afternoon. He'd warned her he couldn't talk long because it was hard, but he was looking forward to it anyway.

Then there was the grand master across the table from her, and the huge brunch in laid out front of them. It'd been ages since Katia had seen this much food.

"Go on, lass, dig in. Mrs. Ayers was up early plannin' this feast and I, for one, am glad of it," Stewart said. He seemed to be in a merry mood this morning, and she suspected it was because today didn't involve planning any funerals.

Mrs. Ayer's offering certainly was a feast: blueberry pancakes, scrambled eggs, sausages, and huge cinnamon rolls. The orange juice tasted freshly squeezed. Heaven, without all the winged ones flapping about. Though, to be honest, Katia actually liked the Divines she'd met so far.

Once she'd finally crawled out of bed close to ten, she'd given her report to a sleepy Riley, who'd also just woken up.

Grand Master Stewart had listened in on that call. When Katia had completed her tale, she'd awaited the verdict, and to her surprise both her master and Stewart had been full of praise. Hearing "well done, Katia!" and "ya did a damned fine job, lass" was like sunshine after a long, frigid Kansas winter.

Then she'd received a call from Simon, who'd also just finished talking to his boss at the Vatican. He'd announced that his demon bite was healing well, that Father Rosetti hadn't fired him, at least not yet, and that his next stop, after a lot of coffee, was to be tested with Holy Water by one of the local priests. Then he was off to church, and finally his parents' church social later this afternoon. Also, would she like to go to Waffle House for breakfast on Tuesday?

His barely awake monologue had made her like him even more. She'd congratulated him, agreed on the Waffle House run, and wished him well at the luncheon. It'd felt like a routine call between old friends, even though that friendship was barely twenty-four hours old.

When the call ended, she turned her attention back to her plate.

"Ya thinkin' of stayin' in Atlanta for a time?" Stewart asked after demolishing his cinnamon roll, then turning to the rest of his meal. He really did have a sweet tooth.

Katia took a sip of her juice, then nodded. "I will, if the local Guild is good with that."

"Ya heard Riley. She's really happy how it all turned out, so yer golden, lass."

"Everyone has been so nice. I honestly didn't expect that," she admitted.

"Well, we do have our share of arseholes, ya just haven't met them yet. For the most part we're a team and watch each other's backs."

"I can see that. Some of the guys in Lawrence were okay, but some were just foul. Didn't matter if you were male or female, they liked being jerks."

"Happens in every Guild," he replied.

"How long can I stay here?"

Stewart shook his head. "As long as ya need. Yer good company. If ya weren't, the answer would be different."

"Oh great!" she said, relieved. "I need to save up some money for a deposit on an apartment. Can I pay you something while I'm here?" She gestured at the meal in front of her. "I eat a lot and that's going to cost you more for groceries."

The grand master thought about that as the rest of his sausage disappeared.

"If ya stay longer than a few months, maybe then. Ya need all the cash ya can save back. Also, ya should know that the local Guild has a fund that helps trappers in case of need. If ya find yer a little short for a rental deposit, talk ta Riley. She'll see what they can do. Ya'd pay it back ta the Guild, bit by bit."

That was great news. "Okay! I don't think we had that in Lawrence." Then she frowned. "Or if we did, nobody bothered to tell me." That was probably the case.

"Are ya good workin' with Simon?" was the next question.

"Yes! He's amazing. He was so calm when we were in Hell. I was scared out of my freaking mind."

"He was too, have no doubt."

"Then he hid it really well. Why isn't he a master? He killed an Archfiend last year. I saw it on one of the videos at the convention."

The grand master grew pensive. "I don't know why he didn't take the master's exam. Personally, I think it would be smart. Some of the trappers are leery of the exorcists, and it's only because of Simon that they'll give them the time of day. If he were a master, that would make it a bit easier for the trappers ta accept them." There was a pause, a slight smile, and then, "Perhaps ya could give it a mention, if ya get a chance."

Katia chuckled. "That was very smoothly done, sir."

"That's the kinda thing we grand masters do. Still, it's a sound idea and perhaps now Simon will be willin' ta consider it. If it came from ya, that is."

"I'll give it a try."

Katia had just started working on her fluffy eggs when her phone rang. A glance at the screen told her it was someone she'd hoped was out of her life, permanently.

"It's Master Kelly in Lawrence. Probably wants to yell at me. He left like four voicemail messages since yesterday."

"Feel free to ignore the man," Stewart advised.

"Better not. He'll just keep calling." She took a deep breath and answered the call. "Journeyman Breman."

"What in the hell are you doing over there?" the man bellowed. "I have had *three* calls about you. One of those was from some asshole named Harper, and the others were the National Guild. Dammit, Breman, they're threatening to audit our books!"

That made her smile. "If you didn't screw over your trappers, then National wouldn't need to audit you. It's kinda elementary stuff there, Master Kelly."

A barely stifled laugh came from across the table.

"Now look here, I'm not taking any of this sh—"

She switched the phone to her left hand and held it out from her ear. The voice on the other end of the phone kept shouting, so Katia took a sip of orange juice and waited him out. He'd have to breathe eventually. A week ago, this rant would have upset her. Now? Master Kelly was a lightweight after the horrors she'd faced with the exorcist.

When the bully finally sucked in a breath, Katia jumped in. "I've spent one day in Atlanta and I'm already part of their team. These people *are for real,* Master Kelly, not just b.s.'ing their way through their jobs and cutting other people down."

"You are a flake! They have no idea what you're like. Wait until they find out about your brother and what he did."

"They already know. Oh, did you hear that Kevin is out of his coma and is just fine? An angel did it. I met *three* Divines yesterday. Isn't that a kick?" And that wasn't even counting Hell's Chief Dickhead.

Absolute silence. Master Kelly usually had a pattern to his abuse: bellow, then berate, then bellow again. She'd managed to jam his brain, but it was time to move on.

Katia looked down at her plate. "I've gotta go. My eggs are getting cold. Have a nice life and don't call again."

She disconnected the call and set the phone aside. Looking up at the grand master, she wondered if she'd gone too far. "Too heavy handed?"

"Not on yer life, lass," Stewart replied. "Harper told me what was goin' on with ya there and that arse deserved all of that."

The phone rang, Kelly again. With a sigh she set down her fork, blocked him for eternity, and then went back to her eggs. A low chuckle came from her brunch companion.

"Yer gonna do right fine here, no mistake. Probably butt heads with people, but sometimes that's the best way to get the job done." Stewart raised his glass of orange juice. "Welcome ta the Atlanta Demon Trappers Guild, Journeyman Breman."

They clinked glasses. "Thank you." And while they were at it . . . "Any chance we can split that last cinnamon roll?"

†*‡*†

Despite Serrah's incandescent anger, protocol demanded she wait for a summons from the Archangel to deliver her report. By the time that happened, her patience was gone. Tempting as it was to ask Rahmiel for advice, she had to do this on her own. She knew exactly what was at stake, and now she needed Michael to understand that as well.

As she arrived in his presence, she gathered her courage around her, much like her wings. Good or bad, she was committed to see this through. To her annoyance Zerath was present, and his condescending expression told her exactly what kind of fool he thought her to be. She made sure to shield her thoughts from him, which led to even more doubts. What if he had acted on the Archangel's orders? Had she read this whole situation wrong?

"I have come to submit my report," she said, careful to look only at her superior.

"And what is it?" Zareth urged, though it was not his place

to do so.

She ignored him, addressing Michael. "During my time in the mortal city of Atlanta, I have found a Divine who is cunning and bent on his own enrichment. He has lied, put mortal souls in danger, and, in his own way, advanced the goals of our adversaries. He is a danger to that which we hold sacred."

"As I have often said," Zareth replied. "Ori the Fallen has not changed in any way. He is still in thrall to the Prince though he claims otherwise. He deserves to be destroyed."

"Ori?" she said, turning toward him now. "I was speaking of you, Zareth, not the Fallen."

"What is this?" the angel demanded. "You dare accuse me?"

"I was tasked with examining the Fallen's actions, to determine if he was stealing souls or killing innocents. I did as instructed, only to find the one I should have been investigating was *you*."

"He lies. How can you not know this?"

"You offered to save the exorcist's life, and his soul, and those of the three young mortals Azagar held in thrall, *if he betrayed the Fallen*."

"Is this true, Zareth?" Michael asked smoothly.

"Ori is a threat. You know what he is capable of."

"I do, yet you were aware that I had assigned Serrah this task. Why would you be involved?"

"To be honest, I did not trust her."

Ignoring the insult, Serrah focused her thoughts. A scene appeared in the air in front of them revealing the moment Azagar coerced the exorcist into a bargain the demon meant to break. There, in the background, was Zareth, just as she had seen him.

Michael gestured and scene repeated itself. Zareth's face paled now. "Explain yourself," the Archangel said. "Why did you not intervene? You knew what that fiend was capable of."

"I was observing the Fallen. It was not my task to help the exorcist. I knew that Serrah would believe Ori's lies. I wanted you to know who you could trust."

"I would say that the Archangel already knew who to trust

as he assigned me the task," she replied evenly. "I would not have watched the exorcist be trapped like that. *I* would have interceded."

"Even if it was forbidden?" Michael asked.

"Yes. Four souls were in peril. Think of how the Evil One would have crowed if we'd allowed Simon Michael David Adler to be lost? If the exorcists cannot trust us to aid them, why should they risk their lives to save those who are possessed?"

"That is a very good point."

"I only did what needed to be done," Zareth insisted.

"When the exorcist took Azagar to the place of execution, the fiend was released from the holy container. No Hellspawn can do that," Serrah said. "The exorcist and the trapper would have died if they had not lured Azagar onto sacred ground. Someone helped the fiend. Someone who could break a holy seal. Someone who wanted the exorcist dead."

"I have no idea what you're talking about," Zareth said, his eyes shifting back and forth between Serrah and their superior. "Clearly the exorcist made a mistake. Mortals are not trustworthy."

"You were the one who broke that seal and turned the fiend loose," she insisted.

"No, Ori must have freed Azagar. He only claims to have left Lucifer's service."

"The Fallen was with me when the demon was freed."

"Has he seduced you as well? Did you believe his flattery, silly one?"

The accusation burned like a whip strike. Serrah felt her anger flare, then forcibly pushed it down. If she lost herself in righteous fury, Zareth would win.

"When the demon was freed, we were in the mortal city of Atlanta. By the time we arrived to aid the exorcist, it was dead. Neither Ori nor I left this behind." She reached inside her robe and removed the feather. "This is one of yours, Zareth."

"Impossible."

Michael's eyes moved to her now. "Is that all the evidence

you have of this alleged crime?"

"Yes," she said, extending the feather. The Archangel took it, holding it as if it meant nothing.

He doesn't believe me.

Abruptly the air swirled, and a scene appeared in front of them. It was the night when the exorcist and the trapper had arrived at the holy place. They opened the building, discussing matters of faith. Then the container was ripped from the trapper's hands, pulling her some distance away from her companion. The box landed on the ground and rolled. When a pale hand touched it, the container exploded. The scene expanded outward revealing Zareth. As he stepped back, smirking, a single white feather fell to the ground.

"Archangel," the traitor began. "I—"

"Silence," Michael commanded. That one word seemed to echo into infinity.

Serrah took a deep breath, refusing to look at the traitor. He had sided with their enemies, willfully colluded with them, as if he were already in thrall to the Fallen in the Pit. Somehow fate, or the hand of the Creator, had ensured that feather had been left behind to be discovered.

When Michael finally spoke, his voice was as cold as the nameless void. "I knew what you were capable of, Zareth, for Serrah is not the first to warn me of your actions. That is why I felt a test was in order."

"You tested *me*?" the angel retorted.

"Yes, even you, Zareth." Michael turned his attention back to her. "Your official report regarding the Fallen, Serrah?"

This would not be easy, so only the truth would do. "Ori is a paradox. He once believed Lucifer's lies, and so he fell. I think he made that decision because he had great animosity toward you."

A stiff nod confirmed her assessment.

"Ori's time serving the Adversary wounded him greatly, for he grew to hate himself for the evil he inflicted upon the mortals."

"And now?"

"Now he fights for them, would willingly die for them. He kills Hellspawn whenever possible." She drew herself up. "He is a Divine in need of redemption, and he is going about that in his own single-minded way, one bloody battle at a time."

"He has not taken a soul since he was reborn?" Michael asked.

"No."

The Archangel turned his gaze on Zareth now. "Did you not tell me he claimed one just this week?"

"He . . . did. The soul of David Elliott Patterson of the mortal city of Minneapolis."

"No, Ori was still in the Prince's chains when he took that one. He has claimed none since he was renewed to life," Serrah said. "I checked with those Divines who keep track of such things."

"Archangel," Zareth began, his voice tighter now. "I can explain."

"You can explain freeing a fiend, one that would go on killing, maiming and stealing souls? You can explain threatening a mortal doing righteous work on our behalf? You would side with the Prince in all these matters just to settle an old score?"

"Ori is evil!" the angel shouted.

"Your hatred of him makes you blind. The evil I see is in you. There will be a reckoning for your deeds. Begone!" With a wave of Michael's hand, the other angel vanished.

Now his eyes studied her, and it took all of Serrah's courage to meet them.

"You used me to test Zareth, to see if the others spoke the truth about him."

A solemn nod.

"Did he recommend that I be assigned this task?"

Another nod.

"I see." She worked that out in her head. "He thought me malleable enough that I would give him what he needed to destroy Ori. You tested me, as well."

One of Michael's eyebrows rose at this. "You are more astute than I assumed."

She let that pass.

"He will be given a suitable punishment. But what shall I do with you? You were to observe, not interfere in any way, yet you did. You interacted directly with the mortals, you assisted Katia Allyson Breman when she was in the Pit by placing words of Latin on her tongue. You were personally *involved* in the mortal realm, not just an observer. That was not your task."

"No, it was not my task, yet I did all of that." The pride she felt was probably a sin, but it was there, nonetheless.

Michael chuffed. "No regrets?"

"None," she said, shaking her head. "The exorcist cast out the fiend and saved the lives and souls of three innocents. That was the most important matter."

Another huff, though much less pronounced this time. Michael closed his eyes, as if listening to a voice she could not hear, then he nodded as his eyes opened. "Because of your actions you will be assigned a new task, one that few would envy."

She had no idea what that might entail.

"Perhaps your new assignment will teach you that mortals are not as we are. They are certainly not as pure as us, nor as important. No, you will very shortly tire of them, I suspect."

She waited for him to reveal her new assignment, but instead he seemed preoccupied. "Wait in the repository of mortal bones where Rahmiel serves."

"Archangel," she said, giving a bow.

Michael vanished to wherever such higher angels went when they weren't chastising the lesser ones.

"Now I've done it," she murmured.

TWENTY-SIX

Serrah found Rahmiel sitting on the stairs that led to a granite mausoleum. This one was quite grand, with stone columns and a gilded gate that led to the old bones stored inside.

"How is the great Archangel this day?" Rahmiel asked, looking up at her approach.

Somehow this angel knew where she'd been. "He was more pensive than usual. I found it unnerving."

"I suspect some influence of our Creator. What of Zareth?"

For someone who spent her days in a cemetery, Rahmiel was remarkably "plugged in" as the mortals would say.

"He has made serious errors and is to be punished."

"Perhaps that will be the final push."

"Push?" Serrah asked.

"To Fall."

She blinked in surprise. "But none have done so since the Prince."

"Are you sure about that?" Rahmiel asked, giving her a sidelong glance.

"Oh . . . " she said, dropping onto the step near the other Divine. As it all sunk in, she repeated, "Oh!"

"We lose a few every now and then, though it is certainly not talked about. I suspect even now Zareth is planning his next move. Dare he Fall? Was that why he worked to destroy both Ori and the exorcist? Has he received assurances that he would be welcomed by a new master in trade for such services?"

"Zareth would be a fool to believe those assurances for they are surely lies."

"If I remember him correctly, he is. You would know him better."

Oh yes, Zareth was more than enough of a fool to listen to the Adversary's gilded tongue.

"Why did Michael send me here? Do you know what he intends for me?"

"In a way, yes." Rahmiel pointed toward Atlanta. "That is your task now."

"I do not understand what you mean."

"Remember I told you that the previous guardian had been reassigned because he was not performing his job properly? Well, now the mortal city of Atlanta has a new guardian. Congratulations! Or perhaps I should say, I am *so* sorry," the angel said, then winked in amusement.

"Me?" Serrah squeaked.

"You."

Serrah stared at the city's skyscrapers in the distance, at Rahmiel, then back at the metropolis. "All of it? All the mortals in that confine?"

"Yes, all the souls within the city borders. There about a half a million of them. Then there are the countless numbers of them who journey into the city every day. Most are righteous, a few are truly wicked. Others are a mix. The usual when it comes to mortals."

"Guardian . . . of a city. But why me?"

"Have you considered that this was not the Archangel's decision, but Someone Else's?" Rahmiel suggested. "That maybe it came about because you and the Fallen work together without bloodshed? Hmm," she said, tapping her index finger to her chin like a mortal. "I wonder Who might want that to happen?"

Serrah was astounded. If Rahmiel's reasoning was correct, it appeared the Creator, for whatever reason, had decided that *she* was to be given this task. An important one, indeed.

"You would be a better choice," she said honestly.

"No, I would not," Rahmiel replied. "I love *this* place too much. I am as much a part of it as the bones I watch over."

"But they are just mortal remains."

"True, but I was here during the great battle, present when momentous decisions were made, both cosmic and personal. I have been a witness to so much important mortal history, and a part of it. I value that as much as these old bones."

"What does a guardian do?" *What if she failed like the other guardian?*

Rahmiel broke into a big smile. "I will show you, but first, I must set a watch."

What she did next made no sense, for the angel made a strange noise that caused several creatures to scurry out from under bushes and down from the trees. A dozen fluffy squirrels formed a half circle in front of her now. When they stopped fidgeting, she knelt and spoke to them in words too soft for Serrah to hear. Then Rahmiel rose, and at a gesture, the squirrels scattered like seeds on a brisk breeze.

"They will be my eyes while I am in the city. They will show me if I need to return here quicker than I plan."

She commands small creatures. "Can I do the same?"

"Oh yes. There are many you can speak with, and some will help you. You also have the trappers, the exorcist and the Fallen to bring you news. That's a good start."

Ori. What would he think of her new job?

"I suspect he will welcome your presence. He will take care of the fiends, you will take care of the mortals. It makes sense."

In truth, it did. "Then show me this city I must guard."

With a knowing smile the other angel took hold of her hand, and in a swirl of air they left the aged cemetery, and the squirrels, behind.

†✷‡✷†

Lucifer drummed his fingers on a knee. His plan had worked better than he'd hoped, though losing the souls of the younger mortals had been annoying. Some might believe that not gaining those of the exorcist or the trapper was a mistake, but not him.

He'd have Simon Michael David Adler's soul one of these days. Let them think they were winning.

Azagar had been easy to manipulate. Flatter him, stroke his inflated ego, then slap him down. As predicted, the fiend had rebelled, seeking to establish himself as the strongest in Lucifer's realm. A more cunning or intelligent demon would have seen the trap. Azagar had been neither.

But in the end, it had worked better than he had hoped, for it had driven a wedge of doubt in the exorcist's mind. Would Heaven watch his back or was that realm just as skillful at deception as this one? Lucifer already knew the answer. In time, Simon Michael David Adler would as well.

Something crashed through the invisible barrier that led to the upper realms, descending in a tangle of body, feathers and rank fear. The angel struck the ground near the base of the throne, and moaned.

Perfect.

Yet another one of Heaven's lot had joined his army, another flawed Divine he could manipulate. Lucifer gestured and two of the closest fiends seized the figure, dragging the angel onto his feet. The newcomer's wings were ripped, turning darker by the minute, as blue blood dripped on the cavern floor. More would soon follow.

"Zareth. Welcome to Hell," he said, gesturing at the cavern around them. He could afford to play the affable host, at least for the moment.

The newcomer stared, at first in horror, then slowly his expression turned calculating. "I have come to serve you, my Prince," Zareth said, his voice unnaturally strong for someone who had just abandoned Heaven. This one would bear watching.

"I had hoped that would be the case. Do you pledge your fealty to me?"

A nod returned.

"Speak the words," he commanded.

A hesitation. A slight one, but a hesitation, nonetheless. Even now Zareth was calculating how he could work this to his advantage.

"I pledge my fealty to you."

"You pledge your service to me knowing that I hold your life in my hands, that only *I* will determine if you live or die?"

"Yes, I so pledge."

"Excellent. Your oath is accepted, Zareth the Fallen."

Ori had made the same vow, but had later learned that the matter of life and death was a crucial one. If one was never permitted to die, it would *eternal* servitude. For a Divine that did not seem to be of much importance, until it was.

Lucifer nodded at the pair of demons. "You know where to put him. Let him rest in chains until I call for him."

"But lord, I thought—"

"You will obey me, Zareth. If you fail to do that, I will have you broken. Then I will heal you and break you again. Do you understand?"

A nod came now, along with fear in the angel's eyes.

As it should be.

"Welcome to Hell, Fallen. I have great plans for you. But first, you need to learn exactly what it means to live in my realm, and to be my servant."

It took only a matter of minutes, but soon Zareth's agonized voice joined that of the others in exquisite torment. It was, in its own way, divine music.

Vanity and the blind quest for power were universal traits of both mortals and Divines. Traits so easy to manipulate, especially in his fellow angels. Lucifer had lied, of course—he broke all his servants before they gained the right to serve him. Zareth was now learning that in the most painful way possible. In time, he might prove useful.

If not, there were always others.

EPILOGUE

Simon rose from the kneeler, settling back on the pew, his mind at peace. It was quiet in the sanctuary today, only a few people in the church. He'd offered his prayers of gratitude for surviving Hell, for Katia, and for Ori. He wondered what Heaven might think of that last part, but that was their problem. The Fallen had served the Light more than one of Heaven's own. Something Simon would always remember.

During their phone call, Father Rosetti had said he had not been surprised by Azagar's strategy, nor that of the Prince. He felt that it said much about Simon's expertise as an exorcist that Hell had gone to so much effort to try to destroy him. In the end, he'd done very well in such a perilous situation that had included treachery by one of Heaven's own angels.

It hadn't hurt that when he'd been tested with Holy Water, Simon Michael David Adler's soul was still his own. Rome would make note of that as well. Still, he knew his report would be shuffled around the Holy See and there might be repercussions down the line. No matter what, he had no regrets.

Two weeks sabbatical. That edict had been dropped on him right before he and Rosetti ended their conversation. As soon as Rome could line up a replacement exorcist to cover the city, Simon was off duty. He didn't bother to argue like he had in the past. He needed a rest, one that would rejuvenate not only his body, but his soul. The time off would allow him to recharge and get his head straight. As his superior had put it, "A tired exorcist is likely to become a dead one."

As Simon exited the church, he found an angel sitting on the steps, though this one did not have a dog at his feet. He paused near Ori, then smiled down at the Divine who had risked his life for him and Katia.

"We saved three young souls and defeated a powerful demon," he said. "I had much to give thanks for this morning."

Ori nodded. "Will you continue to work with Katia Allyson Breman?"

"Yes. The Vatican was pleased at how well we did together." Simon hesitated, then added, "How *all of us* worked together."

One of Ori's eyebrows lifted. "You told them about me?"

"I did. You served the Light, even though some think that's not possible. I know better. Katia's brother is alive because of you."

It took the angel some time before he murmured, "Thank you."

"Stay well, Ori. I have no doubt I'll see you again. Our paths do seem to cross more frequently now."

There was no reply, but then Simon hadn't anticipated one. He set off down the stairs and then along the street. It was a nice day and he needed to walk and think. And he had a vacation to plan.

Ori had begun his day in the heart of the city, where he often sat on these church stairs watching the mortals pass by. Most of the time he was invisible to them, but not today. He liked this place. It was close to Demon Central and the abominations that deserved his wrath. Yet somehow this morning felt different, though he couldn't quite fathom why.

He had known the exorcist was inside the church, and that had pleased him. Simon had learned much during his fight with Azagar and he had grown strong over the last year. It was a good outcome for all. Well, except for the Hellspawn.

What Ori hadn't anticipated was a visitor arriving right after Simon's departure. The moment Michael appeared he'd almost manifested his sword, but held himself in check. If the Creator had decided his time was done on this earthly plane, there was nowhere he could hide from that judgment. Was the Archangel to be his executioner?

Michael walked up the church steps and sat a few feet away from Ori, as if unsure if his presence was appreciated. He was dressed as any mortal might be, clearly wishing to blend in. That was also unusual.

"Fallen."

"Archangel."

A homeless man made his way down the street in front of them. The mortal had in his possession one of the tiny demonic thieves. Earlier he'd used that fiend to steal coins from one of the donation boxes, but rather than keeping the money, he'd patiently distributed it among the other impoverish mortals who lived on the streets.

A sin, followed by penance. Ori understood that all too well.

"A new guardian has been assigned to this city," Michael announced.

That was why Atlanta felt different.

"Serrah?" he guessed. A curt nod returned. "Your way of punishing her?" An angelic version of a shrug was the reply. "I will not interfere with her task as long as she does not side with the Prince in any way. If she does, she will pay a heavy price."

"I know."

Of course, he'd know that. He knew about everything. Or at least he acted like he did.

"You interfered in a mortal's life," Michael asked, then gestured.

It was like one of the moving images that humans were so fond of. This one showed Ori walking down the hallway of the Kansas care home, then slipping inside the room that held the comatose young boy. He'd almost been too late. As he'd entered the room, there was a demon at the boy's bedside, hand over his forehead siphoning out the mortal's life essence.

There had been no battle, Ori too quick for the thing. He'd snapped its neck and then held it just long enough for the body to turn to ash. A quick gesture opened the closest window and the ash trailed outside, and then the window shut.

Leaning close, Ori traced a pattern on the boy's forehead, a warning to any other demon who might try to harm this mortal. The mark would fade quickly, but for now it was needed. As he stepped back, the boy opened his eyes and stared at him.

"Yes, I'm an angel. Yes, you're going to heal, Kevin Damian Breman. You have your sister Katia to thank for that." Ori began to turn away, then hesitated. "No more summoning Hellspawn. That was just stupid. Do you understand?"

A faint nod came from the boy.

"Be well, mortal."

The scene faded away leaving Ori and the Archangel on the street once more.

"Well?" Michael asked.

Some explanation was apparently required. "Katia Allyson Breman was given an impossible choice: save her brother by betraying the exorcist or refuse and have her brother die. She chose the latter, even while in Hell within feet of the Prince's throne. That took immense courage. I chose to ensure that Kevin Damian Breman did not die because she made that most difficult choice."

"Why did you think you had that right?"

"I've had it since the moment I was created," Ori replied. "I was not always Fallen, Michael."

A low sigh returned. "You continue to confuse me," the Archangel admitted.

That was also unexpected.

Abruptly Michael surged to his feet and strode away, only to swivel around, glaring at him. "Why?" he demanded.

"Why . . . what?" Ori asked, confused.

"Why did you follow Lucifer into the Pit? Why would you do that?"

It had never occurred to him that anyone, especially Michael, would ask that question.

"Because of you."

The Divine did not seem surprised at that response. "Serrah was correct, then."

Apparently, there had been some discussion on this subject.

"I was angry at you for being such a . . . " How would the mortals say it? "A stuck-up bastard. You never praised anyone for their work, never spoke with any kindness. You are a cold being, Michael, and that chill permeates all you touch."

The Archangel's shocked expression almost made him regret his outburst, no matter how much it was deserved.

"Yet, I was still to blame no matter your behavior," Ori admitted. "I was angry and stubborn. It was so easy to cast the blame on you, make you the reason why I listened to Lucifer's lies. And by our Creator, did he lie. He fed me everything I wanted to hear, grooming me like one would a pet dog." Bile rose in his throat even now and he forced himself to swallow it down. "It took me a long time to realize just how much I'd lost by leaving Heaven. Still, in the end, it was my decision, and mine alone."

Michael quietly returned to the steps and sat, pensive.

"He offered me similar lies, did you know?" he said. "How I was not valued by our Creator. How I would do *so* much better as his second-in-command." He looked down at his hands now. "I admit, I was tempted."

"Yet you did not give in! For all your arrogance, you were far wiser than me," Ori said honestly.

"You have changed." The angel shook his head. "We both have. I often berate mortals for their poor decisions. I can point to any one of them and say, 'Why are you so ignorant?' And yet, if fate had been different, I would have made the same damning choice as you."

It was an admission Ori never thought he'd hear.

"Such is the power of the Prince's tongue," Michael added. He took a deep breath and let it out slowly. "Do you like guarding the mortals in this city?"

Ori gratefully grasped hold of this change of topic. "Yes, I do. In some ways, it helps to heal my soul. I have much to atone for, as well you know. I shall do whatever I can to stop Lucifer."

He pulled up the quote that had sustained him since his rebirth. "'Long is the way and hard, that out of Hell leads up to the light.'"

The other Divine puzzled on that for a moment. "That was written by Milton, wasn't it? *Paradise Lost*, I think."

Ori stared. He would never have believed Michael would trouble himself with mortal writings. "Yes, it was."

There was silence now as they brooded on what they'd discovered about each other. Another parishioner left the church, unaware that she had passed two Divines.

Finally, Michael spoke. "Please . . . continue to do what you can to help these mortals, for they desperately need your aid," he insisted. "Lucifer will never cease his efforts to control this city, as it refuses to bow to him."

"I shall do what I can."

"I have no doubt that your stubbornness will prove to be a valuable weapon against the Chief of the Fallen. Even *arrogant* Divines such as myself would agree."

Was that humor he heard? Surely not.

When Michael rose from the steps now, preparing to depart, Ori added, "Thank you for speaking the truth to me. Be of the Light, Archangel."

"Be of the Light, Ori." The Divine studied him for some time, his expression changing, even as his voice deepened. "**For though once you were Fallen, you are no longer.**"

It was an unexpected blessing, one that came not only from Michael, but from their Creator. It sank into Ori's heart, and then deep into his soul, burning away the remaining darkness.

He had truly been forgiven.

When he looked up, the Archangel was gone, though the blessing still resounded in his ears. Ori closed his eyes, barely holding back the tears as he offered a prayer of thanks.

He was free.

Throughout the millennia he had not been broken, despite Lucifer's best efforts. Through all the tortures, and the horrors, he had survived. Now he had shed his darkness and reclaimed his own Light. He would ensure that Serrah remained safe so the city, and its mortals, would prosper.

In his own way, Ori would deny Lucifer what the Prince so desperately craved—to rule Atlanta as he ruled in Hell.

"This I vow, for eternity."

The End

From Hell with Love
A Riley Blackthorne Short Story

Originally published in
You Want Stories?
JordanCon 2019 Charity Anthology
www.JordanCon.org

From Hell with Love
A Demon Trappers® Short Story

May 2019
Hartsfield-Jackson International Airport
Atlanta, Georgia

It'd been a day from Hell. Literally.

Even for a seasoned demon trapper like Riley Blackthorne, today had been one for the books—four Hellspawn trapped before lunch, followed by an exorcism at a private girls' school. She certainly had a few tales to tell her husband, Denver Beck, when he flew back into Atlanta this afternoon.

My husband. That was a new thing, just six weeks in the making. Their wedding had been a media free-for-all because only a few days before the happy event, the bride and groom had saved the city from becoming a mass graveyard.

Again.

How often did a Master Demon Trapper (Riley) get hitched to a Grand Master of the International Guild (Beck)? Truly a rare event. As one reporter had blithely explained, it was almost like a royal wedding, except that their matchmaker had been the Prince of Hell himself.

That observation still made Riley's skin crawl.

The newsies had eventually moved on, leaving Beck and her in relative peace, which was why no one noticed when she tucked her car into a slot in the airport parking garage. After a quick application of lipstick and a brush through her hair—at least her gold and auburn highlights were still making her brown hair look cool—she was ready to meet the man she loved. She'd even swapped out her usual trapping clothes—the stained and ripped blue jeans and an equally dilapidated T-shirt—for a bright blue shirt and new jeans.

After double-checking her phone for Beck's flight arrival details, only to find that the plane was delayed by thirty minutes, Riley hauled herself out of the car. She automatically retrieved her worn bag full of trapping supplies and slung it over her shoulder. For a moment, she considered putting it back in the car because it seemed like overkill. As she debated, her late father's voice filled her mind, as clear as if he were standing next to her: *Plan for demons, because they always plan for you.* She took the bag with her.

Riley had just exited the parking garage into the hot Atlanta sun and was about to cross to Hartsfield-Jackson's South Terminal when her phone buzzed with a message. It was Master Harper, her superior, and since he knew she was picking up Beck, this had to be something urgent. Moving out of the flow of foot traffic, she stared at the message—and then read it again just to be sure.

DEMON @AIRPORT. SEE CHAPLAIN @TSA SOUTH TERMINAL. KIDS ON TRAIN AS BACKUP.

"You have got to be kidding me." Riley eyed the huge building in front of her, crowded with passengers, all intent on their own journeys.

A demon here? They always avoided the place. Was this a coincidence?

"Nope." Not with the way the day had gone so far.

She reread the message—unfortunately, Master Harper hadn't indicated the type of Hellspawn—and smirked at the word "kids." In this case, he meant her two apprentices, Kurt Pelligrino and Jaye Lynn. Her year with them was about over, as Kurt would soon be sitting his journeyman exam. Jaye, her training delayed because of family issues, would do so in late June. Riley had no doubt that both would pass, as had her third apprentice, Richard Bonafont. He was currently getting a tan on a Florida beach before returning to Atlanta to start his new job as a journeyman trapper.

Riley muttered to herself as she hiked across the pedestrian crossing, trying not to get her feet clipped by weary travelers and their rolling suitcases. If there really was a fiend at the airport, the actual trapping operation could get ugly. Anytime you put a dense concentration of untrained mortals near Hellspawn, the chance of injuries and deaths rose dramatically.

Since this airport handled over one hundred million passengers every year—her math-adept mind obligingly did the calculation—there'd be an average of a quarter million people through here every day.

Please let this be a hoax. Not that she planned on laughing about it if it was.

Continuing to grumble to herself, Riley was surprised to spy Jaye's red hair near a shoeshine stand. Next to her, Kurt was checking his smartphone, per usual. Their trapping bags sat near their feet.

"Hey, 'kids,'" she said, smirking as she joined them.

Jaye rolled her eyes. "Harper, right?"

Riley nodded in return. Both of them were a bit older than her eighteen years—but then, they'd not faced down the forces of Heaven and Hell on more than one occasion.

"Huh. According to Facebook, we're not at the airport," Kurt reported.

"Then where are we?" Jaye asked.

"The Hartsfield-LaToya Jackson Intergalactic Space Bar and Nail Emporium," he replied. "Who knew?"

"Riiight. Please tell me you didn't check in," Riley said. "I really don't want the entire city freaking out because they know we're here."

"Nope, running in stealth mode, as usual," he replied, looking hurt. "I know better than that."

"Sorry. You do know better. I'm just a little skittish right now."

"Only fair," he replied. "Those trappings this morning were anything but pretty. At least not the one at the brewery."

"That's a nice way to say, 'Thank God we got the damage waiver signed before we trashed the place,'" Jaye replied.

Riley groaned. "Technically, the demon trashed the place, but I'm thinking that the time it'll take to mop up all that beer is going to count against us."

"Yup," Kurt replied. He eyed her nice clothes. "You think the fiend is here because you're here to pick up your dude?"

"I fear so." She looked around, pleased there were no signs of panic in the departing passengers. At least not yet. "You got here quick."

"Mass transit rocks," he said, giving her a thumbs-up.

"Sure faster than I-85. Let's go find out what's up," Riley said. "Pray that someone made a mistake."

If this were for real, a trapping here would be the kind of real-world experience her apprentices needed. Riley shifted to training mode. "How do you suggest we go about this, Oh-journeypersons-to-be?"

It was Jaye's turn to groan, as she was all too familiar with Riley's "teaching" voice. She eyed Kurt, who promptly gestured for her to take the lead.

"Thanks, I'll remember that," she said. Taking a deep breath, she dove in. "Okay, if it were me, I'd locate the reporting authority figure, show them my credentials, try to determine what type of fiend I'm facing, and then get directions to said fiend."

"And if the person in authority has no clue?" Riley pressed.

"Then I'd wait until another legit report came in, because there's no way I'd go through this entire airport, gate by gate."

"There're a hundred fifty-two of them in the domestic terminal alone. That'd take forever," Kurt said. When Riley gave him a look, he added, "I checked Google on the way down."

Of course he did. "Yet that's exactly what might happen."

Jaye winced at that depressing observation. "No way we're getting stuck here forever. We're going to a concert tonight. We almost had to kill people to get those tickets."

"You both know that Hellspawn couldn't care less if you have concert tickets," Riley cautioned.

"Not happening this time," Jaye replied, as if that somehow made it so.

Finding the authority figure wasn't hard—the chaplain was indeed waiting for them near the TSA checkpoint, which was backed up more than normal. An older lady, the reverend had short silver hair and was dressed in all black, except for her crisp white clerical collar.

"You're Riley Blackthorne," she said, smiling. "I've seen you on TV a few times."

Riley barely stifled the grimace. She didn't like being well known, but that's what happened when you took down Hell's worst nightmares in public places—people noticed. And then those same folks uploaded their smartphone videos for the world to see. Apparently, Riley even had her own YouTube channel, though she'd never had the guts to check it out.

But that wasn't this woman's fault.

"Good afternoon, Reverend." Riley gestured toward her companions. "Apprentice Trappers Pelligrino and Lynn."

Polite greetings were exchanged.

"I'm glad it's you they sent," the chaplain said, addressing Riley. She shot a look toward the checkpoint. "They're about to shut down the concourse. The thing won't move, and neither will the people around it. They just keep staring at it and nodding their heads."

"A Mezmer, then," Riley said. "A Grade Four," she added, because most civilians weren't familiar with trapper lingo.

"Apparently, security tried to intervene, and now they're caught up in whatever that thing is doing, just like the others," the chaplain said.

That was typical Hypno-Fiend behavior. Mezmers were particularly adept at tunneling into your mind, then telling you lies so entrancing that you believed every word they said. And the whole time they held you in thrall, they were happily sucking out your life energy. Sometimes they would bargain you out of your soul. On the demonic scale of chutzpah, they rated rather high just for their sheer cunning. Still, when cornered, Hypno-

Fiends could turn lethal in a heartbeat.

Some Hellspawn were benign, like the Grade One Klepto-Fiends who loved to steal shiny objects. Riley had one of those in her house, so finding matching earrings was always a problem. Techno-Fiends, classified as Grade Two, were adept at giving your glitzy big-dollar computer a lobotomy. Others, like the Grade Three Gastro-Fiends, lived to eat everything, including people.

To a trapper, it was simple math: The higher the demonic grade rating, the more dangerous the fiend. Fours were never to be taken lightly.

"I've let security know you're headed to the gate," the chaplain said. "They'll meet you near the train."

"Thank you, Reverend."

"May God watch over you. And good luck."

Since the concourse was still open, at least for the moment, Riley knew there was no way they'd get through the screening process with the stuff in their trapping bags. The X-ray machine would absolutely freak out over the steel pipes and Holy Water spheres. So she headed for the closest TSA agent. Holding up her trapper's license, she smiled to break the ice—because every now and then that tactic actually worked.

"Hi," she said, keeping her voice low to hamper any potential eavesdropping. "I'm Master Riley Blackthorne, and we need access to Concourse C because of a *problem* you have out there. Can you walk us through, so we don't have to be scanned?"

"We're shutting down the concourse," the woman replied. "Maintenance issue."

Not even close. "I know. We're here to handle that *maintenance issue.*"

The agent thought about that and then added, "You can't go out there unless you go through screening."

"As a member of this organization—" Riley pointed at the Atlanta Demon Trappers Guild logo at the bottom of the license "we are allowed to skip security screening if we are on official business."

"You have to go through screening," was the automatic reply. Around them, the news of the concourse's shutdown had now reached the traveling public and wasn't proving popular.

"But I gotta be in Detroit tonight!" someone called out.

Kurt tapped Riley on the shoulder and then handed over his phone. She gave a quick glance at what was pulled up on the screen, then displayed it to the agent. Having a nerd as an apprentice was often a bonus.

"These are the rules regarding trappers and airport security screening. In particular—" Riley glanced at the screen again and then turned it back to the lady "—paragraph three, subsection nine, says you are required by federal law to allow us to pass *without screening* in the fastest manner possible. If you can't make that decision, we need someone who can. No matter what, we're going through security in the next two minutes, because lives depend on it."

There were a few blinks, a quick glance at the information on the phone, then more blinks. "Wait here."

Riley handed back Kurt's phone then began a mental countdown—at the two-minute mark, they were breaching the checkpoint and would deal with the fallout later. At a minute and a quarter, a supervisor appeared—another woman, one no doubt higher on the TSA organizational chart.

"I'll walk you through," the new arrival said, her expression grim.

All of them waltzed past the lengthy line like they were celebrities, which earned them both frowns and grumbling. It was going fine until another TSA agent moved into their path, which led to a heated discussion between the two supervisors. Time ticked away as the conversation dragged out.

Then someone in the line called out, "Hey, isn't that the trapper girl? The one named Blackthorne?"

Heads swiveled. It was a given: If Riley was here, so were demons. That often made life difficult—like clearing out an entire grocery store just because she was buying milk, bread, and pizza.

Since Riley's presence was never a harbinger of good tidings, more than a few people turned and left the line, not even looking back.

The recalcitrant supervisor dude stared at her. "Go on, get going," he said, waving them away.

It was rare that Riley appreciated being a celebrity—and now was one of those times. They sprinted toward the escalator that led into the bowels of the airport and the various gates.

"That went better than I figured it would," Kurt said, hustling to catch up.

"They haven't had this kind of situation here in Atlanta, so it kind of locks up their brains until they work it out," Riley explained. "To be honest, they figured it out quicker than I thought they would."

She hadn't had to yell even once. Part of her was actually disappointed about that.

"Don't we need someone to sign a damage waiver?" Jaye asked.

"Good question. And nope, we don't. Since the beginning of the year, state and federal facilities are required to have Guild damage waivers on file so we're covered in any Hellspawn-related incident," Riley replied. "FYI—questions about those waivers are on the journeyman exam." Her two apprentices nodded solemnly.

At the bottom of the escalator, a single security guard awaited them, a heavyset Hispanic gentleman who looked decidedly spooked.

"I'm Master Blackthorne. You here to take us where we need to be?"

"Yes, ma'am. Follow me."

She'd expected that they'd hop the train to the concourse, but instead there was a shuttle waiting for them. Even before she and her fellow trappers settled onto the bench seats, they were off, rolling down the long hallway that led past the Concourse T gates, then Concourse A and B. The farther they went, the less crowded it became, which told Riley that security had done their best to get the civilians clear of the threat.

By the time the guard parked the shuttle at the escalator that led up to Concourse C, there was no one else around.

"All of C is clear?" she asked. The guard nodded. On a hunch she asked, "Is the demon near gate C48?"

The man nodded again. "Down at that end, yes."

So much for coincidence.

"Thanks, we got it from here," Riley said after they'd disembarked. The guard rolled back down the way they'd come without ever looking back.

"Okay, then," Kurt said. "Let me guess—Beck is supposed to land at that gate, right?"

"You got it."

At the top of the escalator, Riley paused to get her bearings. To their right was the usual collection of shops and restaurants, interspersed with gates. To the left was the same. Plus a demon.

As they hustled along the left corridor, they found signs of rapid abandonment—a newspaper lying on the floor, an overturned piece of carry-on luggage, a Bluetooth headset still blinking away. There was even a child's little stuffed rabbit.

"That's creepy," Jaye said, pointing at one of the video screens. The flight was listed as arriving from "Purgatory." A quick glance showed that all the rest were the same.

In the distance, Riley could see what they'd come for—a Mezmer in full illusion mode, and the dozen people entranced by it.

"There we go," Kurt said, speeding up.

"Wait!" Riley called out, and to her relief, he came to an immediate halt.

The hallway looked like it should, but it felt wrong. *Very* wrong. Someone who hadn't been trained in magic wouldn't have noticed, someone like her apprentices.

Riley held back, testing the edge of the wrongness.

"Some reason we're not busting our butts to get to those people?" Kurt asked, looking first at her, then their destination, and then back again.

It was a valid question.

"What are you sensing?" Jaye asked, less eager than her companion. Her caution would serve her well in the years to come.

"Don't know."

Once again, Riley would have to use her magic, and that annoyed her. It always felt like cheating because the other trappers didn't have that ability. Beck strongly disagreed, and it'd proven to be a constant argument, one of the few they had.

"If it keeps you and yer people alive, where's the problem?" he'd say.

Beck was right, but it still bugged her because the blame for that "advantage" fell firmly on Lucifer's shoulders. His constant screwing around with her life—and her father's life—had led to her learn magic to protect herself and Beck. As well as pretty much everyone else.

Riley spun a low-level spell, hunting for anything that felt like an illusion. There was none. Maybe she was just tired and overcautious. Or . . .

She upped the strength of the spell. Still nothing. Focusing harder, it suddenly became all too clear. "Heads up! We got Threes!"

With a quick burst of magic, she revealed what was actually in front of them. Kurt spat out a swear word as he retrieved his steel pipe from his trapping bag. Riley did the same, minus the cuss word.

A Gastro-Fiend, or Three, had a single goal in mind: hook you on its claws and then eat you, alive or dead. This pair of vicious predators were mature ones—at least four feet tall, covered in thick fur, and with double rows of wickedly sharp teeth. As they lumbered toward the trio, the click of their claws on the floor was barely audible over their deep howls.

"I'm ready," Jaye called out.

They'd practiced this. Since Jaye had better aim than Kurt, she had pulled a Holy Water sphere from her trapping bag. Now they just needed to buy her time to throw that sphere, and then re-arm. That meant Riley and Kurt were going to be the first in line for those teeth and claws.

When the fiends were within ten feet, a Holy Water sphere arced over them, striking one of the Threes in the face. Shrieking in agony, it collapsed to the floor, writhing and clawing at the burning liquid. The second demon had just reached Riley when she slammed her pipe into it, careening it toward Kurt. Just like they'd rehearsed, he swung his own pipe and connected with the Three's head, dropping it to the floor, senseless.

"Score!" Riley called. But before any of them moved, the Threes simply vanished.

"What the . . . ?" Kurt said. "Those were for real, right?"

Riley walked forward to where one of the demons had fallen, then bent to pick up a broken tooth near a small bloody hunk of fur.

"Yes, they were real." She held up the tooth so her apprentices could see it, then pocketed it for later destruction. If it fell into magical hands, a witch or a necromancer could use the tooth to summon that particular fiend. That was always a stupid move that never ended well.

"So, we go from no demons at the airport to three?" Jaye said as she returned the extra Holy Water sphere to her bag.

"Yeah. That worries me." Riley had an idea who was behind this, but right now wasn't the time to share her suspicions, especially not with her apprentices.

She cleared her mind again and went searching for any other cloaked threats, finding only the Mezmer down the hallway. "We're clear from here on."

A quick jog brought them to the Four and its victims.

At first glance, nothing looked amiss unless you were trained in Hellish Tactics 101. A young woman with flowing blond hair stood in front of the gates at the end of the concourse, C48 being one of those. She wore a pristine white summer dress and a bright smile, and she appeared harmless.

"Impressive illusion," Kurt said, nodding in appreciation. Riley had to agree.

What was more impressive was that the fiend had enthralled a dozen people with apparently little effort. As the chaplain had said, two were security personnel, and the rest travelers. Age didn't seem to matter when summoned by this fiend's siren call—there was a slack-faced teenager, earbuds hanging down his T-shirt, as well as middle-aged businessmen, women in crisp suits, a few seniors, and a young couple with a wide-eyed toddler. So far, none of them were unconscious, but that would happen if this demon was allowed to continue.

The victims were neatly arrayed in a semicircle on the terminal floor in front of the Four, just like they were in preschool. Their "teacher" even held a book in her hands, speaking in a reassuring tone while displaying the pictures for all to see.

"Storytime?" Jaye said. "You have got to be kidding me."

"It works," Riley replied. "It's the perfect bait if you're overworked, jetlagged, and just want to chill out. All they need is some juice and crackers, and they're set."

Ignoring the trappers, the fiend continued to read to its victims.

"*Where the Demons Are?*" Kurt said, catching sight of the title. "Maurice Sendak has to be turning in his grave."

"It was my favorite book when I was a kid," Riley said, which meant the Four was already playing with her mind. "We've got twelve victims here, so this one is way strong. Shore up those mental shields now, folks."

The demon delicately flipped another page with a frosted pink nail, then looked up at them with cunning eyes. "Blackthorne's Daughter, come join us! We're almost to the part you love the most."

Riley growled under her breath, but not because of Hell's nickname. She was used to that. What made her angry was the power behind this thing—far more than a Four should possess.

"The only part of this story I love is when you're gone," she said.

The Mezmer scowled and waggled an index finger. "Now who is being a Negative Nancy?"

Jaye snorted. "Really? Where did they get this one?"

Riley ignored the image in front of them, focusing on the power she felt beneath it. The creature was stalling, not trying to suck that last bit of life force out of the helpless souls in front of it.

Was it waiting for Beck?

"Nail it," Riley ordered, and a Babel sphere went flying across the open space, impacting the Mezmer straight on. It'd been Kurt's toss, and this time he'd hit his target. She made a mental note to congratulate him later.

As the magic in the sphere took effect, the demon's glamour withered and then vanished. What was revealed was a five-foot visual disaster. This Hellspawn was female, with saggy breasts and gnarled hands tipped with sharp claws. Pale stringy hair fell onto its sloped shoulders. A pair of crimson goat-slit eyes glowered at them as the book she held disappeared.

"Oh, look, boys and girls, it's time to end the story," the fiend said, her voice still sounding light and airy in contrast to her hideous body. As one, they all rose and turned toward Riley and her companions, some more unsteadily than others.

Would the thing set these people against them? It'd happened before.

"You are free to go," the demon said, and whatever hold it had over them shattered, which left totally bewildered humans staggering their way down the concourse. One woman looked back, saw the thing for what it really was, and let loose a blood-curdling scream, triggering a panicked dash for safety among the others.

Once they were gone, the demon gave a toothy smile. "I am too powerful for your mere magic, trapper."

The sudden push against her mental defenses told her this thing wasn't lying. That meant it had a demi-lord, a higher-ranking demon who used this one for its own purposes while lending it a little more power. Riley spun out a spell of her own, shielding the minds of her apprentices. This situation required it.

"What's your game, demon?" she asked.

"How do you mortals say it?" the fiend replied, tapping a claw against her lips in thought. "Oh, yes. Tag! You're it!"

The she-demon spun on its heels and took off for the nearest exit, gate C48. When it reached the door, it blew the security keypad to pieces in a shower of plastic and electronics. Ramming its shoulder into the portal busted it off its hinges, causing the door to careen down the hall beyond. With one final high-pitched laugh, the horror fled down the jet bridge.

"Go! Go!" Riley shouted.

Pounding toward the exit, then onto the jet bridge, they found the exterior door open and a maintenance crew member cringing in fear against the side of the plane. He pointed a shaking finger toward the open door that led to the tarmac, unable to speak. They ran down the stairs and then stopped, searching for the escapee.

"Where'd it go?" Kurt demanded.

Jaye pointed toward the runway. "There!"

"What's it doing?" he called out as they sprinted toward the fiend. "This makes no sense."

He was right—it did not make sense. The demon hadn't really tried to mess with their heads, so why lead them outside?

Something made Riley look up. *Planes.* None of them were landing because the concourse had been closed, but if one got close enough, did the demon have enough power to . . .

"Oh, God, no," she said, taking off at a dead run.

The fiend came to a halt on one of the wide grass strips between the runways, its smirk even wider. The same taunting laughter came Riley's way now.

As she and her apprentices lined up against the threat, her mind whirled with questions. Who had the kind of power to cloak those Threes and help a Four enthrall all those people? An Archfiend? Maybe, but even that was a stretch. Fallen angel? That was a possibility.

"What is a Four's best weapon?" Riley called out.

"Getting inside people's minds and making them do whatever it wants," Jaye replied automatically. It was one of the first things a trapper learned when they began hunting the things.

"Why bring us out here?"

There was a momentary pause as Kurt made the connection. He stared up as a jet passed by in the distance, in a holding pattern. "Ah, man, no way could it do that."

"If it had enough power behind it, it could," Riley said. Nothing would stop it from latching onto the mind of a pilot and flying that plane anywhere it wanted. Into the ground, into a city full of buildings.

And if one of those passengers was Beck . . .

"We take it down—now," she said, moving a few steps forward. "I want it out of action."

Neither of them had a chance to respond as the ground beneath them began to move.

Geo-Fiend. That was what this was all about.

"Jaye, send out the warning: Five at airport," Riley ordered, trying to keep her voice calm.

The apprentice fumbled with her phone, her hands shaking, but still managed to type the text to all the other trappers in the city. It would only serve as a notice because none of them would get here in time.

As they watched in grim silence, a direct route between Hell and Atlanta formed between the two runways. The massive hole appeared in seconds, the grass and soil turning nearly molten, boiling away. Brimstone and smoke furled upward as a brutish figure slowly rose from within the cloud. When it finally reached its peak, this fiend stood nearly nine feet, one of the most lethal demons Hell could field.

The Geo-Fiend's skin was solid ebony, glistening in the sunlight, with a wide muscled chest to support its equally massive head. Twin horns thrust outward from the sides of that skull, like a bull. As with all the most dangerous Hellspawn, its eyes seared into you, bright orbs of crimson fire.

The hours Riley had spent training her apprentices made their actions rote. Kurt already had a grounding sphere and a shield sphere in hand. After Jaye finished the warning text, she retrieved her own spheres. You didn't trap a Five. You banished it right back to its master before it tore them—and the airport—to pieces.

The Four had stopped laughing now, knowing where it stood in the demonic pecking order. Still, it gave only a half-hearted bow to the newcomer as if it had no worries about this behemoth. It should have been quaking in fear. A lower-level demon would only do that if its demi-lord was significantly more powerful than this monster. That was a very short list.

"Vermin," the Five said—but to Riley's surprise, it wasn't speaking to them.

The smaller demon made a rude gesture toward the Geo-Fiend, causing Riley's jaw to drop at the insolence.

"What's going on here?" Jaye whispered.

"Not sure. This isn't normal behavior for these things."

With a roar, the Five expressed its displeasure at being dissed by scooping up the smaller demon in its claws and cramming the screaming fiend directly into its mouth. A few crunches later, the noise stopped.

"And . . . there goes our trapping fee," Kurt said, shaking his head, eyes wide.

The Geo-Fiend turned its attention back to them now. "Blackthorne's Daughter!" it bellowed, making her ears ache.

"Go home, demon," she said. "You're not welcome here."

"Surrender your soul to me and you will live," it said. "If not, you will die like your weakling of a father, crying and begging for mercy."

The mention of her dad always hurt, but then, that was the point. Paul Blackthorne had died while fighting a different Geo-Fiend, when a small piece of flying debris sliced into his heart. If things had played out differently, Beck would have died that night as well.

For those reasons alone, Riley hated Fives. She felt her magic stir and made no effort to hold it down.

"Let's get it done, demon. The sooner you're back in Hell kissing the Prince's—"

The fiend's roar shook the ground around them as its eyes blazed molten in anger. As the Five rose higher above the pit, pulling energy from Hell itself, it extended a clawed hand. From those fingers came the stirrings of a windstorm, one of the demon's best weapons. A fierce blast of wind struck Riley and the others head-on, tumbling them across the open ground like autumn leaves. Debris flew around them now, hitting their exposed flesh, biting and tearing.

Riley quickly spat out a spell, creating a one-way bubble of protection around her and her trappers. Even as the debris ceased striking them, a grounding sphere arced over her head, straight toward the demon. It shattered before it grew close to the fiend. Another sphere flew by, and this one came much closer to the demon's feet, but still not near enough for the magic to pull the creature back into the pit.

The earth continued to rock as deep fissures opened in the ground around them, spewing dirt, grass, and asphalt high into the air. The nauseating stench of brimstone increased, making their eyes burn and tears run down their cheeks.

Another sphere, better aimed, came within spitting distance of the monster, only to be destroyed when it was flattened by a chunk of metal torn from one of the jet bridges. Around them, the storm grew, swirling in a circular motion like the center of a tornado. If the demon released that storm, it would slice right through the heart of the airport, killing hundreds, perhaps thousands.

"Enough!" Riley cried.

She pulled a grounding sphere from inside her pack, infused it with her own magic, and raised it. Instead of tossing the sphere at the demon's feet, she aimed for its chest. As it flew through the air, the spell around it kept it from being shattered or blown off course. Belatedly, the Hellspawn the missile was incoming and grabbed it.

"A child's toy," it said as it began crushing it in its massive fist.

"Perfect for you, then," she said.

Another of Riley's spheres zoomed toward the Five's feet, rolling across the ground like a bowling ball. Even before the fiend realized what had happened, the sphere fell into the pit beneath it.

"Get down!" she yelled, reinforcing the protection spell around them.

As intended, the sphere in the pit detonated, spewing magic up as far as the demon's knees. The one in its hand enveloped the top of the fiend, then connected with the rising magic. The two spells intertwined, lassoing the Five and dragging it bellowing and howling into the pit. Around them, hunks of tarmac rained from the sky and the screech of anguished metal assaulted their ears.

With a final, tremendous roar, the demon plummeted into the pit and the hole sealed over. Dust and smoke swirled for a few seconds longer, then slowly settled toward the earth. The distinct patter of debris continued for some moments longer, then ended.

"Trappers score!" Kurt crowed, leaping to his feet. Jaye rose a bit slower but didn't appear injured.

The pride Riley felt for these two was almost more than she could handle.

"Good job, guys. You kicked serious butt."

She remained on the ground, trying to let the remaining magic flow away from her fingertips. Finally, the glow from her fingers ended, and she cautiously rose on shaky legs. In the distance, billowing dust coursed across the runway.

Then she felt his presence.

"Heads up, you two. We're not done yet."

The figure that walked out of the dust was clad all in black. Curiously, none of the debris stuck to his clothes, which was the first hint there was something odd about the newcomer.

The Prince of Hell's hair was as inky black as it had always been, though it now had more strands of gray at his temples. Riley knew she'd been the cause of a few of those and that pleased her immensely. The Fallen's eyes were still as brilliantly blue and cunning as ever. He stopped about ten feet from them, then glanced at where the hole had once been.

"Riley . . . " Kurt began.

"This one's mine," she said, her eyes never leaving the angel.

"Riley Anora Blackthorne," the Prince of Hell began. "Or is it Beck now?"

Always pushing. It was his way of getting you to say or do something you'd regret down the line.

Riley ignored the bait. "Some reason you're here?"

"I was heartbroken that I wasn't invited to your wedding," Lucifer said. "Especially after playing matchmaker. Or so I've been told."

"Riiight. Why the airport, after all this time?"

The Prince sobered. "Because you mortals must realize there is no place safe from my servants."

"Well, you've made your point. You were demi-lord to the Four, right?" A nod came her way. "What will happen to the Geo-Fiend?"

"It will be punished for failing in its task, and for killing *my* personal servant. I'll ensure that it takes a very long time to die."

Riley barely suppressed the shudder, because she knew he meant it. "You came here because of Beck, didn't you?" A satisfied nod. "Well, your little drama didn't work. As usual."

"Maybe it worked better than you know."

More head games. It was time to end this.

"Let me help you out, because you seem confused." She angled a thumb over her shoulder toward the city. "This is our home. Great people, good food, crappy traffic, but you can't have everything."

Then she pointed at where the pit had been. "That's your home. It has no good people, totally rotten food, and far too many treacherous Hellspawn. You know, the ones who'd love nothing more than to stab you in the back."

Lucifer's eyes narrowed. "You're getting to your point soon, I hope."

"Yes, I am. Our home isn't yours. You're not welcome here, and neither are your offspring."

"As if you can stop me."

"I can't stop you, but I can stop *them*. And I will. And when I am no longer able to do that, other trappers will continue that job until the end of time."

"Which may be much sooner than you expect."

More bait to ignore.

"What of your grand master? What is his job?" Lucifer taunted.

"Keeping you off guard and preserving the balance between good and evil. I'd say it's working if you're here bugging us."

A frown returned, telling her she was closer to the truth than he wanted to acknowledge. "You think your magic will save you? You have no idea what I could do to—"

He half turned, that frown deepening as if something else had caught his attention.

"Problems?" she asked, barely keeping the grin to herself.

He gave her a glare—which told her she was right—then abruptly faded from sight. The fury radiating off him told her someone, mortal or Hellspawn, was going to pay dearly for interrupting his gloating session.

Fortunately, that someone wasn't her.

Riley let loose a long sigh of relief. When she turned to her two companions, they wore identical shocked expressions.

"That was . . . ?" Kurt began.

"Yes, that was." Riley dug in her memory. "The first time I met His Infernalness was last year in Oakland Cemetery. He introduced himself as—" She paused to ensure she got the phrase correct. "'The Light Bearer, the Prince of Hell, the Chief among the Fallen, and The Adversary.' He suggested I should 'accept no substitutes.'"

The two trappers continued to gape.

"Common reaction," she replied. She looked back toward the terminal, which had sustained some damage but not as much as she'd feared. The rest of the airport was in one piece.

You take your blessings where you can find them.

"I'll cancel the Five alert," Jaye said, tapping on her phone.

"Good. Let's tell the airport people that their *maintenance* problem is solved, at least for today." A glance toward the piles of debris strewn across the runway made her wince—once again, Hell had made an unholy mess.

They'd nearly reached the stairs to the slightly worse-for-wear jet bridge when Riley's phone rang.

"You three okay?" Master Harper's gruff voice demanded.

"We're golden. Demons are history, and I even got to chat with Hell's CEO."

"Huh. Business as usual for you, then. Don't forget the paperwork." Then he hung up. While Harper was heavy on trapping expertise, he was light on manners.

Riley decided to pull rank as a master trapper. "You two go on to your concert. I'll deal with the powers that be and collect my guy." Provided Beck's plane was cleared to land tonight. "We'll do the reports in the morning."

"You're awesome! Thanks!" Jaye said, and after Kurt gave her a salute, the pair trotted up the stairs and out of sight into the terminal. Riley took her time up the stairs and then along the jet bridge. To her surprise, there was no airport official waiting for her as she made her way to the closest chair. She slumped into it, beyond weary.

The flickering of various video screens announced that Hell was no longer in charge, as each showed the proper flight number, followed by a "Delayed" message. When those planes would arrive or depart was anyone's guess.

She would've loved to know what it was that had caught Lucifer's attention. Or maybe she wouldn't, at least not today. It was then that Riley finally noticed her new jeans—now stained and spotted—and her lovely blue shirt with a streak of blood across one sleeve. Every time she moved her head, little bits of debris dropped into her lap.

"Why do I bother?" she muttered.

Knowing Beck had probably had a bird's-eye view of the battle, Riley sent him a message. Maybe hearing from her would keep his worrying to a minimum, if that was even possible.

FOUR DEMONS DOWN, NO INJURIES. THE INFERNAL PEST SENDS HIS REGARDS.

She paused a moment to consider what else to say.

BBQ FOR SUPPER. YOU'RE BUYING.

There was no immediate reply, but she hadn't expected one.

Easing the cramp in her side, Riley closed her eyes to rest. As she did, she sent her mind back to their wedding day, her safe place when life grew too scary. A smile crossed her face now, as she was immersed in memories of love, happy tears, and the joy of marrying the man who owned her heart.

Six weeks and counting.

Maybe Lucifer had done them a favor after all.

The End

Acknowledgements

This book has been years in the making. In fact, Simon's story has always been there, I just had to wait until he told it to me. Katia boldly wrote herself into *Lost Souls*, mostly because she was a lost soul, like dear Simon. If my guess is correct, they will be the catalysts that help broaden the scope of the Demon Trappers' world.

As always, I have many people, real and fictional, to thank for this book, including Simon Michael David Adler and Ori the Inscrutable Angel. When I began this series, I had no idea these two would have an interwoven book of their own.

I wish to thank Tyra Burton who served as cheerleader, beta reader and dear friend throughout this process. As usual her critiques were spot on and much appreciated.

An intrepid group of Kennesaw State University students (Erick C., Zoe R., Lorren D., Lawrence O., and Josh D.) brought fresh ideas to the mix when they assisted in my Demon Trapper marketing plans as part of a class assignment. It was wonderful working with these fine young folks. They are our future, and I'm so glad we're in such good hands.

Clarissa Yeo, the incredibly talented artist at Yocla Designs, (**www.YoclaDesigns.com**) created the perfect cover for Simon's book. I love working with a pro and look forward to the new covers we'll be creating down the line. Thanks, Clarissa!

I must also offer my gratitude to Portugal and its citizens, who have welcomed us despite our elementary language skills. Throughout this hideous plague, they have fought the good fight. Soon we shall gather again in the cafés, on the beaches, and in our homes. Soon . . .

Finally, a big hug for my husband, Harold, who has watched me slave over manuscripts for twenty-three years now. If I had to choose with whom to spend Lockdown, it'd be you, my love.

Is it Wine o'Clock yet?

~ Jana Oliver
April 2021

About the Author

Jana Oliver never planned to become an author. In fact, she told her sixth grade teacher she wanted to be an international spy, which sounded very cool at the time.

That so didn't happen.

After pursuing various careers (registered nurse, disc jockey, travel agent, copywriter) someone flipped a switch in her brain and stories began to pour out. There were so many stories she decided to write them down and publish them. Then someone else published them, in the U.S. and then all over the world.

She's still surprised by all that.

A few years down the line Jana's an international bestselling author with twenty some books to her credit, and has won over a dozen major writing awards, including the Maggie Award of Excellence, the Daphne du Maurier, National Readers Choice and the Prism Award.

Nowadays she can be found writing her tales in Porto, Portugal when not sharing time with her very patient husband and their cranky (ghost) Feline Overlord, Ms. Dali.

Social Media

Website: www.JanaOliver.com

Facebook: www.Facebook.com/JanaOliver

Twitter: @crazyauthorgirl

Instagram: JanaOliverAuthor

BookBub: @JanaOliver

Also by Jana Oliver

DEMON TRAPPERS SERIES
Forsaken (formerly The Demon Trapper's Daughter)
Forbidden (formerly Soul Thief)
Forgiven
Foretold
Grave Matters
Mind Games
Valiant Light
Lost Souls

TIME ROVERS SERIES
Sojourn
Virtual Evil
Madman's Dance

STANDALONE NOVELS & NON-FICTION
Briar Rose
Tangled Souls
Dead Easy
Socially Engaged: The Author's Guide to Social Media (co-authored with Tyra Burton)

WRITING AS CHANDLER STEELE

VERITAS SERIES
Cat's Paw
Killing Game
Broken Dreams

Printed in Great Britain
by Amazon